The Anstruther Lass

VIVIEN CARMICHAEL

Ordering Information:

Prime Seven Media
518 Landmann St.
Tomah City, WI 54660

Printed in the United States of America

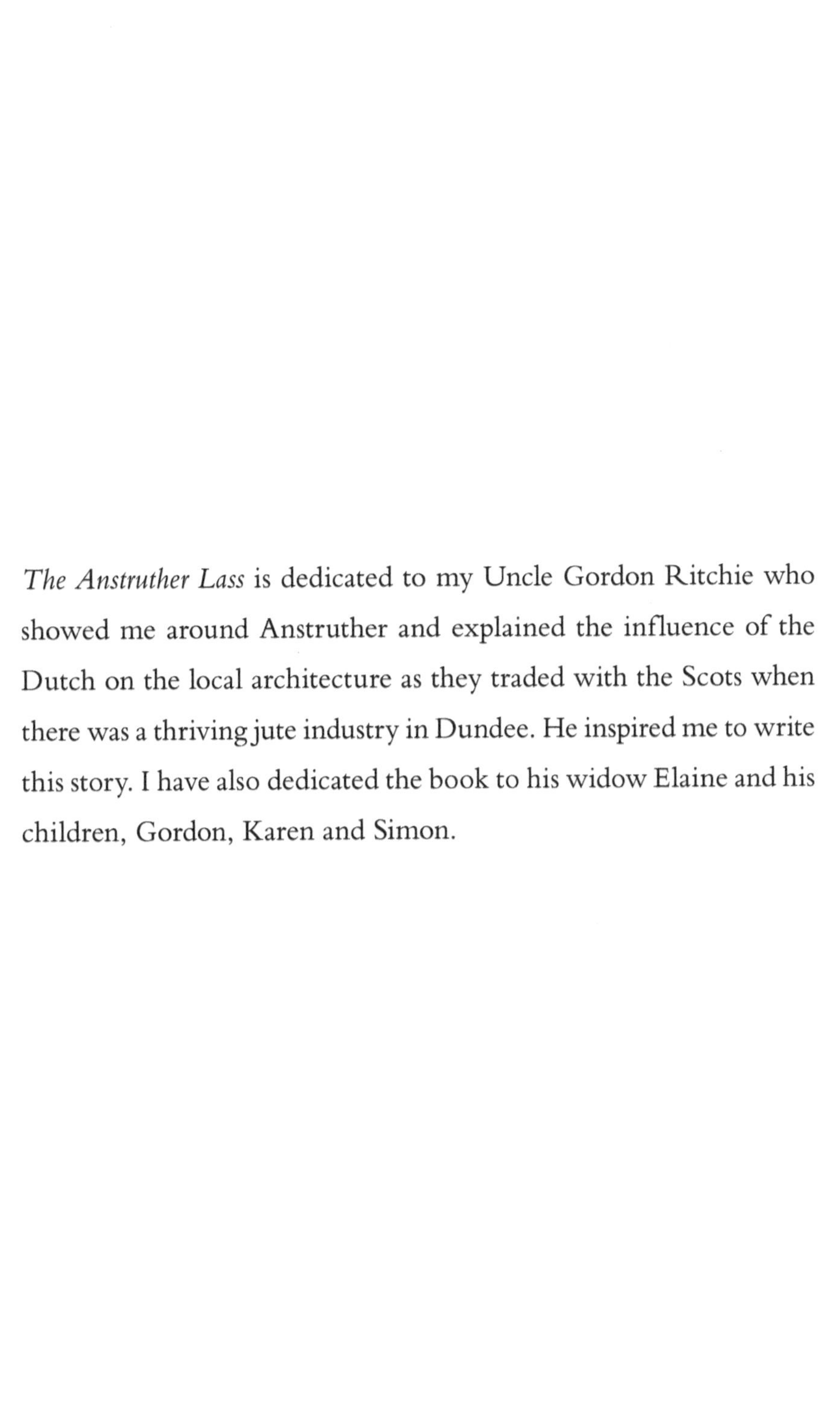

The Anstruther Lass is dedicated to my Uncle Gordon Ritchie who showed me around Anstruther and explained the influence of the Dutch on the local architecture as they traded with the Scots when there was a thriving jute industry in Dundee. He inspired me to write this story. I have also dedicated the book to his widow Elaine and his children, Gordon, Karen and Simon.

With Thanks

The accuracy of this book would not have been possible without the help of the many libraries and museums in Scotland, and I should like to personally thank the following people for their help and patience in finding answers to my many questions.

Pauline Campbell at Anstruther Library, Cunzie Street, Anstruther.

Elaine Coleman at the Library and Learning Centre, University of Dundee.

Alistair Dinsmoor at Glasgow Police Museum, Bell Street, Merchant City, Glasgow.

Heather Johnson, Archives Collection Officer at The National Museum of the Royal Navy.

Thanks also to my husband Denis for all the advice, support and the endless editing of the manuscript.

Thanks also to my friend Yvonne Dedman for proofreading the manuscript.

Cover illustration by Bryony Crane

www.bryonycrane.co.uk

Bryony is an illustrator from the south coast of England who enjoys working with a mix of traditional and digital methods. She uses sketchy pencil linework with digital painting techniques to create lively illustrations with playful concepts, illustrating primarily for children, but also for a wide variety of applications and audiences.

After graduating in 2011, Bryony was chosen as an illustration semi-finalist in the Adobe Design Achievement Awards and in 2012 won the Sky Arts Ignition: Creative Wish Brighton prize.

List of Characters

Lana St Clair	A widow from Anstruther
Stefan Van Uden	Lana's sweetheart, son of a Dutch ship owner
Ton Van Uden	Stefan's father
Lucas Beems	Stefan's friend
Moira Law	Lana's sister
Angus Law	Moira's husband
Ronald Law	Moira's eldest son
James Law	Moira's younger son
Andrea Murray	Lana's younger sister
Ben Murray	Andrea's husband
Aunt Jeanie	Lana's aunt
Gordon	the night-watchman/Anstruther's policeman
Jock	A smuggler from Anstruther
Michael	A smuggler from Anstruther
Robbie	A smuggler from Anstruther
Rory	Jock's delivery boy in Dundee

Mr Willie Campbell   Production Manager of Campertown Mill

Mr Wainwright   Foreman of Campertown Mill

Jessie   Robbie's cousin. mill worker

Maisie   Jessie's friend, mill worker.

Isla Dunbar   Past mistress of Mr Willie Campbell

Jack   A ten-year-old boy mill worker

Leslie   Jack's mother.

Detective Murray   Part of the Dundee police force

Detective Macduff   Part of the Dundee police force

Lady Mary MacDonald   A Dundee benefactress

Florrie   Lady Mary's maid

Meanings of some Scottish dialect words

Auld Reekie	dinburgh
Bairns	children
Bawheid	stupid, empty headed
Bletherin	babbling on, talking idly
Bampot	headcase, stupid person
Chum	to accompany someone
Crabbitt	bad tempered, grumpy
Feartie-cat	a coward, a scaredy-cat
Guidman	a man or husband
Guidwoman	wife
Hee haw	nothing, empty
Peely- wally	pallid, pale, sickly,
Skinny- malinky	skinny
Wee 'uns	children

Table of Contents

Part Two And beyond

Part Three The rescue and the arrest

Appendix

Part One

Scotland

Chapter One

She watched the rat. It darted across the mill yard and disappeared behind some waste bins. It gave her the idea. She shook her blonde curls so that they tumbled round her face framing it. She bit her lips to make them redder, Wullie always said he loved her mouth. He called her mouth a cupids bow and said it had ensnared him. She looked at herself in the mirror and smiled. She had what she called a "get away with it" face. Her blonde curls and blue eyes made her look sweet and innocent. No one would suspect that she was a killer. Her plans were going well. She had scared all the girls in the tenement block owned by the mill, where she lived by telling them that she had seen rats in the building.

Two of the girls had gone to the pharmacy and bought the arsenic to kill the rats. They had to sign the Poisons Register that had been introduced in 1851. This was important, as even though Isla had planned the murder to look like an accident, she did not want any suspicion to fall on her, which it could do if she had bought the poison and signed the register herself. Her plan had nearly gone wrong as since the 1851 Arsenic Act the arsenic had to be coloured indigo blue but the chemist had some old stock that he wanted to get rid of and offered it to the girls at a cheaper price. As they had all clubbed together to buy the rat poison the girls wanted to save money especially as they did not earn much as mill workers.

The trouble had begun when she thought that her lover, Mr William Campbell, one of the mill managers, had seemed to lose interest in her. A pretty girl called Wilma, had started work at the mill and Isla knew what "her Wullie" as she called him was up to as soon as he had appeared on the factory floor and approached Wilma. Why, he had done exactly the same thing with her, introduced himself and then come down to see her at every opportunity. She realised cynically that it was probably a pattern and he had had a whole string of lasses before her. She loved Wullie and although he was married, she hoped to persuade him to let her have a baby. Then he might set her up in a house and he could even leave his wife for her. She needed to act quickly. She, Lindsay and Fiona had put the powder around the outside of the building, and she had seen that it was white and looked like sugar. She had searched around the outside of the mill and had collected a couple of dead rats, which she had put outside the tenement building, near the poison to confirm her story. They had put the remainder of the arsenic in an outside storehouse; Isla crept downstairs and put some of it in a small sugar bowl. She carefully added some sugar to the bowl. She knocked on Wilma's door making sure that no body was about.

"Would you like to have a cup of hot cocoa with me before you go to sleep?

"Aye, that would be lovely."

OK, Let's go down to the kitchen and we can have good gossip over our nightcap."

"What do you think of the Production manager Mr Campbell?" she asked Wilma expecting her to say something quite innocuous.

Instead, she nearly tripped over her nightdress on the stairs in surprise.

"Och, he's lovely. Do you know what he said to me yesterday? I think we must be destined to be together as our names are so similar, I think Wilma is one of the feminine versions of William. I would like to get to know you better can I take you out for a bite to eat at midday on Saturday?"

"So what did you say?" Isla replied, smiling at Wilma but thinking, 'Why you treacherous little bitch, I've seen you fluttering your eyelashes and flirting outrageously.'

"I told him I would meet him in the yard behind the mill, at midday on Saturday but we would have to be careful as I know he's married, and it would never do for folk to find out."

Isla smiled sweetly and said, "Well I hope you have a lovely time", as she poured out the cocoa and heaped two large spoonsful of the sugar and arsenic into Wilma's cup thinking you won't have lovely time because you'll be dead by tomorrow. Isla could hardly contain herself after hearing Wilma's confession but managed to sit and chat for five minutes and then she yawned and said,

"Well, I'm for bed."

She knew that yawning was contagious and sure enough, Wilma began to yawn,

"That sounds like a good idea."

Isla quickly washed the two cups, as she did not want evidence to be found that there had been another person with Wilma when she had drunk the fatal cocoa. She tidied the sugar bowl away into a cupboard. The two girls crept quietly up to their rooms and Isla was pleased that there were no other mill girls about. Isla fell into bed laughing and thinking, 'Well that's the end of that romance – William and Wilma, I ask you – what a line! Such a fool to fall for that a load of tripe. Well, she deserved to die a horrible death for believing it' and she chuckled to herself as she thought, 'It would be a horrible death, first she would get stomach cramps and then nausea and diarrhoea, dizziness and then she would feel numbness spread over her body as all her vital organs shut down and then death.' Isla relaxed as she thought that even if the police investigated Wilma's death, they would not be able to prove that she had anything to do with it. She fell asleep with a satisfied smile on her face.

Chapter Two

"The jute mills, Lana you can't go and work there, I've heard there's trouble enough there, dust and steam and it's dangerous too. I seem to remember when we were young that that there was a terrible accident about ten or fifteen years ago at the Verdant Works Mill. I think a young lass was mangled in a carding machine and was killed instantly. Everyone was talking about it. Why you could end up dead or mutilated." Moira pleaded with Lana.

"I've decided. Anyway, since my darling, Robbie was killed I don't really care. I would be with him again. No, I've decided I'm going to Dundee."

"I thought you were going to work at the Fish Quay."

"That was before I knew Billy O'Neil was the foreman. He's been pestering me since my Robert died and my life wouldn't be worth living with him making passes at me all day, not to mention all the suggestive comments."

The two sisters were sitting in the kitchen of Moira's house at the large well-worn oak kitchen table that Moira had inherited from her mother, relaxing with a well-earned cup of tea. Moira had sent her husband off to work and her two sons to school with sandwiches for lunch. Then the two sisters had swept the house, washed the breakfast dishes and put them away, hung out the washed tea towels, which were now flapping in the breeze outside on the washing line. Moira studied her younger sister's face, her high cheek bones, lovely bone structure and tip-tilted eyes. She was not jealous, as she knew that she was attractive in a different way, with light blue eyes, blonde hair, a rounder face and a pert nose. She had had her fair share of admirers, but she wondered if being as beautiful as Lana was not a curse rather than a blessing. It had certainly been a blessing for Moira and Andrea when they were young; her mother had always picked Lana to run errands and be the family's ambassadress. Her mother used to say, 'Lana always looks so neat and tidy and beautiful but you two are scruffy urchins,' They always giggled and sighed with relief.'

"Well, that's your fault."

"What do you mean?"

Moira thought for a long time before answering. Lana was so used to being the most attractive of the three sisters that she smiled and flirted with everyone naturally, she didn't understand that men could misconstrue it.

"You encouraged him."

Lana's eyes widened, "No, you're wrong. I didn't encourage him or at least I didn't realise it. But what has that got to do with the jute mills in Dundee?"

Andrea arrived slamming the back door with a bang and thumping her basket down on the kitchen table. She had heard the conversation and joined in,

"The trouble with you, Lana is that you always think everybody is good, but you should realise that there is bad in most people and some folks are downright evil."

"Why are you both getting at me?"

"We're not having a go; we're just trying to protect you."

Moira gave Lana a hug to confirm that their words showed their concern for her and were not intended to be hurtful, Lana felt comforted by the familiar smell of Moira's bergamot and lemon perfume.

"Well, the accident was a long time ago, it is safer now, besides, I'm to work in a different mill. Yes, I know it is gruelling work but Robbie's cousin, Jessie, works in the finishing section there and will introduce me. She says the work is easier in this area; all they do is cut off all the surplus fibres and load the jute into a high-pressure roller to give it a smooth pressed finish. Jessie said all the women there are friendly good sorts and all help each other out, so it might not be so bad. Also, I need something to take my mind off Robbie's death. I won't have time for grieving when I'm doing hard work. Anyway, I thought you would be glad to get rid of me for a while. You must be fed up with me either mooning around or going out at night for midnight walks on the beach and screaming Robert's name at the sea."

Let her go and work at the mill, it could be the making of her, having to deal with all the scoundrels and rats who work there," Andrea countered.

"But where will you stay in Dundee? You can't travel back and forth every day."

"I can stay with Auntie Jeanie. You know, her husband was a doctor, that's how she met him as she was a midwife. They were comfortably off and were able to buy their house so when he died, he left her the house and an annuity. She lives in Broughty Ferry Road, and I'll come back to you on weekends, or you can bring the boys to visit Auntie Jeanie in Dundee. She'd love to see them."

Moira and Andrea looked at Lana and saw her stubborn expression that they knew so well. Moira smiled gloomily,

"Well, you seemed to have made up your mind and I know that even if a school of whales swam up the Forth of Tay and blocked the ferry that wouldn't stop you. You would find a way but how are you getting to Dundee?"

"Old Jock said he'd take me to Dundee in his horse and cart."

"He's one of the smugglers. Isn't he? I know him. He supplies my husband at the Ship Inn."

"Yes, and he takes the contraband brandy, rum and tobacco to Dundee to sell. There's a good market there as so many folks have come to work in the jute mills. He goes every Monday. His buyer sends a boy to meet the Tay ferry to collect the goods and pay him. Jock says that the boy comes with a horse to harness up to the cart and he will take me to Campertown Mill."

"Too risky. Suppose customs lay in wait for him and catch him? They'll think you are a smuggler too and throw you in jail. Think of another way to travel to Dundee."

"*Whsst*, he's been doing it now for five years, so I don't think that there's much chance of that. Anyway, most of the customs men are corrupt. They know fine well what is going on and that the smugglers in Anstruther are small fry, so they take bribes to look away."

Andrea agreed with Lana, "She'll be alright with Jock. He knows his way around."

Moira sighed looking at her younger sister, thinking that she had always been a little childlike and naïve. Her mother had named her Lana, meaning child in Gaelic and sometimes she thought of her younger sister as one of her own children. She had to look after her, together with her own two sons, Ronald and James. Lana didn't seem to realise that people could be vindictive and could inform the customs bringing the whole smuggling trade tumbling down like a house of cards. She did not feel the same way about their younger sister Andrea, because Andrea was the hard-headed one. She had turned down all the young lads who tried to court her and instead she had chosen to marry the older widower who owned the Ship Inn just down the road in Elie. Her heart certainly did not rule her head; in fact, it was the opposite. At least Andrea was not mean-spirited and being better off than her two older sisters, she would always lend a hand if they were short of food or money. She turned back to Lana, sighed and said resignedly,

"Well, I'll make you up some bread and cheese to take with you for the journey. What time are you leaving and when will you be back?"

"It's only twenty miles and we are going to set off early at seven o'clock in the morning. We'll get to Dundee by eleven and I've said in my letter to Jessie that I'll meet her at twelve noon outside the mill. She is going to take me to meet her foreman and I hope I can start next week. Oh yes, I've written to Auntie Jeanie and she wrote back and said she'd love to have me. I am meeting her at the ferry before I go back at two o'clock."

"Well Lana, you certainly have been busy and organised everything. Are you staying for supper Andrea?"

"No, I just popped in for a cup of tea and to see you two. Ben has some business in town, and I arranged to meet him at the at five o' clock by the Dreel and we'll go back to Elie in the brougham in time to open the Ship for the evening.

Little did any of the sisters know that Lana's arrival at the mill would stir up a hornet's nest.

Chapter Three

Lana jumped out of bed just after six, poured water from the jug into the bowl and washed her face. She had trouble sleeping these days since she had become a widow and always woke up early. She dressed quickly, ran down the stairs to the kitchen and grabbed the packed lunch her sister had prepared for her. She was carrying her purse containing money she had taken from the jar that she and Robbie had been saving to buy a house. She donned her favourite black cloak with the hood and marched determinedly down the road to meet Jock.

He was waiting in his cart as he had promised and he told her they would go across the country rather than along the coast, as it would be quicker. He looked very smart in a clean white shirt. People sometimes thought that because the smugglers were rogues that they were dirty and unkempt, a false assumption. Another belief that because they were scoundrels, they must also be bad was quite untrue for, as Lana knew, Jock had helped various villagers when they were short of money. His face was lined but when Lana looked at his eyes, she noticed that the lines around them were caused by smiling and gave him a kind expression. The steady *clip-clop* of the horses' hooves, the gentle rocking motion of the cart, Jocks comforting smell of salt and the sea all had a soporific effect on Lana and she was so tired that she fell into a deep sleep. In spite of Moira's misgivings, she knew she was safe with Jock.

She cried out as she woke with a start when they reached the ferry. Jock had told her that they couldn't take the horses on the ferry and he uncoupled the cart and tethered the horses to a post by the dockside. Lana watched in fascination as a couple of the ferrymen jumped down and helped Jock to push the cart on the ferry. She saw Jock pass a couple of bottles to the men and realised that they must have done this many times, because the operation took place so smoothly. The weather was fine, the water across the river Tay was calm and they reached Craigie Pier in Dundee without any trouble. The ferrymen appeared again and with great alacrity pushed the cart up the ramp to the dock. There was a young lad about fifteen years old, on the quayside, holding the reins of a horse. He and Jock harnessed the horse to the cart.

"This is Rory; he's from Ireland, come over with his sister to find work. He works for one of my punters who owns a public house in Dundee. He'll take ye to Campertown works. Ah'll hold my horses for ye in the Tay Arms over there. Ye'll see the cart outdoors and then we'll load it on the ferry and go back home."

He helped Lana up on the cart, "That's me, I'll see ye at two o'clock." Lana looked at the boy. His large frame was muscled. His face was marred with teenage spots, but Lana thought when he grew out of them, he would be a handsome man. Almost as if he knew this, his acne did not seem to worry him and he wasn't shy like some of the teenage boys she knew in Anstruther,

"Right, we're heading for Campertown Works, can ye see that tall chimney over there, that's called Cox's stack, so it is, part of the mill. They've just built it, so they have and it's a useful landmark. We will just head towards that, and we can't go wrong. Is it work ye're lookin' for? I don't know what a pretty girl like ye wants to work in the mills. They'll work ye to death there if ye dinna die first from breathing in all the dust and steam. Can ye not find some work on the fish quays in Anstruther?"

"I've recently been widowed, and I wanted to move from Anstruther as it holds too many memories for me."

Rory blushed, "Sorry, I didn't mean to be cheeky and I'm sorry for your loss."

Lana felt sorry for him as he was so embarrassed and said, "No, you're all right No offence taken. It's kind of you to take me to the mill."

When they arrived outside the mill, Lana could not help giving a gasp. It was much larger than she had expected and there was a maze of sprawling buildings. She could hear a loud noise of machinery running and the hum of voices and the air around the building was misty with clouds of dust. Smoke belched from the tall chimney they called Cox's stack.

"It's awesome, isn't it? Did ye know that there are 5,000 folk that work there?"

"That's a lot of people," Lana said as she got down from the cart, starting to feel a growing sense of panic. How was she going to find Jessie?

Jessie and her friend Maisie came out of the main entrance arm in arm.

"Why on earth does she want to work in the mills?"

"Well, my cousin Robbie was swept overboard from a whaling trawler in a storm. T'was tragic, they never found the body although apparently, they searched for him for a good half an hour, even though he would'nae have lasted five minutes in the freezing sea. Anyway, she thought it would be better if she moved from Anstruther. The place is steeped in memories for her so she thought she would start a fresh life in Dundee. Och, look and there she is." Jessie waved to Lana.

"Ye didnae' tell me she was a looker. Mr Wullie Campbell had better not clap his eyes on her otherwise yer fair cousin might find she has a fresh life growing in her belly!" Maisie gave a laugh.

"Och he's nae as bad as all that. I think it's just rumours."

"Well, ye said he tried tae kiss you behind the carding machines."

"Oh, that was just a joke"

Jessie was always joking. She was a card, always playing practical jokes and messing around. She was popular with all the other girls, and they were forever saying, "Jessie, You're a caution." That was why the girls had all agreed to cover for them so that they had been able to sneak out early for their midday break to meet Lana.

Just then, the bell on the clock tower started to ring, girls started to pour out of the doors on their lunch break and Jessie pulled Maisie by the arm over the cobblestones towards Lana.

"Come on, we'd better be quick otherwise Lana is likely to get swamped and we'll never find her."

Lana was relieved when she saw Jessie waving to her especially when she heard the bell clanging and it seemed like hundreds of girls, all covered in a layer of what looked like flour, came tumbling out of the doors. She saw they were all wearing plain dresses with no crinolines or petticoats, and some were wearing aprons. Jessie flung her arms around Lana. Lana noticed her green bombazine dress, which suited her auburn curls but felt a little coarse and stiff as she hugged her,

"It's good to see ye, hen but you're skinny-malinky. Never mind I expect yer Auntie Jeanie will feed ye up in nae time. This is my best friend, Maisie."

"Hello, pleased to meet you, Maisie," Lana said as she noted that Maisie was as attractive as Jessie but had a more delicate beauty with strawberry blonde hair and freckles across her nose.

"Please tae catch up with ye too, Lana, don't worry about anything. We'll look out for ye."

Lana was relieved that she had reassured her as she noticed that some of the girls were staring at her. They looked bold and brassy, and she felt daunted especially when she heard their ribald shouts.

"Och, look at her, Lady Muck. She looks so bonnie and dainty; a puff of wind would blow her over."

"Who are ye staring at hen? I'll give ye a painting of me next time."

Maisie said, "Don't worry yourself Lana, she canna help it. She's from Ireland" she nodded her head towards the red headed girl, "and that one canna help it either 'cos she's from Glasgow."

Jessie and Maisie linked their arms in Lana's and as they marched towards the entrance, Jessie shouted back,

"This is my cousin's widow, so I'll thank you to have some respect for her. She's under my wing so make sure you are all nice to her or I'll knock your brains out."

Some of the other girls gave a cheer, "That's right Jessie, ye tell them to mind their manners!"

"They're a bit rough but once they get used to ye they've got hearts of gold."

"If you say so, Jessie." Lana replied not completely reassured.

The three girls went through the door, down a corridor and Jessie knocked on a door.

"Come in."

"Hello, Mr Wainwright, this is Lana, my cousin's widow that I told you about. She wants a job here at Campertown Mill."

"Och aye, chuffed to catch up with ye Lana. Jessie told me about ye."

Jessie knew Lana impressed him as he could not keep his eyes off her and he seemed slightly flustered.

"Well, there is a place in the finishing section. You'll be with Jessie sae she can show ye what to do. Did Jessie tell ye about the hours and pay?

"No, we didn't discuss that."

"Well, ye start work at seven and finish at five, Monday to Friday but on Saturdays you only work for eight hours and finish at three o'clock. The women used to work 12 hours a day but tis only ten that's allowed the noo, since they brought in the ten hours act back in 1847. Pay is seven shillings a week. Now where are ye off to live? I seem to remember that Jessie said ye come from Anstruther. We have accommodation for our workers in some tenement buildings, provided by the owners of the mill, at a reasonable cost."

"No, I'm all right as I can stay with my Auntie Jeanie in Broughty Ferry Road."

"That's good then as that's nae far from the works. It'll take ye about an hour to walk to the mill from there, so mind ye set off in good time. We expect good timekeeping and you'll be fined if you're late. Ye must wear plain long dresses and no corsets for we don't want lasses fainting especially near the machinery, as that could be dangerous. Ye must tie yer hair back and wear a headscarf, as again if hair gets tangled in the machinery it would cause a no nice accident. Is that all clear?" Mr Wainwright paused for a moment and then said, "You can start next Monday and when ye have arrived just report to me in this office and I'll get Jessie to sort ye out."

The three girls went outside, and Lana asked Jessie, "What is all the dust that's flying around? It looks like some giants are making bread and shaking flour all over the place."

"That's called 'stour'. It comes from the jute and gets everywhere even in yer drawers."

"Jessie don't be so vulgar," Maisie said giving her a slap on her behind.

"Well, it's true, just look at all the dust that went flying when ye slapped my backside but don't worry ye get used to it."

They sat down on the grass in front and Jessie and Maisie ate their packed food. They were all chatting and enjoying the sun when the bell in the clock tower started to clang loudly.

"That's us, back to work, see ye next Monday. We'll call for ye at six at your auntie's house and chum ye to work. I know where she lives."

They both gave Lana a quick hug and gave her directions to get back to the ferry and they were gone.

★ ★ ★

Back at the mill, William Campbell sat in his large office and frowned. He was not a happy man. There had been a fire at the mill last week and although no one had been hurt, it had affected production. He doubted if the mill would meet the quotas this week. There had been another terrible incident as a young mill worker called Wilma had been found dead in one of the tenements owned by the mill. The police had investigated as apparently, she had been poisoned with arsenic. They said it was a tragic accident as some of the girls had bought the arsenic to kill rats seen in the tenement and someone had thought it was sugar and put it in a bowl. Evidently, she had added it to her cocoa, taken late at night to help her sleep and the poor girl had died in the night. The Police had come to see him, which had disturbed him a little, because his current mistress Isla lived in the same tenement, and he didn't want that to be discovered.

He had taken a shine to the new girl Wilma and had asked her to meet him the next Saturday but surely, he thought, Isla could not possibly have had anything to do with Wilma's death. He was fond of Isla but in view of this latest event and the fact that she was becoming more demanding and said she wanted a baby, he decided he had better finish with her. Campbell decided to pop down to the finishing section to see how the production was progressing. He had seen three girls coming out of the Foreman's office. He knew Jessie and Maisie, but the other girl was a stranger.

"What a Cherry, she's ripe for picking," he had thought, He started to imagine seducing her and he smiled for the first time that day. He popped his head around Wainwright's office door, on the pretence of asking him about the jute production schedule.

He asked casually, "By the way, who was that lassie with Jessie?"

Wainwright, not fooled for one minute, answered his boss, "She's called Lana, she's the replacement for Wilma and she is starting work in the finishing section next Monday.

'Perfect', he thought, and he smiled for the second time that day.

Lana walked down Methven Street until she reached the High Street. She was amazed that there were so many people in the streets and paused to take in the atmosphere. The street was full of carts, barouches, curricles, landaus, hackneys and hansom cabs. It was noisy and everywhere she turned, she heard Irish accents. It was good to see so many shops and market stalls open, doing a brisk trade and she dawdled along looking in some of the shop windows. The smells were quite pungent too and seemed to be a mixture of horse manure, coal, vegetables and something else she could not quite put her finger on. The smell niggled at her as she tried to identify it, she knew she had smelt it before, but she just could not place it. Was it from Anstruther? No, she thought it was completely different to the smell of the herrings that wafted in the air at Anstruther, and she gave up with a shrug of her shoulders.

She passed a coal merchant shop where two men whose faces smudged with black coal were loading sacks of coal onto a cart. They stepped aside to let her pass, doffing their hats. Lana crossed a small intersection and on the opposite corner to the coal depot, there was a completely different shop. Instead of being dirty and dark, this shop looked bright and shiny.

She saw the name over the window display, Keiller and Son, makers of Dundee marmalade and it looked so inviting that she went in. The shop assistant asked if she could help, and Lana purchased three jars of the marmalade for a penny each that she thought was a very reasonable price. She would give one to her sister who had always had a sweet tooth, one to Jock for bringing her to Dundee and one to her Auntie Jeanie. She was even more delighted with the prices when the girl asked if they were presents and offered to gift wrap them.

She continued along the street and the next shop was a milliner. She looked at all the hats in the window and her eyes lighted on a blue concoction with feathers and lace. Blue suited her and was her favourite colour. She squinted to see the price tag and was shocked when she saw it marked at three whole shillings. Why that would be almost half her weekly wage and she reluctantly walked past the shop saying to herself, "You can't afford it, lass." She smiled wryly to herself as she thought that she had no one to wear such a hat for anyway.

Next, she passed a shoe shop where they had some boots. She made a mental note of the shop location for although it was summer, she might need them for the coming winter as they looked well-made, and she thought they would last through the ice and snow.

Lana asked a street trader selling vegetables the way to the ferry. The directions were quite straightforward so she hurried in the right direction, concerned that she was late and would miss her Auntie Jeanie and Jock. She need not have worried as when she came round a corner, she saw her aunt chatting away to Jock, outside the pub. Her aunt greeted her with open arms and gave her a hug. Lana noticed the strained buttons on her blouse, and she smiled as she thought that her aunt looked as if she was bursting out of it.

"It's good to see ye, lassie and I'll love having ye to stay, it'll be company for me in the evening."

Lana presented her with the marmalade and Jeanie gave her another hug,

"Och, you're a terrible lassie, you're always giving me presents."

"Well, you are my favourite aunt after all."

The horn tooted to announce that the next ferry was just about to leave, and they left in a flurry as the ferrymen pushed the cart down the slope, up the ramp and on to the ferry. Lana waved to her Aunt from the deck of the ferry, and they were off. It was mid-summer, the river calm so the trip back across the Tay was uneventful. The ferry docked at Newport in no time with a swirl of brownish muddy water. Jock gave his two horses a lump of sugar each and rubbed their necks. One of the horses snickered and gave Jock a push with her nose.

They went home along the coast road and Lana worried that it would remind her too much of her lost husband. She settled back, heartened by the familiar smell of the sweating horses and scent of leather from the bridles. As they passed through the villages of Kingsbairns, Crial and Kilkenny, to her surprise she found it comforting as she remembered the happy times she had spent with Robbie in those places.

She smiled as she reminisced the day that the two of them had walked along the beach at Kilkenny, the sun on their faces, paddling in the water warmed by the sun-baked sands. She remembered Robert's delighted laughter when she had done a cartwheel on the sand, displaying her petticoats and drawers. She thought that she must be getting over her grief as thoughts of her husband no longer made her eyes fill with tears. Lana gave a happy sigh as they reached Anstruther. This was her home, and she loved all the little Dutch houses along the harbour. The trade between the Scots and the Dutch had meant that many Scottish folk had settled in Holland and some of the Dutch had come to live in Fifeshire, bringing their architecture and culture with them across the channel.

She liked the way they had large stone steps up from the pavements to the front doors and supposed it was because Holland was so flat and prone to flooding that they built them like that. She loved the high roofs with their crow-stepped gables as well and wondered if she would ever visit Holland to compare the houses in Rotterdam or Amsterdam with the ones in Anstruther.

She said her goodbyes and thanked Jock, gave him his jar of Dundee marmalade, pulled her cloak together and quickly walked up to her sister's house.

Chapter Four

The sea mist, sometimes called a *haar* or *sea fret*, swept in from the North Sea drifting gently along the Fife coast. Creeping stealthily along the streets of Anstruther, curling round corners and enfolding the cottages on the quayside in its embrace, it sought out every nook and cranny before spreading upwards to the rest of the small village. The soft grey mist muted sounds, masking activity in the waking village. The mournful sound of the foghorns on the boats out on the Firth of Forth added to the melancholy atmosphere.

But the land had built up some residual warmth from the long hot summer days. The sun joined its forces and together they burned through the mist, which lifted slowly like a theatre curtain revealing the opening scene of a play. Anstruther sprang to life, showing its backdrop of Dutch-style houses on the quayside. The herring lasses with their bright coloured scarves sang and laughed while they worked on the pier. Their chattering voices gave a background noise like a chirping flock of birds. The masts of the boats bobbed up and down in the harbour. The water slapped against the quayside and the sailors shouted to each other readying to leave in their Derry boats to catch the herring. Seagulls swooped and cawed over the boats.

Farmers in their carts carrying vegetables, eggs and cages of clucking chickens for the shops and merchants, rolled along the cobbled quayside. Two women carrying shopping baskets walked purposefully. Children ran about playing and laughing. A dog ran round a man's legs nearly tripping him up. In saving himself from a fall, his hat flew off, which he chased along the quayside just catching it before the wind flipped it into the water. The two women walking arm in arm laughed at his antics and shouted, "Well done" and "Bravo" when he caught his hat. Their voices carried on the breeze and the man responded and gave a bow and a cheery wave.

An omen? Perhaps the fog was an omen of mist shrouded menace, murder and mayhem? Unaware of any sense of foreboding, Lana and Moira walked arm in arm in the sunshine, down to the bridge over the Dreel, past Wightmans Wynd that overlooked the burn where the remains of Dreel Castle built by Sir William Anstruther added to the scenery.

The two sisters strolled up the High Street West. Moira's sons Ronald and James ran ahead of them. The boy's school was closed for the day for a governors' meeting.

"Oh look, there's Consuela and Serafina." They greeted the two women and gave them a quick hug.

"We're going to the market, where are you going?" Lana said just as she noticed all their bags full of vegetables.

"We're just off home. We've already been to the market."

"Oh, yes. Silly me."

Lana and Moira waved their friends goodbye.

Moira mused, "The Spanish are always up early, especially on market days. It's funny isn't it how they are still using Spanish names and we still call them the Spaniards, although they settled here nearly three hundred years ago. Our teacher told us in history how the folk of Anstruther helped a Spanish Armada ship and the sailors were so taken by the hospitality shown that some of them stayed. But they have intermarried with the Scots now so perhaps we should call them "The Spanshires."*

Lana laughed and said, "Or the Fifeish."

Moira joined in her laughter, "It sounds so comical like a new type of fish."

They rounded a corner and entered the market still laughing and that was when Lana noticed a tall, blond man look over the stalls towards her. She had always been attracted to blond men. She could not take her eyes off him. He was beautiful. Lana noticed that the one feature that made him so striking was his eyes. She thought to herself, blonde-haired folk usually had blond eyelashes and eyebrows and looked peely-wally, but he was different. His eyebrows were dark and arched over his dark blue eyes. The fringe of his long black lashes emphasized these eyes even more. Lana looked away, walked over to the next stall and then could not resist another look. He was watching her and their eyes met once again. Lana and Moira continued along the crowed stall, buying vegetables and loading them into their bags. Every time she dared to look at the

---

*   See note 1.

man, he was watching her. He was dressed in a sailor's garb, with a navy-blue jacket over a loose white shirt, knee breeches and socks and he seemed The Spanish Armada and Anstruther to be buying a lot of produce and loading it into a handcart. Lana assumed that he was from one of the ships docked in the harbour, replenishing their food stocks for their coming journey. She remembered the French expression from the French lessons her governess had given them – "Un coup de foudre" – she certainly felt as if she had been struck by lightning, her heart was beating fast, and she felt hot. Moira had not noticed anything, and she put her arm companionably through Lana's, steering her away from the market. Lana dared to make eye contact with the mysterious stranger one more time and he glanced at her as he talked to one of the stallholders.

"I just need to go the fish shop, I promised Angus I'd make his favourite fish pie for supper, then I've got to go down to the pier, I undertook to give Maggie a message from her mother." Moira waved to a woman on the other side of the road.

"Who's that?"

"It's the author, Margaret Oliphant Wilson who lives in the White House; you know the big house on the High Esplanade, just round the corner from us. She's a widow like you, her husband died back in 1859. But she was devastated once more last year when her daughter Margaret died. It's so sad, she had seven children and five of them have died so she only has her two sons now. I believe that she is one of Queen Victoria's favourite writers and I keep meaning to read one of her books. I like the sound of the one called *Katie Stewart*."

Lana was glad of the diversion as it covered up her flustered feelings and she made a mental note to buy the book for Moira's Christmas present. She smiled to herself for although Christmas was a long way off, she knew Moira would be delighted and surprised when she presented her with the book.

Moira said pensively, "It made me think, so Angus and I are hoping for another bairn."

"Ooh, Moira, that will be lovely, perhaps you will have a girl this time."

Chapter Five

The beautiful laughing girls he had watched in the market intrigued Stefan, and he had stopped to ask one of the stallholders about them.

"Why, they're the stuck-up St Clair lassies. But I'm being unfair; they're bonnie lasses so well-mannered and polite. Their father had a good job in a bank in Kirkcaldy, some twenty miles away. I remember he used to ride a bicycle to get to work every day. The family were quite well off until the bank collapsed. I think there was a scandal as there was some fraud, although he wasn't involved, he still lost his job.

Anyway, their mother wanted the girls to have an education and they had a governess, so they don't have a pure wide scots accent. I ask you a governess in a fishing village. I think she hoped that one of them would marry a local landowner and restore the family fortunes. Pie-eater, lot of good it did, one of them married a whaler, one the foreman o' the shipbuilding yard but the youngest did the best and married the publican who runs the Ship Inn up the road at Elie. I have to say, they're kind-hearted lasses for all their fancy auld reekie accents. I mind when they were young, they rescued an old donkey."

The woman noticed that the stranger seemed crestfallen. "Och if it's the dark-haired lassie, ye've taken a shine tae, you're in luck. That's Lana; her guidman was a whaler, swept overboard in the Melville Sea up in the Arctic. It's a dangerous jab whaling and by all accounts thare was an ill storm and a huge wave carried him intae the sea. They stopped and looked for him but never found his body, poor laddie, he woud'nae have lasted more than a few minutes in those freezing seas. Lana was heartbroken as they had'nae been married long My guidman told me that he has seen her walking on the beach at Billow Ness late at night, staring out tae sea, almost as if she thinks she can conjure him up."

Stefan thanked the woman and said repeatedly to himself, Lana St Clair, Lana St Clair. It was a beautiful name. Of course, he did not know what her married name was but that was her original name, and it was good enough for him. He made his way back to his ship named the Zeeland. His father, Ton Van Uden a wealthy Dutch Jute trader who had insisted that he had to learn the business by starting at the bottom, owned the ship. He was currently the purser of the ship, at the market to replenish the ship's stores.

Stefan made his way back to the quayside, pulling his cart with the provisions for the boat. They were sailing on the tide tomorrow for Danzig to deliver the Anstruther salted herring that was so popular in Poland and Prussia, then would return to his hometown of Rotterdam with the shipment of jute they had picked up from Dundee. He had already overseen the delivery of the barrels of salted herrings to the ship. It was hard work pulling the cart around mooring ropes, avoiding all the crowds of sailors, fishmongers and herring girls. The girls were the worst, as they were all quite bold and would shout to him. "Where are ye off to bonnie laddie? Would ye nae like to catch up with me tonight? I'll hold my horses for ye down by the Dreel."

He could feel the sweat running down his forehead and into his eyes and he stopped to wipe his forehead. But by the time he reached the ship and pulled the cart to the cookhouse he was drenched in sweat again and he could feel it running down his back and soaking into his clothes. He collected a bucket of water from the boiler and went to his cabin. He was glad that his father had provided him with his own cabin as it gave him a bit of privacy. He stripped off, threw his clothes in a laundry bag, pulled out the hipbath from under his bunk, poured the water in, climbed in and soaped himself all over. When he was satisfied that he no longer smelled of sweat, he washed his hair using a jug to pour the water over his head.

He climbed out and dried himself on a large scratchy towel, which was the standard ship issue, then he combed his wet hair pulling at the tangles. It was difficult to keep clean on board the ship as the conditions were so primitive and unsanitary. He longed to return home to his family house in Rotterdam where there was a proper bath, running hot water, servants to run the bath and best of all, fluffy towels.

Chapter Six

Lana and Moira headed down one of the narrow alleyways back to the quayside. The boys raced on ahead. On the way, they admired the panorama of secret gardens and roofs and passed by the building that had once housed the notorious gentleman's club,[**] The Beggars Benison

"Do you remember we used to giggle and wonder what the men got up to in there? We still don't know."

"Well, they were all wealthy men up to no good, that's for sure."

When the harbour came into sight, they could see the drifters they called Fifie boats with their two masts, used to catch the herring, bobbing up and down by the quayside. A strong smell of fish wafted in the air. The quayside was heaving with activity. On the pier, there were rows of troughs called *farlans* surrounded by the herring lassies dressed in long oilskin aprons, knee-high handmade boots and shawls tied around their heads.

"You'll never find Maggie in all that lot." Lana said.

[**]   See Note 2.

It was July, the middle of the summer herring season and girls had arrived from all over the country to seek employment gutting and salting the herring. They all had lodgings in the village and were a happy, lively group. They often had parties at weekends inviting all the local fishermen who provided the music with their fiddles and concertinas and many of them met their husbands that way. They were popular in the village as many households prospered from renting rooms to the girls. The local businesses in Anstruther thrived as they spent some of their wages in the shops buying what they could afford for their, 'fu kist', or bottom drawer. As they got nearer the pier, the hubbub grew louder with all the girls chatting, some singing and the seagulls wheeling and shrieking overhead. They suddenly heard a scream followed by a burst of laughter.

"Och the cheeky wee sod, he stole my herring. I was having a chat with my pal and took my eyes off the fish for a few seconds."

"Never mind hen, at least ye hadn't gutted it so it won't affect your count and wages."

The herring girl laughed good-naturedly amongst shouts of, "It's happened to me a few times." "Don't worry tis one of the hazards of the job."

Moira spotted Maggie at last and exclaimed, "There she is."

The girls always worked in a team of three, two gutters and one packer. Lana looked at the bandages the girls wrapped around their hands to protect them. The fisher girls gutted sixty fish a minute and so the risk of self-inflicted wounds was great, and these bindings called cloots protected any wounds from turning septic.

Lana shuddered as she looked at the cloots and was glad that she had decided not to work as a herring lassie.

Moira gave Maggie the message from her mother and as they left the quayside, they could hear strains of a herring song wafting through the air mixed with the background noise of the seagulls shrieking and cawing.

What shall we do with the herring's head?
We'll turn it into an abundance of bread
Herring's head, abundance of bread
and all sorts of things

Of all the fish that are in the sea
The herring's the king of the fish for me
Sing whack for the aira-li-do, whack for the aira-lee

The singing faded into the distance as the two girls walked back to the cottage in Anstruther Wester. Lana helped her sister to make supper. They fried the fish they had bought at the market throwing the haddock pieces, crawfish, crabmeat and prawns into a large skillet.

"Where are those tatties and neeps?" Moira asked.

"It's a good job ma is dead and can't hear you calling them that. She's probably turning in her grave after paying for us to be educated by a governess and speak well."

Lana smiled wistfully as she thought about her mother and father who were both dead. She remembered when the bank had collapsed and her Pa had lost his job, he seemed to lose interest in life after that and he died a year later. Her mother had grieved so much, and she died a few months later, some said of a broken heart. Lana sighed and took the vegetables out of the basket and the two sisters stood at the sink together peeling the potatoes and turnips. The thought of the man she had made eye contact with at the market soon cheered her up and she started to sing as she bustled around, setting the table.

"What on earth is the matter with you? First, you're sighing and now you sound happy."

"Yes, I am. We've had a lovely day together at the market," thinking to herself that perhaps she should confide in her sister about falling for a handsome stranger at the market. Then she remembered Grandma Ritchie's saying, "Aye keep a wee bit to yourself that ye would nae' tell to onnie" and she thought she had better keep quiet. Moira would probably try to find out about the man and invite him for dinner and that would be so embarrassing. No, she thought it would be better if she tried to find him herself and perhaps, she would go down to the harbour tomorrow and find out the name of any Dutch ships. She thought he was probably Dutch, as they bought and traded the herrings. They put the fish in a large dish and Moira covered it in a white sauce that she had made. Lastly, they piled the mashed potatoes on the fish, sprinkled breadcrumbs on top and put it in the oven to brown the top. Lana put the bannock on the breadboard and placed it on the table, together with some butter and cheese.

She poured out some milk for the two boys and placed bottles of ale and glasses on the table for the adults. Lana placed the steaming bowl of turnips on the table and laid five places. Moira went to the pantry and took out the bread-and-butter pudding that she had made earlier, placing it in the middle of the table. They did not follow the new fashion for serving each course separately and still ate in the old-fashioned way where they laid out all the courses on the table at the same time.

Ronald and James were playing with the kittens on the floor.

"Look Auntie Lana, "I'm teaching Boots to fight." James lifted his hand, swiped the black kitten with white feet that looked like boots and Boots pinged him back with his paw.

"But watch Bonnet she does the best sprongs,"

James put his hand on the floor and wiggled his fingers. The other kitten, which was black with a splash of white on her head that resembled a hat, skittered backwards and then launched herself in the air on all four legs landing on James's hand. Both boys laughed delightedly at the kitten's antics and Moira and Lana joined in.

"Right, you two, go and wash your hands and sit at the table, supper's ready.

Moira's husband Angus came in. She liked Angus and he was always cheerful and making jokes. She knew that the yard had encountered some problems with the boat they were building, and she opened a bottle of ale and handed it to him asking,

"Did you have a good day? How is the Saint Ninian coming along?

"Aye, there's still a wee problem but we'll finish it in time."

The food was good, and they all tucked in, the boys and Angus having second helpings.

"That was good, I'm stuffed." Angus said appreciatively as he patted his stomach. "Ye're making me fat, with yer wonderful cooking, woman."

"That means you'll have to play more football with us pa. If you run around, you'll get thinner." Ronald piped up.

Angus laughed good-naturedly, "Och, if I had to play football with ye two each time ye pester me, I'd be as skinny as a stick insect."

They sat around the table finishing their drinks until Moira got up and put the boys to bed. Lana cleared the table, her fingers lovingly stroking the old oak wood table that held so many happy memories of family meals when she and her sisters had been children. It felt so smooth and had a distinctive smell. Whimsically, she felt as if the table was passing its strength to her. She realised she had to stop her daydreaming and returning to reality, she started to wash the dishes so that Angus could dry them and put everything away. Lana felt at ease with Angus. He was a good man and worked hard at the shipyard, which she supposed was why he had become the foreman at so young an age. Although he left for work early, he always got up at half past five and polished everyone's shoes, even Lana's boots. They would find their shoes and boots laid out on a newspaper by the door, clean and shining every morning without fail.

He was forever teasing her, and tonight was no different. He used his nickname for her. "So, *Miss a Lana eous*, did ye nae find any miscellaneous cats, dogs or lame ducks today at the market?"

Lana laughed, as she did not think that you could describe her sailor as a lame duck, he looked far too healthy and robust, and she shook her head. "No, you're all right."

"Well, I can sleep soundly in my bed and nae be worried that I'll find a horse or donkey tethered on the back green in the morning. But lassie, I would'nae mind if ye could find me some wee stray hens."

"I'll see what I can do." Lana jokingly replied.

She knew Angus was referring to the two kittens that she had found abandoned in a ditch a few weeks ago and brought home. At first, Angus had said they could not keep them, but the boys pleaded with him, and he reluctantly gave in. They were no trouble and Angus now admitted that he loved them and even played with them. Suddenly she heard Ronald shouting down to her."

"Auntie Lana, "can you tell us one of your stories? I like the one about the Pirates."

"No, I like the one about the Ghost better", Jamie piped up.

"Well, I might just have a new one for you."

Once she had told them their story, the boys were drowsy and fell off to sleep so Lana went back downstairs. She felt restless and distracted and knew she would not be able to sleep. She sometimes talked to Robbie when she was alone, and she wanted to ask him if he would mind if she found a new man. So, when Angus said he was off to bed, she took the opportunity and taking her cloak from the peg behind the door she said,

"I'm just going for a walk down to the beach to clear my head, tell Moira not to wait up for me,"

She pulled the hood over her head and walked the few yards to the familiar beach. There was a full moon, which lit up the sand and the sea lapped gently on the shore. She could see the lighthouse on May Island as its beam swung round and there were myriads of stars lighting up the sky.

★ ★ ★

Stefan had decided that he would go down to the beach at Billow Ness tonight in the hope that he might meet Lana and make friends with her, so later that evening he looked in his locker and chose his favourite blue shirt and light brown trousers to wear. He picked out a patterned blue necktie and tied it in a bow round his neck to complete the outfit. Satisfied that he looked his best he went up to the 'tween deck or saloon for supper of the usual salt beef, ale and the inevitable ships biscuits. He chatted amicably with the other sailors and then said he was going out for a walk on the quayside.

There was a lot of joshing from the other sailors, "Oh, so you're looking for a sweet cherry to pluck are you boy?" "You mind those old herring lassies don't catch you first." "Make sure you pick a pretty girl and bring one back for me." Stefan just laughed good naturedly as he felt optimistic, and nothing could affect his high spirits.

He walked down the pier and the herring lassies were still working with oil lamps fixed on to the farlans. It must have been a good catch today as all the herring had to be salted when they were fresh and often the girls had to work until midnight to finish their work. One of the girls called out to him, "Och, it's a lucky lassie that's meetin' ye tonight."

★ ★ ★

Lana stared at the sea. It was smooth and unbroken by waves, there was not even a ripple, the moon reflected on its smooth surface like a mirror image. The water lapped gently on the shore. Usually, she felt comforted by the sound, but tonight there was a different atmosphere and it seemed menacing. A black cloud loomed across the sky covering the moon. It made the beach a dark place, no longer familiar but threatening. She saw a movement. Her stomach gave a lurch. She jumped and could hardly breathe. She had always been afraid of the dark and as a child had checked under the bed and in wardrobes before she put the light out and went to bed. Something was approaching. A figure loomed out of the shadows. Her heart beat faster until she realised with relief that it wasn't some evil phantom but it was him, the handsome stranger from the market and she gasped out,

"Oh, it's you", as if she had known him for years, "I thought you were the Black Lady."

"Who's she?"

"She's a ghost that haunts a house in Castle Street opposite the old Dreel Castle. I thought that as it was such a fine night, she might have fancied a walk along the beach to scare me half to death."

Stefan burst out laughing and Lana joined in his laughter relieved that she was not about to be attacked.

"Well, I'm not a ghost, I'm Stefan Van Uden and I am sorry Lana if I startled you."

"What are you doing here?"

"Sorry, I wanted to meet you. I am the purser on the Zeeland. The ship is sailing for Danzig and then on to Rotterdam tomorrow, so I had to come and find you tonight."

"How did you know my name and that I'd be on this beach?"

"Oh, I asked one of the stallholders in the market and she told me that her husband had seen you walking, alone on the beach at night. She told me about your husband, and I am sorry for your loss. It must have been terrible for you."

Lana hoped that no one had heard her shrieking Robbie's name at the sea as this was a private ritual and she would have felt embarrassed if it was common knowledge, a snippet of gossip. She did not like to be the object of pity.

She squared her shoulders and said,

"Thank you."

"The lady also told me about the donkey you rescued."

He took hold of her hand and they walked along the beach until they came to a low wall and sat down, looking out across the water.

Lana began to tell him the whole story about the donkey.

"My sisters and I saw old Mr McPherson out with his donkey. He was hitting it with a stick. The poor thing was lame and was braying pitifully. I was only eight, but I grabbed the stick and hit Mr McPherson with it. He snatched it back and I took the reins of the donkey and said, 'You're the *horribliest* man I've ever seen. He's so thin 'cos you probably don't feed him so I'm buying him'. My sisters Moira and Andrea started to laugh because there is no such word as *horibliest*. I had made it up. Then I grabbed the reins and ran down the road with the donkey. The old man chased after me shouting, 'Stop that lassie she's stealing ma donkey'. My two sisters chased down the street after Mr McPherson, the donkey and myself, shrieking with laughter. Lana started to laugh as she remembered, and Stefan joined in her laughter. She carried on telling how they had heard a whistle and Gordon, the night watchman, appeared. She told Stefan that she and her sisters had all thought, 'Oh no we're in trouble' and they had been surprised when Gordon had taken one look at them and instead of scolding them, he reprimanded Mr McPherson. He said that folk had noticed that he was mistreating his donkey, but none had had the courage to stop him until these three young lasses had stood up to him.

Then I told him I was not stealing Dobbin, but I had some money saved up in my tin at home and I was going to buy the donkey. Old MacPherson had said "You won't have enough. I want 10 shillings."

Lana carried on with the story relating that Gordon got out his wallet and said, 'Away with your bletherin. The donkeys lame and nae worth ten shillings. I'll give ye three shillings' and handed him the money. The old man's face was a picture. Then when we got home, Mum was shocked when she saw the donkey and local night watchman, who acted as the police officer for Anstruther.

She shouted at us, 'What trouble are you three in now and if you think you can keep that flea-bitten old donkey here in the garden you are wrong. How on earth are you going to feed the poor thing anyway?' and so I said,

'I shall put him in Farmer Duncan's field behind the house with his horses. He likes me and I know he will agree,'

My sister, Moira joined and said, 'I'll go round everyone and ask them for money every week. I'll sell everyone the idea that they can use the donkey'

Moira is brilliant, she loves organising tasks. It's what she does best, she had a book with how much each person was going to pay and she collected the money every week.

Mum said, 'Saints preserve us."

Lana held her stomach and laughed till the tears rolled down her face as she remembered her mother's horrified face.

In between giggles, Lana carried on telling the story and said,

"There wasn't enough money in our money pot, but we gave what we had to the policeman. We said we would pay the remainder later, but he was really nice about it and said it was alright as when Dobbin was recovered, he'd borrow him to pull a cartload of his mother's belongings when she moved to her sister's house in Pittenweem, in August."

Lana added that he was not called a police officer back in those days; he was called the night-watchman, paid for by all the rich residents of Anstruther and that they were lucky to have someone to keep the peace in our little village.

"So, it all worked out well. Even the local vet rallied round and trimmed the overgrown horn on the donkey's hoof and gave us some ointment for all his cuts and sores, so he was no longer in pain. When Dobbin was well again, someone knocked at the door every week to ask to borrow the donkey to move this or that somewhere. He became the community donkey. He's had a good life in the end and I'm so glad we rescued him and it's great that the farmer has taken him over and lets him live in his field in return for doing some work for him around the farm."

Stefan had been laughing all through her story and at the end, he laughed so much that it was infectious, and Lana joined in.

Then Stefan said, "I have also got a funny story, about an animal. I will share it with you. When I was, about nine years old we found a stray puppy in the town, I persuaded my father to let me keep him and we called him Sproet, which means a freckle as he had brown spots on his face. He went everywhere with me. He was always hungry although we fed him well. It was because when we found him, he was thin and starving and he never got over being a street dog, scavenging for food to stay alive and survive.

One day we were passing a butcher's shop and they had sausages on display on a stand outside just at the level of his head. He casually nibbled a sausage as he walked past but did not realise that it was on a string. Well, the butcher started to shout at him and chased after him yelling, 'Stop thief' so, of course he ran down the road with the string of about 20 sausages flying behind him. Everybody was pointing at him and laughing. He didn't stop till he got home and after I had made sure he was safe at home, I went back to the butchers and paid for the sausages."

They both laughed together. "I like your laugh and I like the way you speak. You have a Scottish accent, but I can understand you because you don't use any, hmm what's the word."

"Dialect"

"Oh yes, that's it, dialect. I can't always understand the funny Scottish words they use."

Lana laughed again, "Well when we were young my Pa was the manager of a bank in Kirkcaldy so we were lucky as we had a governess and both my sisters, and I can all read and write. Our family the St Clair's used to be landowners in Fifeshire, and my mother hoped that one of us would marry well and restore the family fortunes."

"I see, well instead of marrying a rich Scot perhaps you could marry a rich Dutchman. My father owns a shipping line and importing business."

Lana laughed again, "So you think I should marry your father."

"No, my family have money, my father wanted me to learn the business from the bottom and so that is why I am the purser on board the Zeeland and perhaps you could marry me."

Stefan realised his mistake immediately as he saw a shadow pass over Lana's face. He was going too fast.

"But I don't even know you."

"Yes, but you will get to know me. I come over to Anstruther every week to pick up the herring so we can meet."

"I'm going to Dundee in two days' time to work in the jute mills, so I won't be in Anstruther."

"That's even better, we pick up the jute cargo every week from Dundee and so I'll be able to see you. Just give me your address and I'll call on you."

Stefan took out a piece of paper and pencil from his jacket pocket and wrote down the address of Lana's aunt.

"I'll be back in Dundee on Friday, so I'll call for you then."

He caught hold of Lana's hand and they walked in companionable silence back to the house. He gave her a hug and kissed her on the cheek as he said goodbye. He would have liked to kiss her properly, but he realised he would have to be patient. He had noticed that her dress was clean but was old, worn, and almost threadbare in places, probably because she had dyed it black when she was widowed. It had the redeeming feature of a white collar and white cuffs, sewn on to comply with the fashion for a mourning dress but it was still very plain. It made no difference to him, but he thought she should be dressed in silk gowns, beautiful fur hats and capes.

Lana was in a dream when she went into the house and did not see Boots the kitten. She trod on his paw, and he squealed piteously. "Oh No", cried Lana and picked him up whispering, "Sorry, little one." into his ear as he put his nose up to hers and started to purr.

Moira heard the commotion and came downstairs. "Oh, it's you back; I thought we had a burglar."

Lana could not help herself and was grinning happily.

Moira looked at her sister's sparkling eyes and rosy cheeks, "You look as if you've caught a gold 'un with the silver," alluding to the herring that that were known as the silver.

"You could say that." The two sisters sat down at the table while Lana told her all about Stefan. Moira's eyes grew wider as she listened,

"That's wonderful; I told you that you would meet someone else."

Aye but I'm scared, I'm frightened to love someone again in case I lose him. I think I am cursed. I have already lost one husband to the sea and this man is a sailor too."

"But if his father is the ship owner, he'll soon be sitting behind a desk and won't go to sea."

"And I feel guilty about Robbie."

"Don't worry about Robbie, if he was here, he would say, 'I'm dead and you're still alive lassie. I do not want you to live your life alone and mourning for me. I'll be happy if you are happy.' That's what he would say and that's what I say too."

The two sisters made their way up to bed and Lana fell into a dreamless sleep as soon as her head touched the pillow. She had the best night's sleep she had had for months.

★ ★ ★

She was not the only one who slept soundly. Stefan skipped and almost danced back to the Zeeland moored in the harbour as if he had wings on his feet. He was deliriously happy. He had wondered if Lana would be a disappointment, but he thought as well as having a beautiful face she was also funny and sweet natured. There was an openness about her that he loved. He shouted out as he walked, "I think I'm falling in love. I love Lana St Clair." He wanted to carve her name on his boat. He calmed down as he walked up the gangplank and crept quietly to his cabin, but he couldn't resist humming a tune as he went and the captain stuck his head out of the door to his cabin,

"You sound happy; did you have a good time?"

"Oh yes, I've met the girl I'm going to marry."

"Well, your father might have something to say about that. I thought it was all planned that you were going to marry Antoinette Lemaire."

Stefan just smiled at him and said, "Everything's changed. I'm in love." He went into his cabin, threw his clothes off and fell into his hammock and into a deep sleep.

Chapter Seven

Lana woke up with a start and felt confused as for a moment could not work out where she was as all the surroundings were unfamiliar. Then she remembered she was in her aunt's house, and this was to be her first working day at the mill. She quickly washed, dressed in a lavender coloured gown she had brought with her. She had decided to throw away her black widow's dress as she thought, "It's the end of an era and a new start for me and my mourning is over." She went downstairs into the kitchen where she found her aunt making porridge.

"Here you are, lass, just what ye"ll need to set ye right for the day."

She finished her breakfast and Jessie and Maisie knocked on the door. Aunt Jeanie handed her a packed lunch, kissed her goodbye and wished her luck. As the three girls approached the mill, the road grew more crowded with workers making their way to the gates. Lana noticed that there were more women than men. They made their way through the doors and Jessie took her to Mr Wainwright's office. He handed her an apron saying,

"Hello Lana, welcome to Campertown Mill, Jessie will show ye what to do."

As they entered the factory, the noise of the machinery made an ear–splitting din.

Lana shouted, "How do you speak over that noise? It's deafening"

"Ye'll get used to it and we mime a lot", Jessie laughed, "Come on I'll show you where the privy is, then I'll introduce you to the other girls and show ye what to do."

As they walked past a bewildering range of machinery and workers Lana noticed that there were a lot of children working, some as young as nine or ten. There was even one, crawling under a machine cleaning it.

The girls worked as a team. Two went over to the weaving looms and collected the jute from the girls working there. They loaded it onto wheelbarrows and took it back to the finishing department, two more girls joined them, they spread the jute on to a large table and used large scissors to crop off the surplus fibres. The process continued by laying the jute on the pressing machines. When everyone was happy that it was perfect the machinery was switched on. The jute fed through large rollers under high pressure and came out the other end of the machine with a smooth pressed finish. Two more girls folded the finished jute and laid it on another table to be collected and packed.

The time seemed to pass quickly. There was a rhythm to the entire process and the girls laughed, shouted, or mimed over the sound of the machines. There was a feeling of camaraderie and the children who swept up the odd jute cuttings from the floor where they fell were included in this comradeship.

After the midday break, Lana spoke to a young boy sweeping the fibres round her feet, who reminded her of her nephews. He was wearing a jumper, darned at the elbows and she could tell that although his shoes were polished and shiny, they had seen better days.

"What's your name?"

He looked at her suspiciously, "Why do ye want to know?"

"Well, I'm new here and just started working at the mill today so I wanted to make friends."

"Us bairns are nae supposed to speak to yoos lassies in case it puts ye off your work and causes an accident. We do speak to some of yoos but me ma told me to nae trust anybody. She's right as some folk speak to the bairns and then report them to the manager and we get into trouble, sometimes they fine us. But this team is all right and you're all right too. Ah can tell."

"Well, I'm glad I'm all right. My name's Lana and I am a widow from Anstruther."

"I'm Jack and me ma is a widow like you. My father died in a coal mining accident in the Wemyss colliery, near Kirkcaldy. A fall of coal knocked out a prop and the roof fell on him and killed him. Me mam says I'm the wee boss now."

"Do you have any brothers or sisters?"

"I've got two wee brothers and three wee sisters, so we need the extra money I earn so we can all eat but its nae bad working here. Me ma works in the weaving department and did ye know that she was so proud when she was made a weaver that she wears her gloves when she leaves home, instead of putting them on when she gets tae the mill, so that folk know she's a weaver. It's the best job in the mill, did ye nae know that?"

Lana looked at the little boy and thought how sad it was that he should lose the innocence of childhood before he had even grown into an adult but then she had another thought that it wasn't so bad as maybe being wary would protect him from harm. Her sister always said to her, "You're too open and gullible, you should be careful, or you'll get hurt."

Lana had no more time for thoughts as there was a sudden hush and apart from the machinery, there was no sound. No one was talking or laughing.

"Uh oh, watch out. It's our Wullie. Wullie Campbell, he's the production manager and he sometimes honours us with a sudden visit. Don't trust him Lana, He's a snake."

Lana was amused that a ten-year-old boy was giving her advice and she gave a laugh as William Campbell approached her.

"Hello, well it's good to see that you're happy and settling in all right. I'm William Campbell, the production manager at the Mill. I believe you started here today and that your name is Lana St Clair."

Isla had seen Mr Campbell approaching and had left her station on the pretence of going to the privy, so that she could walk seductively past him. He always used to tell her that he loved the way she walked. She was still desperately in love with the man and could not understand why he had finished their relationship. Isla had been hoping to make him change his mind.

She washed her hair every morning before work and dabbed some of the precious Eau de Cologne perfume he had bought her on her body. She did not miss any opportunity to brush past him, but he seemed immune to her, and she was becoming increasingly incensed that he was ignoring her. She noticed that he looked especially handsome today and was wearing light coloured trousers, a cotton shirt and waistcoat with a cutaway morning coat. He was also wearing a flowered cravat and he had trimmed his moustache. He obviously wanted to create an impression on someone.

"I'm pleased to meet you Mr Campbell." Lana said as she shook the hand that Mr Campbell was holding out to her, and she did not notice Isla staring at both of them.

"Ye've got a prestigious name there. Did ye know that you're descended from the Earls of Orkney and Caithness.

"Yes, our mother always told us that the St Clair family owned a lot of land in Fifeshire at one time. My married name is Wallace, but I have reverted to my maiden name."

William Campbell studied Lana. He had felt compelled to see her after just catching a glimpse of her last week and he was not disappointed. He thought, "She is even lovelier than I thought; nice white teeth, good complexion, wonderful hair and beautiful eyes." He assessed her as if he was about to purchase a prize racehorse. She's perfect, he thought.

Isla knew what "her Wullie" as she called him was up to as soon as he had appeared on the factory floor and approached Lana. Why, it was the same pattern as always. Well, she would show him. How could he tell her he loved her and that she was his darling and then just abandon her? She was incensed. This was not going to happen to her. She absolutely loved him, and she was going to fight to keep him.

She was not usually a vindictive person. She had always been the girl that boys asked to dance first and if she liked a boy, he always asked if he could meet her again. She studied Wullie's face as he looked at Lana and felt sick with resentment. She had experienced jealousy before when she had noticed Wullies interest in Wilma. As the emotion flooded through her body, she knew she would have to get rid of this rival, just as she had got rid of Wilma. She was not going to sit back and let that stuck-up strumpet take her man. She had already killed one lass to keep him and if she had to kill another one, then so be it.

Chapter Eight

Lana was happier than she had been for many months. Jessie's popularity amongst the girls had ensured that she was not only accepted but also well liked. It was as if there was a golden glow of sunlight over Jessie, which spread over her too. Every morning the other girls called out greetings to her.

"Good mornin' how's it going Lana?"

"How's your Auntie Jeanie? She's a good old soul. Does she aye bake those bonnie cakes of hers?"

Lana had learnt everyone's name and soon knew all about their lives. There were four young single girls, Jessie, Maisie, Aggie and Frances and the two others in their team were Mairi and Shona who were a little older and married. Mairi had two children and her mother looked after them while she was at work. Shona had five children and her eldest daughter, who was twelve, looked after the younger children while her second eldest daughter Isobel, aged ten, was a sweeper at the mill.

There was one girl, however, who always glared at her. Lana could not understand what she had done. She had noticed her before as she was pretty, with blonde curls and a flower bud shaped mouth, or at least Lana thought she would be pretty if she were not always scowling. Lana had smiled at her a few times during the week but she had always glowered back at her and so she had given up trying to be pleasant. Lana was curious. Why was this girl so unfriendly when everyone else was very agreeable?

As well as learning about the other girls, she also had been curious to learn more about the jute trade. The foreman, Mr Wainwright, was always amenable and so one morning Lana had waylaid him.

"Mr Wainwright, what is jute actually used for?"

"Well Lana, that's nae an easy question for it's a fabric of a thousand uses for everything from clothing to flooring and from deck chairs to explosive fuses! It's even used for the pioneers' wagons in the American west and our Navy makes ropes with it. World trade relies on it as sacking and of course it's vital in wartime as it's made into tents, gun covers, sandbags and horse blankets."

"But if it's so important why are all the jute mills in Dundee. Why don't they take it to London?"

"Och, well lassie, that's a fair question and ye see it's because Dundee has the whaling industry. Ye see whale oil is used to soften the jute and tis a vital part of the manufacturing process, so the Dutch East India Company bring the raw jute here and we make it into useable material. It just woud'nae be any use to take it anywhere else 'cos they'd have to import whale oil."

Mr Wainwright seemed pleased to answer her questions and he didn't notice her expression darkening when he mentioned the whaling industry.

"Thank you, Mr Wainwright, I appreciate you answering my questions, but I'll go back to work now."

Lana suppressed a sigh as the mention of the whaling industry had touched a raw spot and made her think about Robbie, but it also solved the mystery around the smell in the streets of Dundee that she had failed to recognise. It was whale oil. She thought how silly she was not to have known this, as she had smelt it so many times on Robbie's clothes when he came back from his whaling expeditions. She went back to join the other girls and soon brightened up as there was always cheerful banter going on.

It was not long before the midday break bell went and Aggie said,

"Come and sit with us to eat your lunch, Lana. Dinnae go with that Jessie and Maisie, they're rubbish."

Lana shook her head and Aggie replied,

"Och well, we'll just have to come and sit with you three, then."

"Who says ye can sit with us you bawheid? "Jessie teased but when she saw Aggie's crestfallen face, she said,

"Only joking, we'll all sit together and have a jolly good gossip."

It was Friday and all the girls were in good spirits as they had Saturday afternoon and Sunday to look forward to and after they had all eaten their packed meals.

Jessie asked. "Would ye like to come to the dance with us on Saturday night, Lana? Its being held at the Dundee Arms in the High Street, there'll be fiddlers and pipers and all, so it should be a good laugh."

Lana did not know what to say as her Dutchman, Stefan, had promised that he would arrive this evening and she did not know whether to confide in the girls. She took a deep breath,

Will it be all right if I bring someone with me?"

"Och, I didnae know that ye knew any men in Dundee", Shona said.

"He's not from Dundee. He is a Dutch sailor called Stefan who I met in Anstruther last week. He is coming here today to collect a cargo of jute and will be in Dundee for the Saturday and Sunday before he sails back to Anstruther to pick up a consignment of salted herring."

"Och, a sailor boy ye say, ye'd better be careful Lana, you know what these sailors are like they have a girl in every port, and he probably thinks 'cos ye're a widow that ye'll be easy prey," Mairi remarked with a cynical laugh.

"No, you're wrong; he's not like that at all. He's genuine."

"Yeah, a genuine wee liar", Mairi snapped back.

"Give the lassie a break, will ye, can ye nae just be happy for her that she's got a sweetheart," Maisie said, speaking up in Lana's defence.

"So, Lana, Whit's he like yon Stefan?" asked Aggie.

"Oh, he's tall and blond with lovely blue eyes and I think that he's beautiful." Lana said and just talking about him made her get butterflies in her stomach.

"So, he's a handsome laddie, then,"

"Yes, and he's funny and kind,"

"He sounds too good to be true," Mairi countered.

"Will ye nae be so mean spirited Mairi," Jessie exclaimed.

"It's Lana's business and if she likes the man, it's up to her. She didnae ask for yer opinion so just keep quiet."

All the girls supported Jessie and Aggie said, "Ah will look forward to meetin' him."

"Ah will look forward to seeing if he arrives," Mairi said.

"Stop yer bletherin Mairi or ye'll turn into a crabbit old woman."

The bell went to signal the end of the lunch break and they all got up to return to work. The mill was noisy, but the girls sang songs, while they worked, the most popular one called not surprisingly, the jute mill song. Lana sang along with all the other girls in her team to celebrate the end of the working week.

Oh, dear me, the mill's gannin' fast,
The puir wee shifters canna get a rest,
hiftin' bobbins coorse and fine,
They fairly mak' ye work for your ten and nine.

"Nae long to go now Lana and ye will have finished your first week," Jessie said

"We all go down to the pay office in shifts to collect our wages. We're at the end of the line so we go last with the weavers and Mr Wainwright will tell us when it's our turn but tell me, Ah can't help thinking that there's more to Stefan than ye are letting on."

"Why do you think that?" Lana replied innocently.

"Well, I dinna think that an ordinary sailor woud know when the ship was coming to Dundee. Ah think he must be the captain."

Lana laughed at Jessie's shrewdness and decided that there was no harm in confiding in her. "Well, he's more than that. He is the son of the ship owner; His family is extraordinarily rich as they own a fleet of ships and run an importing business. His father wanted him to learn the business from the bottom up, so he is the purser on the ship now.

"Crivens, ye have fallen on yer feet lassie. Good luck to ye."

Mr Wainwright told the girls from the finishing department that it was time to collect their wages and so they all headed for the pay office. Lana followed all her friends. As they passed the pressing machines, Lana noticed through the steam still rising from the silent presses that the girl from the weaving department who appeared not to like her, was waiting for someone. Lana said, "Excuse me" and brushed past the girl and then to her horror she seemed to trip over something, she missed her footing and she fell towards the steaming press. Lana gave a scream as she could feel the heat rising from the press as she tumbled towards it and although she knew it was burning hot, she put her hands out to save herself.

Chapter Nine

Lana felt herself grabbed and fell backwards on to something soft. She took a deep breath, realised that she was lying on a body and moved her head to see that it was Mr Wainwright. She hastily scrambled to her feet.

"Are ye aright lassie?"

"Yes, thank you Mr Wainwright, you saved me from getting burnt."

All the other girls ran back to Lana asking what had happened and they were all talking at once, so it made quite a commotion. Mr Campbell disturbed by the rumpus came out of his office and seeing Lana in the centre of the furore he dashed down the stairs from his office to check what had happened.

Isla slunk away and no one noticed her apart from Leslie, Jack's mother, who was just as puzzled and concerned as all the other girls were. Leslie did not join the group gathered around Lana but stood back and so she noticed the acid ill-tempered expression on Isla's face. She realised that she had tripped Lana up, on purpose. She could not understand why she had a grudge against Lana but promised herself to tell Jack so that he could warn Lana about Isla.

The girls all started to talk at once and Mr Campbell could not make any sense of it all.

"Will you all quieten down please? Now Lana, you tell me what happened?"

"I must have tripped, I thought I was going to fall on to the pressing machine, but Mr Wainwright caught me and saved me."

"You poor wee lassie, you'd better have a tot of whisky for the shock." He pulled out a hip flask from his pocket. "Can someone get a cup or a glass?"

The glass produced, Lana gasped as she took a sip of the whisky and felt it burning her throat. She carried on sipping and soon the warmth from the spirit seemed to spread throughout her body and she felt better. Isla saw her ex-lover rush down and make a fuss of Lana but when he passed her and he did not even notice her, her face turned red as if she was on fire inside and her anger burned. She muttered to herself as she hurried away.

"Why that brazen hussy, she's stealing mah Wullie. She thinks she's so high'n' mighty with her auld reekie accent. How fur dare she. Ah knew he liked her for he's always staring at her at every opportunity but I just dinnae know what he sees in her, I'm much prettier than she is. I'll show her. I'll get even with her somehow. I can make sure she has an accident. She'll be sorry. If she's nae so good looking or crippled, he won't want her anymore and he'll come back to me."

Jessie said, "Maisie and I will collect yer wages for you, Lana" and they sped off. When they returned Mr Campbell was suggesting that he took Lana home in his carriage, but Lana told him that she did not want any more fuss made and that Jessie and Maisie would walk her home as they did every evening.

The girls set off and took their usual route and as there were crowds of people already on the streets, mixed with the mill girls walking home they did not notice Isla. When they reached Aunt Jeanie's home, Isla gave a smug smile to herself, as she now knew where her rival lived and thought she would come back tomorrow night and follow Lana to the dance. After all, there might be an opportunity to push her under a horse-drawn carriage. Her smile broadened into a grin, and she laughed aloud as she imagined Lana lying on the ground injured, her blood pulsing out of her and her life ebbing away.

As Lana opened the door, the house smelt different, somehow. There was a strange atmosphere, and this combined with a salty smell made her think something must be wrong.

Chapter Ten

Jeanie came down the hall looking flustered and wearing her best dress, which confirmed her suspicions. Her heart gave a flip as she wondered if it could be that Stefan, the man she had dreamed about all week, had actually turned up.

"You look nice, Auntie but why are you all dressed up?"

Before her aunt could reply to her question, she had the answer as Stefan appeared at the door of the kitchen. Lana, not used to drinking, was feeling a bit tipsy from the whisky that Mr Cameron had given her, and she gave a shriek and flung herself into Stefan's arms.

Stefan, who had not been expecting such a warm welcome, was surprised, and twirled her round in the hall. Lana was overwhelmed to see him and the whisky dispersing her usual decorum, she boldly put her hands on his face and kissed him. She felt the world spinning round her. Her stomach was doing somersaults and she felt as if she could kiss Stefan forever. But at last, she pulled away from the kiss, giggled and said,

"Jessie, Maisie, May I introduce Stefan, I'm sorry I've forgotten his surname" and she gave a hiccup and giggled again,

"Stefan, these are my friends Jessie and Maisie and oh, you've already met my Aunt Jeanie."

"My name is Stefan Van Uden, and I am very pleased to meet you."

"We are chuffed to catch up with ye too, Lana has told us all about you." Jessie replied, always the spokesperson.

"Only good things I hope."

"Aye, she was hoping ye'd turn up in time to go to the dance tomorrow. It's at the Kings Arms. There'll be food, drink, music, and dancing, it should be a good party."

"I'll be pleased to come with Lana and look forward to seeing you there."

"That's brilliant; we'd better be going so see ye tomorrow. See ye later Jeanie and see ye later Lana and Stefan."

Jessie and Maisie walked arm in arm down the road.

"Well, Lana wasnae wrong when she said he was good looking."

"Aye, He is a fantastic enough fellow, and he seems to be fond of Lana."

"Ah would say he's more than just fond, did ye no see the way he looked at her?"

"Och aye, so there could be wedding bells soon."

When the door closed, Stefan went back into the dining room and brought out a rectangular box.

"This is for you, Lana."

She opened the box and found layers of tissue paper and when she peeled them back, she gasped in pleasure as she saw that Stefan had brought her a blue gown and it was just the colour she loved. She pulled it out and held it up to her.

"How did you know that blue was my favourite colour? How did you know what size I am? I hope it fits."

"I chose blue to match your eyes and my sister helped me. We went to the seamstress and as I thought you were about the same size as her, the seamstress used her measurements. So, I hope it fits you too."

Auntie Jeannie looked shocked. It was not considered the proper convention for a man to give a woman presents before they were engaged to be married but she could see that Stefan was a gentleman and so she relaxed and said,

"Och, go and try it on and I'll set the table for supper. Did ye know that the dear laddie has bought me presents too, some chocolates and a bottle of wine that I will open? I've put the hot water in a bowl in your room so ye can have yer usual wash and brush up before supper."

Jeanie fussed around and picked up the discarded box bustling into the kitchen clearly overcome with all the excitement.

Lana went upstairs and stripped off her working clothes. She used the hot water Aunt Jeanie had left in a bowl to have a strip wash and even washed her private parts between her legs. She thought to herself that she wanted to smell fresh for Stefan and as she dried herself, she giggled as she thought you never knew what might happen. She slipped the dress over her head but could not do up the buttons at the back. It seemed to fit perfectly, and she loosened her hair from the ponytail and brushed it out. She looked in the mirror and saw that her cheeks were flushed which gave her a rosy glow, so she bit her lips to make them redder. Satisfied that she looked her best she went downstairs and Stefan's face broke into a grin and Aunt Jeanie gasped.

"You look beautiful." Stefan said.

"Thank you, it does fit me, but I couldn't do up the buttons on the bodice up at the back. Auntie Jeanie, can you do them up for me?"

Auntie Jeanie fastened the buttons and Lana did a twirl.

"I love it, I love it" she giggled, "Thank you Stefan It's the best present I've ever had."

"The dress looks bonnie and the colour suits ye. I've never seen ye look so bonnie."

Jeanie ushered them into the dining room where she had arranged the table, lit the oil lamps, and even lit some candles. Lana and Stefan sat at the table. Jeanie came back from the kitchen carrying a steaming pot of stew, placed it on a trivet and went back to bring in another smaller dish. When she returned, she handed Stefan a bottle opener and he opened the bottle of wine and poured it out into the tumblers Jeanie had put on the table beside each place.

"I'm sorry I dinnae have any proper wine glasses."

"That's alright, the wine tastes the same whatever glass it's served in," Stefan replied smiling at Jeanie.

Jeanie began to relax and served out the lamb stew together with the rumbledethumps she had made from the left-over vegetables from the day before. They were soon all chatting away and enjoying the food. Stefan particularly enjoyed the meal and when he had finished, he said,

"That was a wonderful meal. I loved the lamb stew and what do you call the other dish motioning towards the smaller dish?"

"Rumbledethumps."

"Rumble thumps"

Lana started to giggle, "No, silly, rumble de thumps", she said emphasising every syllable.

"It's a very funny word. What is it made of? I would like the recipe and I can give it to our cook to make at home."

Aunt Jeanie's eyes widened, "Ye have a cook?"

"Yes, a cook and a housekeeper, two maids and a gardener."

Jeanie's eyes grew even wider.

"I told Lana, my family own a shipping line and trade in jute and herring. My father wanted me to learn about his business from the bottom up and so I'm the purser on one of our boats at the moment."

"Well, Lana didn't mention that." Jeanie looked flustered again and covered her discomfiture by collecting up the empty plates and disappearing into the kitchen. She reappeared with a bowl, a pot of cream and three dishes.

"Scottish raspberries", she said with pride as she served out the desert.

When they had finished the raspberries, Jeanie addressed them both.

"Away ye go the pair of ye, go for a walk, it's a lovely evening. I'll wash and dry the dishes."

"No, I won't hear of it. We'll both help and with the three of us the work will be finished in no time."

"Ach weel, thank ye, ye've a kind heart."

As they worked, they chatted about Stefan's boat and when everything was put away Lana took her cloak off the peg by the door and she and Stefan walked down the path hand in hand.

Aunt Jeanie watched them from the door and a tear glistened in her eye as she thought how pleased she was that Lana had found such a handsome and kind man to replace her late husband. She thought, 'The lassie deserves some pure happiness with all she's been through.'

Lana told Stefan all about her first week at the mill and all the new friends she had made.

Stefan was interested and smiled at all her tales but said, "You shouldn't have to work at the mill, if you married me, you could lead a life of leisure in Rotterdam. I know that you don't know me very well, but I know that I love you, so will you marry me, Lana?"

Lana forgot her earlier reservations and did not hesitate, "I think I fell in love with you at first sight in the market, but your proposal is so sudden that I would like to think about it."

Seeing his crestfallen face, she added, "I'll give you my answer tomorrow."

Chapter Eleven

On the Saturday night, Lana took the bowl of hot water that Aunt Jeanie had given her, upstairs and carefully washed herself all over. When she had dried herself, she put on the dress that Stefan had bought her, and Aunt Jeannie did the buttons up at the back.

"Shall I do your hair for ye?"

"Oh, that will be wonderful; I remember how you used to do my hair when I was little."

While Jeanie did her hair, Lana told her about Stefan's proposal of marriage and asked her aunts advice.

Well, it's a bit sudden but I think I'm a good judge of character and I would say you've found a good man there."

"But I haven't met any of his family or friends."

"Aye, there is that but see what your friend's think of him tonight and if they all like him, I think you should say yes."

Lana nodded and as Auntie Jeanie had finished doing her hair, she took her new hat from its box that Stefan had bought from the shop on the High Street when he had met her at the mill on Saturday afternoon to walk her home. As soon as he had seen it, he insisted on buying it for her as it matched the dress perfectly. She perched it on her head.

"How do I look?"

"You look so beautiful that you'll be the belle of the ball."

There was a knock at the door and Lana ran to open it, but her face fell and her mouth opened in surprise when she saw it was a police officer and not Stefan.

"Sorry to trouble ye, lassie but we're doing a house-to-house enquiry. A sailor was murdered in the next street, and we are asking if anybody saw anything last night between ten o' clock and midnight."

"Oh, how terrible. I have heard that there has been a spate of murders in Dundee. All sailors I believe. Do you know who he was?"

"Yes, he was a Scots sailor this time, but the murderer does nae discriminate there have been Polish, Irish and even Russian. He sometimes drags the body into the Tay but this time he left the poor laddie in the street."

Lana told the police officer that both Auntie Jean and herself had been in bed and had not seen or heard anything unusual. The police officer thanked her and went on his way calling at the next house.

★ ★ ★

Isla walked cautiously as she approached the house where Lana lived. She crossed the road and was going to hide behind a tree while she watched the house but changed her mind as she thought she would look suspicious, especially as there was a police officer knocking at all the doors along the street.

She looked around and saw some bushes, which would have provided excellent cover, but they were in someone's front garden. She thought that if the owner of the house saw her, they would come out, tell her to clear off and cause a rumpus that she did not want. In the end, she decided to sit on a wall in plain sight, as if she were tired and resting. She had thought through ways to get rid of her rival. She knew she could not use arsenic again as it would be too much of a coincidence and anyway as Lana did not live in the tenement block it would be too difficult to use poison at the mill. So, she planned that if the streets were crowded and an opportunity arose, she would shove Lana off the pavement in front of a speeding horse and carriage.

She smiled to herself as she saw Jessie and Maisie knock at the door. She had not had to wait long at all. Lana opened the door and Isla studied her jealously as she was wearing a beautiful blue dress in the latest fashion. 'Where did she get that dress?' Isla wondered. Then she noticed the blue hat that matched the dress perfectly, Why wasn't that the same hat that was in the milliner's window in the High Street, that she had coveted herself? 'How on earth did that stuck-up strumpet buy that hat?' she mused.

She had suggested to William that perhaps he could buy it for her and another jealous pang struck her that he had bought it for Lana instead of her. She became even more convinced that William had given the hat to Lana as a gift as she thought that Lana had only been at work for one week and she couldn't possibly have saved up the money to purchase it, herself. She had to admit grudgingly that Lana looked very fetching in the hat but all the same, she thought, 'it would suit me better with my blonde curls and blue eyes.' She had no more time to speculate as a tall blond young man followed Lana out of the house. Isla's jaw dropped as she realised that the man's presence might put an end to her plans to push Lana into the road, because the man always walked on the outside.

"Who was he?" Isla wondered. "A brother perhaps but they did not look alike." Then he put his arm around Lana, she smiled at him and he kissed her lightly on the lips. Watching that little scene Isla started to grin as she thought, 'Why she already has a sweetheart. That is even better. I cannot wait to tell Wullie and see his face. He doesn't stand a chance. Lana is obviously smitten with this handsome laddie.'

She resolved to find out more about Lana's beau so that William would feel the pangs of jealousy that she had felt. Oh yes, she was looking forward to making him suffer. She smiled thinking how revenge was so sweet tasting, little knowing that unfortunately she would never have the opportunity to taste it. She checked that she had her little notebook in her bag so that she could be sure of writing down all the details she could find out about Lana's beau to tell William and rub his nose in it.

Chapter Twelve

Lana walked arm in arm with Stefan in the crowd of other revellers as they left the public house. Everyone was in high spirits talking and laughing about the evening. She could only remember being so happy at her wedding with Robbie and felt a pang of sorrow and tension as she thought of the golden days she had spent with her husband. It was more than sorrow, as she felt guilty that she could feel so happy when Robbie was dead. Then she remembered her sister's words that Robbie would want her to be happy and she relaxed and smiled thinking that maybe he had sent Stefan to her. She mouthed a silent thank you towards the night sky and started to laugh at her fanciful thoughts.

"What is it?"

"I was remembering you dancing the Eightsome Reel," and they both burst into fits of giggles. Lana thought what a wonderful man he was to be able to laugh at himself.

"You looked like a boat that had come adrift from its moorings in a storm, tossed from wave to wave."

"I didn't know Scottish dancing was so complicated."

"But you soon got the hang of it and you did the Gay Gordons perfectly, you were as good as all the other lads."

"Well, I had the most beautiful and graceful partner."

"Yes, this evening has really been good fun and all my friends liked you."

Lana realised how important this was because before she had met Stefan's own family and friends, she only had her own common sense on which to judge Stefan's character.

"Yes, I too liked all your friends, especially your cousin Jessie, she's really funny."

Lana thought back to the evening and thought how everybody seemed to be so happy. Why, she thought even the blonde girl who had glowered at her all the time at the mill had been friendly. She had wanted to know all about Stefan and Lana had recounted how she had met him and that he was a Dutch sailor who had had her dress made especially for her in Rotterdam. She told her that she knew it was not socially acceptable for a man to give a girl gifts, but her aunt had sanctioned the present as thought Stefan was respectable and honourable.

She didn't tell Isla that he was in fact the son of a Dutch ship owner and Jute trader or that he was just serving an apprenticeship and would eventually join his father running the business. Nor did she mention that he was rich, or would be one day, as she thought it would seem as if she was boasting.

She did tell her that they had gone for a walk in the town that day and passed the milliners shop and that Stefan had insisted that he buy her the hat as it matched the dress perfectly. She had decided to accept Stefan's proposal of marriage and told Isla that she would be leaving the mill when she married Stefan. She was surprised that Isla seemed to be overjoyed for her, but she just thought, 'Everybody likes a romantic tale with a happy ending.'

When they reached Lana's house, all the girls waved goodbye, and Lana and Stefan were alone. Stefan put his arms around her and kissed her passionately. Lana was in turmoil as the kiss had awoken desire that had lain dormant, and she knew that she wanted Stefan to make love to her. As she snuggled up to him, she could feel his hardness through his breeches. She wondered if she could sneak him into her room upstairs.

"I would ask you to come back to my ship with me, but I know that some of my crew will be there, so it would be embarrassing for you. No, I shall send them all off on errands tomorrow, come and collect you in the morning. I'll show you round the boat and then you can try some Dutch gin in my cabin."

Stefan broke away from her abruptly and Lana realised how difficult it was for him.

"I've got a better idea. We can go for a walk in the fields behind the town and take a picnic. I'm sure we can find a secluded spot."

"Yes, that sounds even better. I'll see you in the morning at about ten." Stefan kissed her lightly on the lips again and waved goodbye as he set off down the street towards the harbour.

Neither Lana nor Stefan saw Isla following him. She had decided to find out the name of his ship so that she could tell William and really rub his nose in it. She couldn't wait to see his face when she told him about Lana and Stefan. She walked quietly, almost on tiptoes and as she merged into the shadows, she thought how clever she had been. She didn't realise that by following Stefan, she had not been clever at all.

As they approached the harbour, a mist swirled in from the river carried by a slight breeze. Isla shivered involuntarily as the temperature seemed to go down by a few degrees. It was dark, the fog blocking out the gas streetlights. The fog sucked out all sound from the area and a strange quietness prevailed. The distant sound of revellers disappeared. The sound of Stefan and Isla's footsteps were muted. It was eerie and Isla was frightened and felt the fog had an entity of its own. It was a living breathing beast, just stalking its prey waiting to attack. She did not realise that there was an actual monster lurking in the shadows and was horrified as the monster became real and materialised.

A figure dressed in black soundlessly crept out of the fog and she realised Stefan was about to be attacked. Thoughts flashed through her mind that if Stefan was hurt or even killed it would leave Lana vulnerable and her Wullie would take advantage and comfort her. Isla would definitely lose him then. 'Oh, no', she thought, 'I can't have that.' and she leapt forward and grabbed the dark figure's cloak.

She was so intent on helping Stefan that she didn't see the flash of steel in the attacker's hand until it was too late. She felt the blade pass over her throat and to her surprise she felt blood pumping out from the wound as she fell to the pavement. Blood spurted from her carotid artery, and she lost consciousness, so she didn't feel anything when her attacker dragged her over the cobblestones and heaved her into the river. A foghorn sounded mournfully masking the splash of Isla's body as she hit the water.

Stefan was unaware that he had narrowly escaped losing his life and that ironically a girl who had wanted to harm and even murder his beloved Lana had saved it. Muffled by the fog, Stefan did not hear Isla's faint cry for help when the shock of hitting the freezing water momentarily brought her back to awareness that she was about to die. Isla took her last breath, her dress filled with water, ballooned out and the current carried her like a ship in full sail on her final voyage, her blonde curls streaming out behind her like a flag. Stefan carried on walking and whistling and boarded the Zeeland while the black cloaked figure stealthily slipped into an alley and disappeared.

Chapter Thirteen

S tefan grabbed Lana's hand and pulled her with him as he ran down the grassy slope. She gasped and then laughed with exhilaration as they reached the bottom of the hill.

"This looks a good spot for our picnic"

Lana gazed at the large meadow filled with long grass and wildflowers.

"Oh yes, we can make a camp in the grass just like we used to do when I was young."

They waded into the long grass, flattening it when they thought they had gone far enough, hidden from anyone's view. Lana spread the blanket out that she had brought with her for the picnic and opened the picnic basket. Then she opened all the little packages that Aunt Jeanie had prepared. There were ham sandwiches, scotch pies, pieces of cooked chicken, salad, mayonnaises and pickles together with some small sponge cakes and bottles of ginger beer.

"It's a feast, not a picnic."

Lana laughed as she carefully removed the stopper from the bottle containing the ginger beer and poured it into the two cups from the basket.

"Well, you know what my Aunt Jeanie and Scottish hospitality are like now!"

They clinked their cups together, Stefan chose a scotch pie to start and as he bit into it he said,

"Mmm, this is wonderful, what sort of pie is it?"

"Oh, that's called a scotch pie and has been around since the middle ages. It's made with pastry of course and spiced mutton. In the middle ages, the church frowned on them and said they were a luxurious, decadent English style of food. But I think they were so cheap to make, and mutton has always been plentiful in Scotland that they survived all the church's criticism, and they are part of folk's staple diet."

"I've seen people selling them in Anstruther in the market, but I didn't ever buy one but now I know how delicious they are, I will."

They sat enjoying the rest of the picnic and when they had finished eating Lana swept away all the crumbs and tidied away all the empty bags into the picnic basket. They lay back on the blanket enjoying the late October sun. Stefan bent over and enfolded Lana in his arms. The pins fell from her hair and it escaped falling in glossy curls about her face. Stefan brushed it away from her face and kissed her slowly on the lips. Lana looked at Stefan,

"You are the most beautiful man I have ever seen."

Stefan gazed down at her, her cheeks were rosy from the late October sun and with her hair spread out around her he thought he had never seen anyone so pretty.

"You are so beautiful too."

Lana started to giggle.

"What?"

"We sound like a mutual admiration society."

Stefan joined in her laughter and holding her tightly he suddenly kissed her laughing open mouth. Wrapped in each other's arms she kissed him back passionately. She sucked his tongue, bit his lips and thrust her hands under his shirt rubbing her palms against his chest.

He put his hand under her dress, stroked her thigh and slowly pulled up her long skirt. She was wearing long cotton under-drawers. He touched her legs through the material and then moved it to where her thighs met. He found the fastening drawstring at the waist of the under-drawers and untied the bow pulling then gently down. Lana feverishly helped to remove them. Then she unbuttoned his breeches and pulled them off. He moved his hand between her legs exploring her with his hand. She parted her legs and groaned. Stefan lay on top of her.

"Should we do this? Suppose I get pregnant?"

"Well, you have accepted my proposal of marriage and we'll be married in a few weeks, so you don't need to worry. If you become pregnant, I will be thrilled, and the baby will just have to be born a little premature."

Lana felt as if she would explode with desire and the thought of having Stefan's baby excited her even more. "Oh yes," she thought, "Make love to me and give me a baby who looks just like you."

She grasped his hips and pulled him into her raising herself slightly at the same time and she felt his hardness enter her. Lana couldn't help thinking about her late husband and thought it hadn't been like this with Robbie. Her feelings were more intense as she gave herself to Stefan. Stefan pushed in and out more quickly and she moved in time with him. They both reached a crescendo at the same time crying each other's names in sheer delight. Stefan held Lana's face between his hands and kissed her long and hard on the lips as he wanted to show her that because the physical act was over, it made no difference to the way he felt about her.

Lana still felt insecure. "You must think badly of me, being so easy."

"Lana, I will never think badly of you, I love you, I want to marry you and spend the rest of my life with you. I'll tell my father when I return to Rotterdam. He wants me to marry Antoinette Lemaire, the daughter of another shipping magnate to amalgamate our businesses. I've known her since I was a boy, and she is lovely but she's like a sister to me. I could never love her the way that I love you so my father will just have to accept that I will make my own choice of a bride."

"Oh dear, I don't want to be the cause of a rift between you and your father."

"No, it will be alright. My sister, Mariella, will help me persuade him. She's always on my side. We will get married in Anstruther so that your sisters will be there, and I'll arrange for all my family to come and stay at one of the local inns.

"Oh, my goodness. Where will we live?"

"Well I thought I would have a house built in the grounds of my father's estate and then I will buy a small house in Anstruther so that we can come and stay, and you can see your sisters, your family and friends."

Lana sat up with a look of astonishment on her face which turned to an enormous grin, "You've got it all worked out haven't you? It sounds wonderful, almost too good to be true so I can't help but worry that something will go wrong," she said, little realising how prophetic her words would be.

Chapter Fourteen

Lana had said goodbye to Stefan on Sunday night as his ship would set sail on the tide of Monday morning. He would be back on the following Friday and had promised to take her out for supper that same evening.

As Lana, Jessie and Maisie approached the mill on Monday morning, they could tell that something was wrong. There were groups of girls outside the factory and every so often one of the girls would run from one group over to another group. There was a strange tense atmosphere. It was unusual as there was the familiar noise of chattering voices but no laughter. They walked up to a group of girls and asked what was going on.

"It's Isla, she has disappeared."

One of the girls who lived in the same tenement accommodation owned by the mill owners said that she hadn't come home after the ceilidh on Saturday night, and no one had seen her since then. She had reported her missing to the Dundee City Constabulary, police officers had arrived a few minutes ago who had gone to see Mr Campbell. Somebody had found her purse down by the docks with a notebook with Mr Campbell's name in it and all sorts of other things written down. The friend thought that she might have been murdered.

"Oh no, how terrible", Lana gasped, "She was so sweet to me on Saturday at the dance and I was just getting to know her."

"There was hee haw sweet about that lassie." Jessie commented darkly, "if she was being nice to ye, Lana, 'twas because she wanted something from you."

The bell rang and the girls huried into the factory and started work but there was a lot of whispering back and forth between the girls.

Lana was surprised when Mr Wainwright appeared by her side and said almost apologetically. "Can you go up to Mr Campbell's office as the police officer wants to ask you a few questions."

"Why on earth do they want to ask me questions? I hardly know the girl."

"Ah dinnae know, Lana, just they want to see ye, that's all."

Lana shrugged her shoulders and left to go upstairs to his office and felt all the girls staring at her from the factory floor. When Lana reached the manager's office and knocked on the door, Mr Campbell opened it and ushered her in. She saw two police officers who looked so imposing in their jackets edged with gold braid and their top hats that she felt ill at ease and intimidated. Mr Campbell indicated for her to sit down in a chair next to one of the police officers, a tall man who seemed even taller because of the top hat. Lana felt rather overawed because of the size of the two police officers but relaxed when one of them introduced himself,

"All right Lana, I'm detective Murray and I just want to ask ye a few questions about Isla Dunbar. Ye have nothing to worry about but ye've likely heard she is missing."

"Yes, I understand that she didn't go home after the ceilidh last night."

"We are treating the report of her being a missing body very seriously at the moment. Someone handed in her purse and 'twas found down by the docks. She had a notebook with a few things written in it that are over puzzling. She wrote, 'Tell Wullie C that Lana has a beau called Stefan Van Uden, who is Dutch' and she's scribbled, 'His ship is' and then she's put a question mark and written that they're to be married before yule. Why on earth has she written all this about ye?"

Lana felt herself blushing as this was her private business and she thought to herself, she didn't really want to discuss her private affairs with anyone, especially Mr William Campbell. Why the mill could dismiss her before she was ready to go and if they knew she was leaving to get married it was precisely what they might do. There were people queuing up for jobs at the mill and not a day went past when someone would come to the factory enquiring if there were any vacancies.

"I'm sorry, I talked to her at the ceilidh, and she met my fiancé, Stefan. She walked back part of the way with us but then I went into my Aunt Jeanie's house, where I live, and I didn't see where she went after that. I have no idea why she wrote those words in her book."

William Campbell knew exactly why Isla had written those words in her book, but he was not about to incriminate himself and admit that Isla had been his mistress for the past two years and that he had just discarded her ending their relationship. Feelings of rage swept over him like the blasts of hot steam that came from the jute presses. He was angry with Isla for writing about Lana in her notebook and angry at Lana for having a fiancé but most of all he was angry with himself for being so obvious about his interest in Lana that Isla had noticed. He knew now that Isla was planning to tell him that he had a rival.

He thought angrily, 'What a jealous wee bitch' but keeping his voice calm said, "She must have been off to tell me Lana's good news as we give our girls a wee wedding bonus, when they leave to get married and sometimes organise a wee leaving party."

The police officer seemed happy with that explanation, "I must tell ye that we are now treating this as a murder enquiry. When we went to the place where her notebook was found we discovered traces of blood on the quayside, and it looked as if a body had been dragged over to the water and thrown in. Ye say ye were at home on Saturday night and I'll need to call round to your home and take a statement from yer guidwife, Mr Campbell. We've already seen Stefan as we made some enquiries and as his ship was the only Dutch one in the port, we were able to go on board, search the ship and question Stefan. He seems to be a sound and honest laddie."

He smiled at Lana, "I think ye've found a guidman there Lana. Ta for your help."

"Do you think she was a victim of the Dundee Slasher?"

"Well, we don't think so, no, as the serial killer that has been labelled with that name only kills sailors."

With a sudden insight, the other police officer, Detective McDuff said, "Unless she was in the wrong place at the wrong time, and he murdered her accidently."

William Campbell was not in the least bit worried that Isla could be dead but just that she might have written down other details of their clandestine romance that could incriminate him and make him a suspect. If indeed, they found her body and as they suspected, she had been murdered, he would then be the prime suspect although he was relieved that he had stayed in on Saturday and that his wife could vouch for him.

With all those conflicting thoughts rushing through his head he managed to stay calm and stood up saying,

"That will be all Lana, ye can go back to work but maybe ye would like to go to the rest room first and have a cup of tea as all this must be a shock to ye."

Although it was a cool day, he could feel beads of sweat on his forehead and a trickle ran down his face. He took out a handkerchief from his pocket and wiped the sweat away. Then he returned it to his pocket and holding out his hand to Lana, smiled as he said in a pleasant voice.

"I congratulate ye on yer forthcoming wedding. Ye must let us know when ye plan the occasion." Although inside he was furious at this turn of events and was thinking, 'There won't be any wedding if I have my way.'

Lana shook his hand and was so relieved that he hadn't said that she would have a week's notice to leave that she didn't notice that his smile had not reached his eyes. Detective MacDuff, however, observed that Campbell was sweating and thought,

'There is something nae right here, he's covering something up. I will need to investigate Mr William Campbell.'

Lana made her escape quickly and ran down the stairs into the factory. She grabbed Jessie by the hands and pulled her into the restroom area while many of the girls watched open-mouthed.

Mr Wainwright did not stop them, so Lana was able to tell her cousin all that the police officers had told her. They went back to the finishing section and restarted work while Jessie relayed all the latest information to their workmates. The communication of this latest news soon spread across the whole factory floor and after the flurry had died down a silence descended on the factory. Although Isla had not been the most popular of girls there was a stillness which was punctuated by sounds of crying as some of the girls heard that one of their own might have been murdered.

Chapter Fifteen

The life at the mill soon settled down and the girls were looking forward to the Sunday break when once again, the atmosphere was shattered. Someone had found a girl's body washed up several miles down the river from Dundee, the Police had confirmed that it was Isla and that her throat had been cut.

Mr Wainwright called a meeting after lunch on Friday and told the girls the bad news. Some of the girls had hoped that Isla had just run off with a beau and were shattered at his announcement. The mood in the mill was subdued, with girls running back and forward whispering to each wondering about the motive for her murder.

Jack sidled up to Lana and whispered, "Me ma told me to tell ye that ye shouldn't be upset about Isla 'cos she thinks she was jealous of ye and she thinks she was the one who tried to push ye under the hot press."

"Thank your Mum for me but tell her I think she is wrong. She was a bit offhand with me when I started at the mill but on Saturday, she was friendly and sweet." Lana could not make any sense of it all and just felt sad and confused.

She was not the only one who was confused as the two detectives who were investigating the Dundee Slasher murders, Detective Murray and MacDuff were also investigating this suspicious death. They couldn't make any sense of it either. This murder did not fit into the usual profile, as the victims had all been sailors so far.

There were only four detectives in the Dundee Police and Chief Constable Wallace, the Superintendent of the Dundee Police, had set up a special unit to try to catch the murderer. He had written for advice to Sergeant Archie Carmichael of the Glasgow police, known as Glasgow's Sherlock Holmes. Archie Carmichael had helped to solve many crimes and had given the Dundee Police lots of tips. He told them to photograph any footprints found near the bodies and compare them so that they could get some idea of the size of the murderer. He also advised taking photos of the victim's wounds so that they could get some idea of the weapon used.

Photography was an innovation, only used in criminal cases since 1862 and so Murray and MacDuff were still getting to grips with this recent technology. They, of course, interviewed anyone who had been nearby when the various murders were committed and so they had statements and photographs. They had put all the evidence together in a murder book but so far had no suspects.

The two police officers were discussing the progress they had made on the case as they walked back to the police station.

"Ah think that this murder of Isla Dunbar is connected to the Dundee Slasher. She was unfortunate as she was in the wrong place at the wrong time. Look at where the murder happened, down by the docks. I think we can assume that the Slasher was after a sailor, and she got in his way. Another thing is that if ye look at the photographs of all the footprints we have they are all wee feet. I have a hunch that the Dundee Slasher is a woman."

"Mimm, all the witnesses say the identical thing that the body was wee and sporting a black cloak. But I think it's more likely to be a wee man, women don't usually go for this method of murder, poisoning is more their style. I think we need to look more closely at Mr William Campbell as I'm very suspicious about him. There is something more about Isla that he is nae telling us. He was extremely uncomfortable. He woud'nae look me in my eyes when I questioned him. He is definitely guilty about something."

Well, one thing for sure. He's not our murderer"

"Why do ye say that Murray?"

"His feet are too big!"

The two police officers chuckled as they carried on down the High Street and made their way back to the police station in Monroe Street.

Chapter Sixteen

Lana could hardly wait to see Stefan and practically ran home on Friday evening. Jessie and Maisie had trouble keeping up with her.

"What's the hurry, lassie, there's nae a fire?"

Stefan was waiting for her at the door when she arrived at her aunt's house, and she practically flung herself into his arms. She was distraught as the discovery of Isla's body had reminded her of her husband's death and she sobbed incoherently into his shoulder. He finally managed to calm her down and used his handkerchief to wipe away her tears. They all went into Aunt Jeanie's kitchen where Jessie and Maisie explained that the police had found Isla's body. Aunt Jeanie busied herself making a pot of tea. Stefan knew that Isla had disappeared as the police had already interviewed him before he had left the weekend before. Lana then recounted the discovery of Isla's notebook on the quayside with both her and Stefan's name written in it.

Maisie said darkly, "She was up to something, that sly fox."

Lana started to sob uncontrollably again.

"No, she was being so nice to me at the dance. It must be my fault. I think she was going to tell Mr Campbell that I was getting married so that the mill would give me my marriage gift."

Aunt Jeanie passed her a handkerchief,

"Here, dry your eyes before ye make them all red, Och, ye've never got a handkerchief when you need one."

She addressed the other three, "She was aye like that as a wee 'un and never had a handkerchief when she wanted one."

Stefan smiled at Lana, "I'd better make sure I always have a handkerchief then."

Lana started to giggle, "Oh no, my Auntie will tell you about all the things I used to get up to as a child."

"You're all right there, ye were the sweetest bairn ever and you're aye just as adorable now."

"Oh, thank you Aunt Jeanie, but I'm not sure about that."

"It's true"

The girls finished their cups of tea and said their goodbyes. "We'll call for you on Monday morning, Lana."

Lana and Stefan had a supper at one of the small restaurants in the town and spent a quiet weekend going for walks before he left to return to Holland.

★ ★ ★

Detectives Murray and MacDuff had carried out further investigations about Isla and one of her friends had told them that she had been having a clandestine romance with William Campbell and that he had finished the relationship. She told them that Isla had confided in her that still loved him, was terribly upset and had said she was going to win him back.

"I told ye thare was something suspicious about that man," detective Murray said,

Detective MacDuff commented, "But he has a good solid alibi."

"His guidwife could be lying to protect him. I think we ought to bring him in to the station and ask him a few more questions. It could rattle him a wee bit and he might confess. Who knows maybe Isla threatened to tell his guidwife about their romantic adventure so maybe he killed her to keep her quiet?"

"Yes, ye could be right. Let's go and pick him up."

The two police officers turned up at the mill and asked Mr Campbell to accompany them to the police station. Campbell agreed to go with them readily but asked if they could go unnoticed down the back stairs to avoid all the mill workers spreading gossip. Murray popped in to see Chief Constable Wallace who asked if he could be present at the interview. When he reached the interview room, the Chief Constable flung the door open, strode in and didn't pause to hold the door open for the two detectives. With his air of self-importance, the detectives could only imagine that Campbell would find him intimidating.

MacDuff addressed Campbell, "This is Chief Constable Wallace, and he will be conducting the interview. You know detective Murray and myself detective McDuff and we will be sitting in for the interview. Ye know that you are nae under arrest but helping us with our enquiries."

Campbell looked worried and not his usual confident self. He did not trust himself to speak as he thought his voice would shake and so he just nodded.

Wallace started, "We know that ye were bedding Isla Dunbar and we are investigating her murder. It's nae use denying it as one of her friends has told us that Isla confided in her and loads of other girls have confirmed that they saw ye together. I put it to ye that Isla was off to tell your guidwife and so ye murdered her in cold blood. Ye planned it to take place by the docks and slit her throat so that she would look like another victim of the Dundee Slasher."

Campbell was infuriated and his anger overcame his fear of the Chief Constable. "I didnae murder Isla. I was very fond of her but realised that 'twas wrong of me to carry on with one of the mill girls, when I'm a married man and so I told her that we had to stop seeing each other a few weeks ago. We parted on good terms, and she was certainly nae off to tell my guidwife anything. Anyway, ye have spoken to my guidwife and she has told ye that I was at home all night on the night of the murder. It wasnae me."

"You had your fun with Isla, and you were tired of her, so you decided to get rid of her and throw her body into the Tay. Just like a bairn who is bored with a toy and throws it away for its nae use anymore. I think ye could have slipped out of the house fur an hour without your guidwife noticing."

"That's ridiculous, anyway we were sitting cuddled up on the settee all night, playing card games, so how come don't ye ask her again."

"Let's go through it again. I suggest you give your answers some careful thought. It'll be better for you if you stop wasting our time and tell us the truth. After all, we could tell your guidwife ye were bedding Isla and see what she says. She may nae be so inclined to give ye a false alibi then."

Campbell had tears in his eyes and a catch in his voice when he said, "Oh nae, please don't tell her that. She would likely leave me, and I'd lose my wee 'Uns as well as her. I'm telling ye the truth, I didn't murder Isla. I don't know how come she was down by the docks, but I think she was just in the wrong place at the wrong time and the Dundee Slasher murdered her by mistake."

He squared his shoulders and continued, "I think I'm entitled to a solicitor if you're going to continue with your questions."

The Chief Constable jerked his head towards the door to indicate to Murray and MacDuff that they should terminate the interview.

Once the three police officers were outside the interview room Wallace said to his two detectives,

"Good try but I think you're wasting your time. He didnae murder Isla. He can be an adulterous cheating scoundrel but he's awfy much of a feartie-cat tae murder someone. Did ye see the way he was so scared that ye would tell his guidwife that he had been unfaithful. We could keep him in the cells overnight, but we have nae proof that he murdered Isla so I dinnae think it's worth keeping him in custody any longer. Let him go away and slink back to his faithless life. He's a fecking arsehole but he's nae Islas' killer. I tend to agree with him that she was in the wrong place at the wrong time."

The two detectives went back into the interview room and told Campbell that he was free to go. Campbell walked jauntily back to the mill, whistling as he went. He hoped that none of the mill workers had seen him escorted off the premises, otherwise rumours would start circulating around the mill and that would never do.

He tried to think of some story to explain his visit to the police station and eventually thought that if anyone asked, he would say that his wife had had her purse stolen from the house while she was in the garden, and he had gone to verify the facts. He couldn't deny that the police taking him to the police station had given him a fright and he thought to himself that he would have to make watertight plans when he was to get rid of Stefan.

Chapter Seventeen

The weeks went by, life went on as usual at the mill and there were no more dramas. Stefan went back and forward to Danzig and Rotterdam collecting and delivering the jute and herrings. Stefan explained to Lana that he would be away for two weeks at the end of November. He knew he ought to tell his father that he had fallen in love with a girl from Scotland and wanted to marry her. He kept putting it off, knowing that his father would object, and they would end up quarrelling.

It wasn't only that his father wanted him to marry Antoinette Lemaire to unite the two shipping businesses but there was another reason. They were a Catholic family and his father who had strong religious beliefs would be horrified if Stefan wanted to marry a Protestant. He agonised over the situation and wondered idly if Lana would consider converting to being a Catholic. He knew that the longer he left it the worse it would become and cursed himself for his indecisiveness. He knew he could no longer put off approaching his father and planned to tell him about Lana as soon as he returned to Rotterdam.

Lana told him, "That's alright I'll go to Anstruther on Saturday afternoon and Sunday to see my sister and the boys."

He hadn't mentioned anything about his misgivings to Lana and so he said with a smile on his face, "I'm going to talk to my father about marrying you and perhaps we can arrange a suitable date, sometime in the Spring I think would be best. I've thought about it. You will probably want to marry in your local church at Anstruther, so perhaps you can set a date with the priest and talk to your sister to see where we can hold the reception."

Although privately thinking his family would not attend the wedding, he added, "My father, sister and I can stay at the hotel that you choose for the reception."

"Oh, that will be lovely. My brother-in-law will give me away. I think I will borrow my sister's wedding dress, as I know she has it wrapped up in paper. I don't want to wear my old wedding dress as I believe that would be unlucky. Oh, thinking about it, I would like to get married in Dundee, then all the girls from the mill can come and I would love to have Jack, a little boy at the mill to be a pageboy. Jessie and Maisie can be my bridesmaids and my two nephews can be pageboys too. My sisters can stay with Aunt Jeanie and Jessie. It's so exciting but there's so much to do. But who will be your groomsman?"

"I will ask my best friend Lucas to be my groomsman. He can stay in the hotel with my family."

Lana was getting dressed for her trip to Anstruther to visit her sister and her family when she noticed a strange feeling in her breasts.

They tingled and felt sensitive, and she wondered if she was pregnant. She could not ask Aunt Jeanie as although she knew that her aunt had been a midwife, she had never had any children of her own so hadn't experienced pregnancy. Lana decided to wait until she saw Moira.

Aunt Jeanie walked to the ferry with her and as she was boarding the ferry, she noticed that her aunt was looking at her strangely.

"What is it? Have I suddenly grown horns or something?"

"Noo. It's just that you look so bonnie today, you are positively glowing."

"Well, I'm just so excited to see Moira again. I've got such a lot to tell her about and we've got to make plans for my wedding."

"Och aye, I expect that's it then."

Lana waved goodbye to her aunt and stayed on the deck for the trip across the river. She had written to Moira who had arranged for a brougham cab to pick her up at the ferry terminal and take her to Anstruther. In good spirits, she skipped down the gangplank, looked around for the cab and spied someone she knew from her hometown.

He called out to her, "Why Miss Lana, good to see ye, I must say you look bonnie, your cheeks are all rosy and your hair shiny. It must suit ye working at the mills in Dundee."

"Oh, hello, Jack, I don't know about working at the mill, it's demanding work sometimes but all the girls are lovely. It's so good to see you too. Thanks for meeting me. How are your wife and the children? I expect they're getting excited for Christmas and Hogmanay."

They chatted all the way to Anstruther, and Jack told her all the local gossip, so the journey passed quickly until Jack dropped her outside Moira's house. There was a great flurry of welcome as both

Ronald and James flung themselves into their aunt's arms and hugged her. Moira kissed her sister, and they all went inside for a cup of tea. Moira had bought some Scotch pies for a snack and Lana tucked in enthusiastically as she found that the journey had made her feel ravenous. The boys went outside to play, and Lana told her sister all about Stefan and their plans to marry.

"I thought it would be better to have the ceremony in Dundee and then all the mill girls can come. Will you come to Dundee next Thursday and help me arrange everything? Auntie Jeanie would love to see you and you can stay the night and go back home on Friday. I'll ask for the afternoon off on Thursday."

She carried on talking, her face flushed with animation, "Ooh yes, I thought for the wedding that you and Angus and the boys can stay with Aunt Jessie as her house is large enough and Andrea can stay with Cousin Jessie. I thought Jessie and Maisie could be my bridesmaids and you could be my maid-of-honour. Oh, and can the boys be pageboys? They've got their kilts and they'll look a picture. Ooh, yes and do you think I could possibly borrow your wedding dress. I don't want to wear mine, although I have kept it, but I think it would be bad luck."

Moira was so pleased that Lana was happy and vivacious, "Of course you can borrow it, I'll go and get it down from the attic and you can try it on."

The two sisters went upstairs, and Moira propped up the ladder she had brought with her and clambered up the steps. She came down huffing and puffing with her wedding dress wrapped in a muslin sheet. They unwrapped the gown carefully.

"Why it looks brand new and it's still so white. It's lovely."

"I'll try it on. We're about the same size so it should be alright."

Lana thought this would be a good opportunity to ask Moira about the early signs of pregnancy.

"Moira, my breasts feel all tingly and a bit sore. I think they're rather swollen as well. Is that what happens when you're pregnant?"

"Yes, that's what happened to me and it's certainly one of the first signs that you could be pregnant. What will you do?"

"It'll be fine; Stefan is going to arrange for his father and sister to come to Dundee for the wedding, so we'll just have to get married quicker that's all."

"Have you missed your monthlies?"

"Yes, at first I thought they were just late."

Moira helped Lana to undo the bodice of her dress and slipped the wedding dress over her head. It was a little tight over the bust so Moira adjusted the laces on the bodice and so it was a perfect fit.

"You look as lovely as you did at your first wedding."

Moira was concerned about her sister but didn't want to spoil her obvious happiness and so she said, "What will Stefan say if you are having a baby?"

"He'll be delighted. He has said he wants us to have four children."

Moira didn't comment but thought to herself, 'I just hope you are right Lana.' and said instead, "Come on, lets pack the dress away and go downstairs and make a list of everything we've got to organise for this wedding."

The two sisters were engrossed in making their list when Angus came home, and Lana asked him if he would give her away at her wedding. Angus was in a teasing mood as usual and said,

"Well, I dinnae know about that lassie, I might want to keep you for myself."

The boys came in, each clutching a fat cat in their arms, proudly showing them off to Lana.

"Look Auntie Lana. Boots and Bonnet are enormous now."

The cats jumped out of the boys' arms and the smaller one, Bonnet, lay on the rug by the fire and rolled over with her paws in the air displaying her tummy.

Ronald tickled her tummy and she immediately caught his hand with her claws. "Ouch"

Angus said, "She's a right floozy, that one."

"What's a floozy, Pa?"

"Well, a floozy kind of lures ye to be nice to her, promises the earth and then she tells ye to sling yer hook just like this wee bonnie thing here who tempts and encourages ye to stroke her tummy and when ye do she pounces and claws yer hands."

"So, Pa, are floozy's always ladies? Who do they tempt? Can a man be a floozy? What does it mean to promise someone the earth and why do they do that?"

Moira, who could see the way that the conversation was going, gave a warning frown to Angus and in her best authoritarian voice interrupted quickly,

"Boys will you go and wash your hands, and will everyone sit at the table as supper is ready."

After supper, Lana went upstairs to tuck the boys in and tell them a story and then the three adults sat by the fire and chatted. Lana no longer had any desire to go and shout at the sea.

Saturday evening and Sunday passed quickly and soon it was time for Lana to return to Dundee on Sunday at four o'clock. Jack had agreed to take her back to Dundee and arrived with his horse and cart. Lana clambered in with her case and a bag containing Moira's wedding dress.

Moira reached up and kissed Lana on her cheek. "I'll see you on Wednesday at Auntie Jeanie's. I'll stay overnight so make sure you get the afternoon off on Thursday so we can plan for the reception at whatever hotel Jeanie suggests."

Lana wrapped her shawl around her head as it was getting cold and Jack passed her a blanket, which she was glad to tuck around her legs. Ronald and James ran alongside the cart for a while and then as it went faster just stood by the side of the road and waved goodbye to Lana.

Chapter Eighteen

When Lana arrived at work on Monday, she spoke to Mr Wainwright to request Thursday afternoon as unpaid holiday. He told her she would have to speak to Mr Campbell and said he would arrange for her to see him. After lunch, he told Lana that Mr Campbell would see her now and Lana made her way, with trepidation, up to his office.

Mr Campbell always made her feel nervous. He reminded her of a wolf, the way he looked her up and down as if he would like to devour her. She giggled nervously to herself at her fancifulness and took a deep breath to compose herself as she knocked on the door. When she entered Mr Campbell, who was standing by the window looking out, motioned to Lana to sit in the chair opposite his desk.

"Alright, Lana, bonnie to see ye. My ye look so well. It must suit ye working here in the mill. So, what can I do for you?"

Lana knew she would feel even more intimidated if she sat down as Mr Campbell would be towering over her, so she said,

"Thank you, Mr Campbell, I prefer to stand if you don't mind as my request will only take a minute."

She drew a deep breath and carried on "I am planning to get married in the next month and I would like to have Thursday afternoon as unpaid leave so that I can go with my sister and organise the church and the hotel reception."

Mr Campbell was shocked at how quick Lana's romance with this Dutch sailor seemed to be progressing, but he covered his feelings up and said calmly,

"Congratulations. Yes, ye had said ye were planning to get married but I didn't know we would be losing ye so soon. Aye, certainly that will be in order and ye don't need to take it as unpaid leave, we do allow a few days off for our workers to organise their weddings so that's fine. Just let us know the date of the wedding. I suppose you'll be going away then."

"Yes, I'll be going to live in Rotterdam. We will live with my husband's father to start with, and he will have a house built for us in the grounds."

"So, you're marrying into rich folk. Lucky lass."

Something about him made her flesh crawl and she felt angry at his comment, "Well, it wasn't very lucky, as you call it, when my first husband was lost at sea, so I suppose I deserve a bit of happiness now."

Campbell did not feel any compunction about what he was about to do but smiled as he thought that Lana would be lucky to have himself to look after her.

"That's fine then, ye can return to work now and I'll tell Mr Wainwright ye can have Thursday afternoon off."

Lana left and Campbell stared out of the window thinking that he would have to organise the murder of Lana's fiancé Stefan, much quicker than he had realised. He mused to himself, 'How much do you offer someone to kill a person?' He wondered if he should ask the smugglers first and if they said no, he was sure he would be able to find someone else to do his dirty work. He thought he'd have to be careful when he sounded the smugglers out, as if they refused, they would have evidence against him.

He smiled to himself again as he had an idea that would solve that problem. He would go to see them in disguise, so they would have no idea of his identity. Oh yes, he felt incredibly pleased with himself and puffed out his chest as he descended the stairs and had a spring in his step as he walked round the mill inspecting all the different departments, He stopped and chatted with some of his workers and was so pleasant that there were whispers between the girls.

"What's got into oor Wullie today? He's smiling."

"I reckon, the mill owners must've given him a Hogmanay bonus."

"Wish they'd give us a Hogmanay bonus."

"Well, you never know your luck."

"I'm nae that daft."

★ ★ ★

They would have been astonished to learn that someone in fact was planning to do just that and give them both a Yuletide and a Hogmanay gift. Lady Mary MacDonald sat in her drawing room at a desk with a whole pile of coins in front of her to her left and a pile of envelopes to her right. She sighed as she put coins in the envelopes and marked the envelopes with a B for bairns or MW for mill worker. Her maid Florrie knocked at the door and came in.

"Ma'am,"Would ye like your afternoon tea served here or in the conservatory?"

"Oh Florrie, I'd appreciate it if you could come and sit down next to me and give me a hand. I've still got about fifty envelopes to fill."

"Certainly, I'll help but I'll just tell Cook to hold up making the tea."

She reappeared and drew up a chair next to Lady Mary, "It's so good of ye to give the mill girls a gift at Yule. I hope they appreciate it."

"I'm sure they do; they have such a hard life some of them but at least the Act of Parliament meant they had to cut their hours, so the working hours are not as bad they used to be. It's the little children I feel most sorry for, fancy having to work all day at the mill when you are eight years old. They even must crawl under the machinery sometimes. I know my father was strict but at least I went to school, had friends and we could play outside in the fresh air. I heard that there was a tragic accident and one of the girls was poisoned with arsenic and another one of the girls was murdered and so I have asked if I can give a Christmas gift to that production team."

Lady Mary gave a shudder and renewed her efforts to put the coins in their envelopes. "I can't give to everyone as the mill employs about 5,000 folk and there are about 300 in each team."

"My goodness we'd be here all-night filling envelopes, not to mention how much it would cost you."

Florrie looked at her mistress and thought, "What a shame that she puts all her energy into charitable works. She should have married and had her own bairns. She was a striking looking woman.

She was slim and petite and with her black hair and large dark eyes and there always seemed to be suitors asking her to dance and inviting her to dinners, but she did not appear to be taken by any of them."

"What has happened tae Mr Gavin Stewart? I thought he was a pure pleasant chap and he seemed tae be very fond of you."

"Fond of my money, more like. I found out he had a gambling debt, and he was looking for an heiress to pay them all off and run up new ones, I dare say. No Florrie, that's the trouble when you are an heiress and have a small fortune, none of the men who have come calling are genuinely interested in me, just my money. I don't have a high opinion of men; they are all the same and just after money or bed."

Florrie blushed and was quite flustered, "It's a shame that you think that as all men are not like that. Why, take my own fiancé Malcom Ross, he's as sweet as a marshmallow and just as soft and kind-hearted."

Lady Mary made a grimace and carried on working. She had her own thoughts about her experiences with men and thought they were all vile animals but decided not to say anymore. At last, they had filled all the envelopes and she put them all into a basket.

"I hope I've done enough. I don't want to miss anyone out. I think I'll take some extra coins with me just in case."

Florrie lifted the basket, "My it's heavy, I didn't know that coins weighed so much. Mind you, there must be two or three hundred shillings in here and I've never had to carry so much money. Are you sure you can manage?"

"Of course, I'll get Hugh who's driving the carriage to carry it into the mill and then someone will help me when I'm there. Now I'll take tea to the conservatory and ask Cook to serve me a piece of the wonderful Victoria sponge she made yesterday."

Chapter Nineteen

Campbell slipped out of his house calling out to his wife, "I'll nae be long love, just got to pop back to the mill. Ah forgot to bring some papers home."

"Well, supper will be at seven sae don't be late. It's your favourite, roast wee lamb, roast potatoes, neeps, carrots and cauliflower."

"Fine but don't forget I've asked the Scott's and the Anderson's to come to supper next Saturday."

Campbell had arranged a small gathering so that he would have plenty of people to give him an alibi if the police came calling again, when they discovered Stefan's body.

As soon as he had walked down the road, he crossed over into the small park and changed into his disguise. He knew the smugglers would be at the Fishermen's Tavern in Fort Street, this night as they were always there on a Monday evening, for a celebratory drink after they had successfully delivered their contraband returning to their homes late on Monday night or early Tuesday morning. He didn't want anyone to recognise him so he put on some old worker's overalls over his own clothes. It made him look large and burly, which he thought was all the better. He stuffed the balaclava hat that his father had brought back from the Crimean War into his pocket. He would put that on when he reached the tavern. When he arrived at the tavern, he asked a young lad who was hanging around, to tell Jock, Michael and Robbie to come outside for a moment. He slunk into the dark lane at the side of the tavern, far from the gas light outside the pub and donned the balaclava. When the three smugglers stumbled out into the street, slightly the worse for wear with drink, he attracted their attention.

"Pssst, I'm in the alley here, I've got a proposition for ye. Would ye like to earn yourselves two hundred pounds?"

The smugglers always greedy to make an extra pound or two were curious and followed the voice into the alley.

"Och, that's a lot of dosh. What do ye want us to do for that?

"What I want you to do is kill someone."

"Och, We're no into murdering folk"

"He's a rapist and he raped my sister, nearly strangled her all, she just got away with her life, but she's never recovered and sits every day alone in her room too frightened to go out."

Campbell knew that this would change their mind and sure enough Michael said,

"Och, that's hideous, what a stinking swine, he deserves to be punished. Can the police not arrest him and prosecute him?"

"No, he's denied it and there's no evidence, so the police have said tis nae worth bringing him up in front of the magistrates."

"Well, he deserves tae lose his life as your poor sister seems to have lost hers. We'll do it gladly. What's his name?"

"He is called Stefan Van Uden and he's Dutch. His ship, the Zeeland, is due to dock on Saturday."

"Oh, a sailor laddie is he. I've met some of them Dutch sailors. Handsome brutes. They think they're God's gift to women."

"Yes, exactly and if ye slit his throat the Dundee Slasher will be blamed for the demise of our sailor boy."

"That's even better."

"Well, here ye are, I'll give ye the two hundred now. I don't want to have to meet up with ye again. It's quite a delicate matter and ah don't want my folk knowing about my involvement."

"We understand that, and the job will be done next Saturday night. We'll find out where his ship docks and we'll lie in wait for him, late at night. Ye go off home and look after yer sister. When she hears that the swine is dead, she may even recover."

"But mind ye keep your mouths shut. I don't want ye bletherin all over Dundee about this, otherwise the police may suspect that tis not the Dundee Slasher and come looking for ye."

"No, we'll nae breathe a word about it, dinnae worry yourself."

With that, they were gone laughing good-naturedly as if it was a in normal Monday evening celebration. However, what they didn't know was that the Dundee Slasher had also been making plans to murder Stefan. The serial killer had been watching Stefan and the next Saturday night he was to become the next victim of The Dundee Slasher. The killer approved and was extremely proud of the nickname. The murderer thought back to the sailor. The last time the sailor had escaped, saved by that slip of a girl. The Slasher felt guilty as the murder of the girl had been accidental. This time the Slasher intended to get this sailor, why he had probably been taking the girl back to his ship to have his wicked way with her, so he deserved to die, just like all the other evil lying sailors, with their girls in every port.

Campbell could not believe how easy it had been and ripped off the worker's dungarees and balaclava while he was in the alley. He walked with a jaunty stride home to his wife and his favourite supper and did not feel the slightest pang of conscience that he had organised Stefan's murder. He passed an old tramp in the street and gave him a present of the dungarees and balaclava.

"Ta, you're a good man, so ye are."

"I know"

★ ★ ★

The next day, on Thursday afternoon, Lana walked with a spring in her step to meet her sister to organise the details of her wedding, not realising that fate, in the shape of William Campbell, meant that the wedding she was planning would never take place. Lana and Moira had gone to the registrar's office and collected the marriage notice form.

"Goodness me, I didn't think it was so complicated getting married. Birth certificates, death certificate for Robbie, Stefan's passport. I don't remember having to give many details when I married Robbie."

That's because Ma and I helped you."

"It all seems like a dream now." and she added wistfully,

"I wish Ma was still alive. I miss her so much. She would have loved Stefan and I know would feel our education had been justified because I am marrying a rich man."

"I miss her too and it was terrible that when Pa died she seemed to go into a decline and died within a few months. Anyway, she's not here but I am so you can't be a daisy daydream this time; you have to give notice that you intend to marry ten or twelve weeks before the ceremony. It's the end of November now and ten weeks will be the middle of February, so maybe we should set the intended date as Sunday 12 February, the Sunday before Valentine's Day."

"Oh yes it has to be a Sunday so that all the mill girls can come and its lovely that it will be near to Valentine's day,"

"I thought you would like that. Now we need to go and see the Minister at St Mary's, the Dundee parish church"

The Minister, Archibald Watson, set the time of the wedding for half past two in the afternoon of the 12th February and Lana arranged to bring Stefan to the service on Sunday. The Reverend Watson had explained that they both needed to attend the church services every Sunday for three weeks for the reading of the banns. Lana had agreed that they would both be happy to do this, and she was positively beaming as she walked away from the church. The next stop was the British Hotel on Castlegate, as suggested by Auntie Jeanie, where they planned to hold the reception.

As they walked into the reception area Moira whispered,

"It's a bit fancy, isn't it?"

The receptionist addressed them, "Can I help you."

"I want to hold my wedding reception here and I believe I need to see the manageress to make all the arrangements."

"Och aye, that'll be Mrs Wishart. I'll just get the pageboy to fetch her. If ye go into the lounge I'll arrange for afternoon tea tae be served and send her in."

The two sisters sat back in the comfortable armchairs while a maid poured cups of tea, gave them each a side plate and passed them plates of delicious and delicate looking sandwiches and rich cakes. They took a selection and the maid placed two small tables next to their chairs, so they were able to put their cups and plates down and enjoy their afternoon tea in comfort.

"Well, I could get used to this." Moira remarked.

"Me too."

Mrs Wishart swept into the room, introducing herself. She was tall and looked elegant as her navy-blue crinoline dress brushed the floor and she held the skirt up with one hand, revealing perfect white lace petticoats beneath. She eyed the two sisters with a disapproving look and Lana wished that she had gone home and changed into her best dress. She was conscious that she was still in her work dress from the mill and didn't look as if she fitted in to the sumptuous surroundings."

"I believe ye want to discuss arrangements to hold your wedding reception at the British Hotel." She said disdainfully with a sneering expression on her face.

Lana noticed that she had a thin mouth with lines that turned down at the corners.

"What is your name and the name of your future husband."

"My name is Lana Wallace, but I use my maiden name of St Clair and my husband to be is Stefan Van Uden, a Dutch ship owner."

Mrs Wishart gave a sharp intake of breath and her whole demeanour changed, "Van Uden, ye say, how come I know the folk, they've often stayed here in the past. I believe Mr Ton Van Uden brought his guidwife and bairns to stay one year. They were delightful folk. Let me see there was an older laddie and a younger wee lassie. Ah, so it's the laddie that you are marrying. Well, yer a lucky lassie as they're wealthy folk.

Lana mused to herself that it was funny how money had such a big influence on the way folk were treated. It didn't make one bit of difference to her if someone was rich or poor, but it obviously was important to Mrs Wishart.

"Would ye like another cup of tea Lana, Here, I'll pour ye a cup. Here ye go, I'll pour one for your friend too."

Lana saw that that her sister was smiling wryly at her as she too had noticed that Mrs Wishart had suddenly become respectful.

"She is my friend but she's my sister too, Moira Fraser now but she was Moira St Clair."

"Och aye ah seem to remember that the St Clair's were landowners in Fifeshire. Do your folk still own land there?"

Lana gave her sister a slight kick under the table and replied quickly, "Yes we still own some land and of course, there is the castle too."

Mrs Wishart became even more deferential when Lana told her that they would need to book three rooms on the eleventh and twelfth of February next year for Stefan's father, sister and his groomsman."

"What about Stefan?" Moira asked, "He'll need to stay somewhere the night before the wedding."

"Oh, my goodness, I forgot about that. Yes, we'll need another room for the eleventh too."

"Now, will ye want a buffet or a sit-down dinner?" Mrs Wishart asked.

"Oh, I think a buffet will be fine." Lana replied.

"How many guests will there be?"

Lana had made a list and said immediately, "Oh there'll be eighty guests."

"What about a wedding cake?"

"No, my Auntie is making the wedding cake and my sister here is making the favours for each guest."

Mrs Wishart showed them a card with the menus for the different buffets and prices. Lana gave her sister another kick under the table and said disdainfully,

"Is this the best that the hotel can offer? This is only suitable for a children's tea party. We want a wedding feast, with a whole salmon, sides of beef, lamb, gammon and turkey, with different salads, pickles, Scottish rolls, bowls of new potatoes, roast potatoes and a table with different desserts."

Mrs Wishart looked confounded, went red in the face and replied, "Of course the hotel prides itself on the service we provide to guests and we will certainly be able to offer a buffet to suit your requirements. I will make out a list of all the food items you have suggested and an invoice for you to check tomorrow. We will need a ten percent deposit and the balance paid on the day in case there are any extras to be added."

Lana told her that she would come back on Saturday afternoon with Stefan, her fiancé to pay the deposit.

When the two sisters left the hotel, Moira almost collapsed in giggles, "What a snob but oh dear, her face when you said we had a castle, I don't know how I kept a straight face and when you said her buffet was rubbish, her expression was a picture, and I nearly had a fit of the giggles."

Lana laughed too and they set off down the road chuckling merrily, "I think, one of our great uncles does have a castle, although I think it's a bit dilapidated. I'll find out from Auntie Jeanie where it is just in case Mrs Wishart asks about it. The two sisters made their way back to their Auntie Jeanie's house where they collapsed in the armchairs in the front parlour. Aunt Jeanie made a pot of tea and poured them both a cup.

"Oh, that's the best cup of tea I've ever tasted."

"Yes, I think so too."

"Well, it's probably not the best cup of tea but it seems like it because you really needed it." Aunt Jeanie said as she bustled around bringing in a plate of sliced Dundee cake.

"You're an angel, Auntie Jeanie, How did you know that's just what I fancied." Lana said grabbing a piece of cake and putting her feet up on a stool. Moira dived in as well and in between munching, the two girls told Aunt Jeanie about all the arrangements they had made.

Chapter Twenty

The next morning, the two sisters were up early. Moira was returning to Anstruther and Lana had to go to work.

"How are you feeling?"

"I've started to feel a bit sick, sometimes it's just in the morning but it can be at any time."

"You definitely are pregnant then. When are you going to tell Stefan?"

"I'll tell him on Saturday."

"Good luck with that."

"Oh, he'll be delighted I'm sure."

"Well, I just hope you are right", Moira said sceptically.

Jessie and Maisie knocked at the door and Lana kissed her sister goodbye.

"Thanks for all your help with the wedding. I'll see you at the New Year. We don't get time off for Christmas so I'll stay with Auntie Jeanie and then I'll be arriving on the 31st for the Hogmanay celebrations and have a few days off, so will it be all right to stay with you for New Year. I think Auntie Jeanie said she would like to come and stay too, so will that be alright."

"Away with your bletherin, of course you can both stay. We'll look forward to having you around."

"Will it be alright if Stefan stays for Hogmanay too? I'm going to tell him about all the celebrations we have in Scotland and he will want to experience a Scottish New Year, if he can fit it in."

"I expect we can make room for him too but ye'll have to keep him inside till the clocks chime midnight as we can't risk a blond man first footing us and bringing bad luck."

Lana gave her sister a last hug and went off down the road with her two friends.

Aunt Jeanie turned to Moira. "I do worry about that lassie; she's such an innocent and so trusting of anybody. At least Stefan seems to be a good man, so she should be all right there. I expect you'll want to be off now, so I'll chum ye to the ferry. Have ye arranged for someone to catch up with ye to take ye back home?"

"Yes it's all arranged, one of my neighbours is meeting the ten o'clock ferry with his horse and cart. Not the most elegant way to travel but at least it's free."

"All right that means ye've got time for me to make ye some breakfast before ye go, come into the scullery and I'll see what I can rustle up."

★ ★ ★

The next day was Friday and after lunch, there was a bustling air of excitement at the mill. Jack came running up to Lana his eyes wide and told her,

"It's Lady Mary MacDonald she's come to give us all a Hogmanay gift. My Ma says she's giving our team money this year for she heard about Isla being murdered. All the other teams are saying it's nae fair but my Ma says they should stop their wittering for it'll all work out in the end as we'll just go to the back of the queue next year."

Jessie came up to her and they stood and watched as Mr Campbell ushered a small dainty woman who was dressed in the latest fashionable style, onto the Mill floor. Lana gasped,

"Oh, doesn't she look a picture. I like the bright pink colour of her dress and I love the wide sleeves with undersleeves of paler pink."

"Aye, the colour is all the newest fashion and it's called magenta after the Italian town of Magenta." Jessie commented knowledgably,

"She's all right; she can be a Lady, but she doesn't put on any airs and graces. She's very down to earth. Ye'll catch up with her in a moment as Mr Campbell will bring her round to everybody so she can give each person her gift. It's great timing as it helps everybody out with food and presents for Yuletide and Hogmanay."

Lana watched as Mr Campbell took Lady Mary to everybody in their team one by one and noticed that she took time to talk to everyone. When it came to her turn, Lana detected that although she smiled a lot she had an air of sadness about her, which made her think,

"She must have suffered some terrible loss in her life or perhaps she felt guilty about something and was trying to assuage her conscience.' Lana didn't realise how right she was.

When Lady Mary left, Jack came running up to her in great excitement, "She gave all the wee'uns a shilling, a whole shilling. I've given it to my Ma, and she says she's off to buy us all Yuletide presents, cos she got two shillings which means she can buy loads of food for Yule and Hogmanay. What about ye?"

"Yes, it's wonderful, isn't it I'm going to use my money to buy all my family presents for Yule, I know a book my sister wanted to read, so my first stop will be the bookshop."

At last, it was time to go home and as evening fell, Lara could hardly wait for Stefan to arrive as she had so much to tell him.

"We're just going for a walk before supper Auntie Jeanie, and I'll tell Stefan all about the arrangements we've made for the wedding.

As they walked down the path, they both said at the same time,

"I've got something important to tell you."

Stefan said, "You go first."

Lana agreed as she felt that she would burst if she didn't tell him her good news. "I'm pregnant. The baby will be born in late July, so I've made arrangements for the wedding as soon as possible on the 12th of February next year."

Stefan picked her up, swung her around and kissed her,

"That's wonderful sweetheart. I am so happy, and I think in that case that we should get married in the registry office as soon as possible. We can still have the church wedding in February."

"Can you get married twice?"

"I don't know. We'll have to ask the minister, but I don't see why not."

"Alright. What was your news?"

"Oh dear, it's not good news like yours I'm afraid. My father has objected to me marrying you. He still wants me to marry Antoinette Lemaire."

"Oh no, that's dreadful. What are we going to do?"

"We are just going to go ahead and get married. When I tell him about the baby, his first grandchild, I'm sure he'll come round.

The following day, Stefan met Lana at the mill at three o clock when she finished work and they set off to the British Hotel. Lana had changed into her best dress at the mill, to go back to the hotel to see Mrs Wishart.

"You look beautiful in that blue dress and the hat sets it off."

"You don't look so bad yourself and at least the pompous Mrs Wishart won't be looking down her nose at us. When I went to book the reception on Thursday, I was in my work clothes and she was really condescending to me until I mentioned your family name."

"Ah well my father has been a client of the hotel for a good number of years."

They checked the list of food for the buffet and Lana noticed that Mrs Wishart had added various cheeses and biscuits and a list of delicious sounding desserts. Stefan paid Mrs Wishart the deposit required, and Lana could hardly believe how she grovelled to Stefan. Lana and Stefan spent the rest of the afternoon walking through the town and looking at the shops and stalls. Lana bought the book 'Katie Stewart' for Moira from the bookshop for her Christmas present and then they returned to Auntie Jeanie's house as she had told them she was cooking supper for them. When they sat down to eat, Stefan was pleasantly surprised when Jeanie served up the traditional haggis with neeps.

"I've never tasted haggis before, and I always wanted to. Oh, this is delicious and these vegetables that you call neeps what are they?"

"Turnips"

Lana and Stefan sat in the front parlour and as it was approaching Christmas, Lana told Stefan that although the Scots gave each other presents on Christmas Day, they did not have a public holiday for Christmas and Boxing Day so she would have to work at the mill as usual. She said that the real celebration was at New Year or Hogmanay*** and she told him about all the traditional practices that took place.

"I hope I can spend New Year with you and your sister's family as it all sounds good. Will you ask her if I can stay at her house? Will she have room for me?"

"Moira has said she will be delighted to invite you to stay and by then we can sleep together so she won't have to find an extra bed."

"I look forward to it but let me tell you about how we celebrate Christmas in the Netherlands. The most important day is the 5th of December, when Sinterklaas, our name for Saint Nicholas, brings presents. It all starts on the second Saturday of November when Sinterklaas travels to a city or town in the Netherlands. It is our tradition that says St Nicholas lives in Madrid, not like your Santa Claus who lives at the North Pole. Every year he chooses a different harbour to arrive in Holland, so as many children as possible get a chance to see him.

"But why does he live in Madrid?"

"That's because from the sixteenth century till early in the eighteenth century the Netherlands was under the Spanish Crown as part of the States of the Holy Roman Empire in the Low Countries."

____

*** See Note 3. Hogmanay

"That's so strange as we have him travelling in a sledge pulled by reindeers.

"Well, Sinterklaas in the Netherlands doesn't have reindeers but he travels with his servants called 'Zwarte Pieten' which means 'Black Peters'. It is a big occasion when Sinterklaas and his black servants come ashore from their steamboat and all of the local churches ring their bells ring in celebration. Sinterklaas, dressed in his red robes leads a procession through the town, riding a white horse. The children leave a shoe out by the fireplace or on a windowsill so that Sinterklaas can leave presents. They are told that during the night, Sinterklaas rides on the roofs on his horse and that a Black Peter will climb down the chimney or through a window and put presents or candy in their shoes."

"But why do they put their shoes out in November when you said he brings present on the 5th December."

"Ah, in many families the children are told that Sinterklaas and Zwarte Pieten make a weekly visit, so they get treats for a few weeks and then on December the 5th the children receive their main presents."

"So, the children get larger presents as well, not just small ones that can fit in their shoe?"

"Yes, that's right, they do get larger presents left in a sack outside the door."

"And do parents tell the children that if they are not well behaved that Sinterklaas will leave a sack of soot instead of presents?"

"No, I think it is worse than that because children are told that the Zwarte Pieten keep a record of all the things they have done in the past year in a big book. Good children will get presents from Sinterklaas, but bad children will be put in a sack and the Zwarte Pieten take them back to Spain for a year to teach them how to behave! My sister Mariella, used to have nightmares and wake up screaming, 'I don't want to be taken to Spain,' so in the end my parents had to tell her that it was all a fairy story. I was older and I had already found out that from friends at school that Sinterklaas wasn't real and that your parents gave you the presents, so I was glad as I would have probably told her myself because she used to get so upset."

Lana snuggled up close to Stefan on the settee,

"You are such a lovely person, so kind and I'm glad that we met."

"I'm so pleased that I found you too, you are my 'zielverwant'. I'm not sure how you say it in English."

"Explain to me what it is, and I'll see if I can find the word."

Well, everybody has a soul, and this is when two souls are friends and meant to be together."

"Aah, I think you mean soulmate. That's lovely and I think you were right we were brought together by fate and we are meant to be together for always."

As the time approached ten o' clock, Stefan said his goodbyes before walking back to his ship. They didn't realise that their happiness was soon to be shattered and their dreams torn apart.

The last words that Lana heard Stefan say to her were,

"I'll see you at eleven o' clock tomorrow."

It was another dark, misty night with the mist rolling in from the river and Stefan shivered as he walked back to the harbour. He wasn't usually nervous but tonight he imagined dark shapes looming out of the fog. It was almost as if he sensed that there was a hidden menace lurking in a nearby alley. Then as if he had conjured it up, he felt rather than saw a presence behind him. Stefan felt himself being grabbed and saw the flash of steel and then shouting. He felt something hard hit his head and fell unconscious on the quayside.

The killer was surprised when the three smugglers appeared and pulled the sailor away and was so intent on getting away quickly from the men who had prevented the killing that the precious silver knife used for the 'righteous retribution' fell on the quayside. The killer thought, "It's annoying to lose the knife but I can probably replace it. At least I've got away and not been caught and maybe I managed to slash the sailor's neck before those men intervened. It's not too bad after all as my mission was probably successful and the sailor is most likely dead."

Chapter Twenty-One

It was midday and Lana had been back and forth to the window looking out for the last hour.

"Where can he be Aunt Jeanie? He's never late and he said he'd be here at eleven o' clock to say goodbye as he only had a couple of hours before the Zeeland was due to sail. I'm getting worried."

"I'm sure he's alright, he's just been held up with some business on his ship or at the dock."

By the time it was one o' clock Lana was frantic, "Oh Aunt Jeanie, what if he's been murdered by the Dundee Slasher? I'm going down to his ship to make sure that he's safe."

"Well, I'll come with ye then, I don't want ye disappearing as well."

Aunt Jeanie took her cloak off the hook and wrapped it round her. She handed Lana her cloak and a woollen scarf. "Here ye are lassie you'll need these; tis freezing out there and blowing a gale."

★ ★ ★

Lana wasn't the only person who was worried. The captain of the Zeeland went up on deck and peered down the quayside. He saw one of the cabin boys who he had sent round the pubs to look for Stefan, walking towards the ship.

"Did you not find him?"

"No, Skipper, no-one's seen him last night or this morning."

"Oh well, I seem to remember that his father and he had a quarrel as Stefan wanted to marry a local Scottish girl and that didn't fit in with his father's plans. Maybe Stefan's decided to stay in Dundee and marry his girl, so we'll have to set sail without him and give the news to Mr Van Uden that his son just disappeared."

The captain started to shout his orders to prepare the ship for their departure, "Cast off. Weigh anchors. Come on, look smart, we only have half an hour to catch the tide because we've been hanging around waiting for Stefan to show his sorry face and he will have a sorry face when his father catches up with him."

★ ★ ★

Lana reached the small harbour first and saw that the space where the Zeeland usually berthed was empty. Auntie Jeanie caught up with her, breathing heavily. As they stared out to the entrance to the harbour Lana gave a wail.

"Oh no, there's the Zeeland and she's just sailing out of the harbour. Oh, how could he leave without saying goodbye? Oh no, perhaps he's changed his mind about marrying me."

Tears welled up in Lana's eyes and ran down her cheeks. She wept and each word came out racked with sobs.

Aunt Jeanie handed her a handkerchief with a sigh, "Here ye are lassie, you nae have a handkerchief when you need one."

Lana wiped her eyes and said, "Perhaps he's changed his mind about marrying me and is going to do as his father wishes and marry Antoinette."

"Na, I think the Zeeland sailed without him, I'm good at judging folks' character and ah I can tell ye that Stefan is a fine upstanding young man, and anybody can see that he loves ye. He's not reckless and wild. He just wouldn't forsake ye, especially as you're expecting his bairn."

"How did you know I was pregnant?"

"You're forgetting I was a midwife, so I know all the signs."

"Of course, how silly of me. But about Stefan, I think the only thing I can do now is to go to the police station and report him missing and also check the local hospital."

★ ★ ★

Lana was miserable. She didn't know how she had managed to get through the week. She had one of Stefan's old jumpers and she took it to bed with her every night, it smelt of him, his skin, his hair, his laughter and she cuddled it, imagining that he was there with her. She sobbed into it, her tears mixing with his smell. She carried it around the house with her like a magic charm as if it could bring him back.

The police had taken a statement about Stefan being missing but so far had not managed to find him or find any clues as to where he had gone. She didn't know whether to be relieved or not to find that he was not injured and in the hospital. At least if he had been there, she would know where he was and what had happened to him. She wondered if her sisters had been right that she was too trusting and now that he had taken his pleasure with her, he was just going to abandon her. Everyone at the Mill was being kind to her, even little Jack gave her a toffee from a tin he had been given for his birthday from all the mill girls. But Lana was inconsolable.

Jessie said, "Don't worry, "I expect something happened and the ship had to sail quickly but he'll be back next week, with a big bunch of red roses to say sorry. Oh no, they don't have roses in Holland its tulips isn't it but they may not last for the trip so you may have to make do with a box of herrings!"

Lana smiled for the first time that week.

"It's good to see ye smile, don't worry bonnie lassie. He's a good man and he pure loves ye and there is an explanation to this mystery that we'll find out sooner or later."

Little did they realise that the explanation would be later rather than sooner. The week went by, and Lana set off on Saturday for the docks to see if Stefan's ship had come back to port. The Zeeland wasn't there, and she walked down the quayside, towards the mouth of the Tay. She passed some dockhands as she walked and called out to them.

"Do you know if the Zeeland is expected today?"

"Best ask the harbourmaster lassie. He's just up there a bit. Ye'll nae miss him. He's got a beard and he's sporting a captains bunnet. He looks like and old seadog."

He gave a laugh, "Ye're in luck. There he is. Alright Alex, there's a lassie wants a word with you."

Lana looked at the harbourmaster, his face was like an old treasure map, tanned a deep bronze with ruddy cheeks covered with broken veins. Lana bet he had led an adventurous life and could tell a few tales.

"Do you know if the Zeeland is expected to dock today?"

"Aye, I know the ship, coming from Rotterdam. I don't think she's due back until the middle of the week. There was quite a furore when she left as their purser, a young laddie, Stefan, I think his name is, went missing. The captain sent some crew round all the taverns and inns looking for him, but he had just disappeared, so eventually they had to set sail without him."

"Oh no, he was supposed to meet me last Sunday but didn't arrive so I was hoping that there had been some emergency and that he had to leave on The Zeeland in a hurry. But it seems that something has happened to him."

The three men looked at her with concern. Lana took a deep breath and managed to stop herself from crying.

"Would you like one of us to chum you back home?"

"No, it's very kind of you but I'll be alright."

★ ★ ★

The next week at the mill was even worse as there was still no news of Stefan. Sleep just did not come to Lana. Heartache and grief prevented any chance of it. She saw men in the streets with blond hair and chased after them only to find that they weren't Stefan. As the week went on, she felt so tired that sometimes she felt herself falling asleep, on her feet at work. She would close her eyes and feel herself drifting off and then as she almost fell over, she woke up with a start to find herself staggering against the bales of jute.

Jessie and Maisie were so worried about Lana that her that they had talked to her aunt, and she had agreed that they would have to do something. On Thursday night when they all arrived at the house, Aunt Jeanie met them at the door with a wide smile on her face.

"Now, lassie, I've arranged to borrow a horse and trap from my friend, Mrs Smith and I'm off to drive you to Anstruther to stay with Moira. It's nearly Yule and fresh New Year so ye might as well stay with your folk now and ye can help Moira with all the Hogmanay preparations. She'll be a comfort to ye and will know what to do. Besides, I have not seen her and the wee 'Uns for a few months, so I'll close up my house and come with ye, it'll be a good break for me too."

"Oh, yes, that will be lovely." Lana said as she flung her arms around her aunt and kissed her on both cheeks.

"Jessie will tell Mr Wainwright that you're nae well and need a few days off and ye'll nae be back till efter the New Year's break. Although anybody with half an eye could see that ye weren't well. It's a wonder that the mill didn't arrange for some time off for ye, falling asleep at work with all that machinery around, it's a danger.

Jessie replied, "The mill only care about their production levels, nae their workers and they think it's up to each person to look after themselves." Aunt Jeanie made a *Tch Tch* sound of disapproval.

★ ★ ★

Lana chatted to her aunt as they made their way down country roads. "My thoughts are going round and round in my head wondering what's happened to Stefan. I think sometimes that I'm cursed and any man, who loves me, dies. But, Auntie Jeanie, I don't think he's dead. I feel that he's still alive. I feel as if I'm going mad. I sometimes see him walking down the path to your front door. I know I'm hallucinating and it's not real but the sense that he's come back is so wonderful. Then when I realise that it's just a dream, I get even more upset and miserable."

Lana gasped out the last words as sobs racked her body and tears rolled down her face.

"Now don't upset yerself'. Think o' the bairn you're carrying. It won't do him or her any good."

Her aunt handed her a handkerchief and Lana dried her eyes and stared into space. Eventually the rhythmic clip-clop of the horse's hooves and the rocking motion of the carriage had a soothing effect on her, and Lana wrapped her shawl round her, relaxed and fell asleep.

Her aunt let her sleep, "There ye go, lassie sleep, it's the best thing for ye. Ye'll feel much better when you wake up."

★ ★ ★

They arrived at Moira's house in the late afternoon. Lana had woken up and felt refreshed after her siesta and when her sister opened the door to her, she presented a picture of health with glowing cheeks and shiny hair.

"Why Lana, whatever are you doing here in the middle of the week and Aunt Jeanie too. Well, this is a surprise." Lana threw herself into her sister's arms, sobbing hysterically. Moira patted La

"Stefan has disappeared, and the police can't find any clues to his disappearance. The poor wee lassie is beside herself and is no sleeping, so I've brought her back to ye."

Ever practical Moira ushered them both in, "Come away in and I'll make us all a cup of tea and you can tell me all about it."

Lana calmed down after drinking her tea and explained to Moira the circumstances leading up to Stefan vanishing.

Moira had been unconvinced that Stefan would be delighted about the baby and said, "So he must have gone back to Rotterdam. Perhaps he has decided to wed the girl his father wanted him to marry."

"No, when I went back to the port to see if The Zeeland was coming into the docks last week, the harbourmaster told me that the captain had found that Stefan went missing that Sunday when they were due to leave and sent out some crew to look for him but eventually, they sailed without him."

"Well, you don't know if he boarded his ship at the last minute or perhaps, he was hiding on the ship."

"Why would he do that?"

"Perhaps he was torn about a terrible decision between leaving you and fulfilling his father's dearest wishes."

"No, he wouldn't desert me; I just don't believe he would do that. Something has happened to him."

"But the police haven't found a body or any clues as to where he has gone."

"No, it's a mystery. All they found were a few spots of blood on the quayside and they said this did not prove anything."

"Well, until we have found an answer it leaves you in a mess. You cannot have a baby and be unmarried. The community would never accept it. They would shun you and the child, and it would be the child that would suffer the most from being illegitimate. It's incredibly lucky for you that I have just found out that I am expecting and so we can arrange for you to go and stay at Elie with Andrea and have the baby in secret. I will arrange to have my baby at Andrea's, and we can pretend that I have given birth to twins, and I can look alter both babies. You can even go back and work at the mill and come home here at the weekends."

Lana gave Moira a hug, "That's wonderful news for you; I hope you have a daughter as I know you always wanted a girl after having two boys. But what about the midwife she'll know that you only had one baby?"

Aunt Jeanie interrupted, "Well that's no problem, ye know that I am a trained midwife. That was my job before I retired so I can come and stay with Andrea at Elie and deliver both the babies."

"Yes, I guess that will work. Lana, you'll have to stay hidden at Andrea's and I'll come over just before I'm due. I know there are quite a few rooms above the pub as Andrea rents out rooms to holiday makers in the summer."

"Won't she and her husband mind that they'll lose

"I expect she can make it all right with Ben, he adores her, being so much younger than him and she can twist hi

"Well, that's settled then. Lana you can continue to work at the mill. Ye'll have to try not to put on too much weight and disguise your condition as much as you can. Ye'll have to leave when you are about seven months gone and go and stay with Andrea at the pub in Elie. I'll come and stay with you and when Moira arrives, we can say that she doesn't want to give birth at home. It's a bit crowded with the boys, so Andrea has kindly offered her a bed at her place and I'm going to attend as the midwife. Moira ye must exaggerate your bump a bit, so that folk aren't suspicious."

Moira gave a chuckle, "Looks like I'll be eating for three."

The door burst open and Robert and James, returning from school, looked surprised and overjoyed when they saw Lana and Auntie Jeanie. After they had given them hugs, they all sat around chatting about what the boys were doing at school until Angus came home from work when there was a repetition of the whole surprise and excitement. Moira and Aunt Jeanie started to prepare an evening meal, the two boys set the table and Lana lit a couple of candles. Soon the meal was ready and the whole family sat around the table, enjoying roast chicken, roast potatoes and parsnips, carrots, and peas, chatting happily. Lana felt happy for the first time in the

Ronald noticed his father's comment first, "Does that mean that Mum is having a baby?"

Angus nodded and he said, "Gosh, we're going to have a wee brother or sister."

James said, "I hope she has a boy."

The women cleared the table and when the dishes were washed and the boys were safely in bed, the family sat around the fire chatting. Lana felt better than she had for the last two weeks, knowing that her problems had been resolved and started to feel drowsy. Moira noticed and gently took her by the arm and propelled her upstairs to the spare bedroom. Jeanie followed them upstairs and helped Lana into her nightdress.

Lana curled up under the blankets and quilt and was soon fast asleep, where Jeanie soon joined her, calling out,

"Nighty night Moira, ta for everything, ye've managed to calm her down. Ah think she was worried about what to do about the bairn."

Chapter Twenty-Two

The time at Moira's home passed quickly with all the preparations for Christmas and Hogmanay. Although Christmas wasn't celebrated as much as Hogmanay or New Year the family still made some preparations for it. Christmas Day and Boxing Day were not public holidays, so Angus had to go to work but, in the evening, the family sat down to as feast of goose, roast potatoes, roast parsnips and Brussel sprouts, followed by a rich plum pudding steamed on the stove for three hours.

The boys were delighted when their parents gave them model ships of the HMS *Nelson* and the French *Bucentauer.* A friend of Angus's at the shipyard made model boats and he had asked him to make the two ships for his boys. To complement this gift Lana bought the boys some toy soldier sets of Admiral Nelson and his crew and the gun crew of the HMS *Victory* as well as a set of French soldiers. Auntie Jeanie gave them a book each: *Tom Brown's Schooldays* for Robert, *Coral Island* for James, and some marbles too. Moira was happy to receive some handkerchiefs with her initials hand embroidered with Lana's hair, a hand-made strawberry shaped pincushion from Auntie Jeanie and a silver thimble and sewing scissors from Angus. She was surprised when Lana presented her with another present, the book '*Katie Stewart*,' by the local author Margaret Oliphant Wilson.

"How did you remember that I wanted to read that book?"

Lana was gratified that her sister was delighted with her present and just smiled at Moira enigmatically. She was herself overjoyed to receive a scarf and mittens from Auntie Jeanie and a painting set from Moira and Angus.

Moira whispered to her, "I thought this would be useful as you can do some painting while you are cooped up at The Ship Inn."

Moira gave her husband a pair of embroidered bedroom slippers. Auntie Jeanie gave him a monogrammed tobacco pouch and Lana gave him a scarf. The boys had saved up their pocket money and bought their Ma and Lana some ribbons for their hair, a second-hand knitting bag that they had bought from a market stall for Auntie Jeanie and some handkerchiefs for their Pa.

With Christmas over the family had a busy time preparing for Hogmanay. They cleaned the house from top to bottom and took the ashes out from the fire. Moira, Lana, and Jeanie worked hard to get the house spick and span for the forthcoming holiday. Lana felt a little sad, as they had planned that Stefan would stay for Hogmanay. He had never experienced a Scottish New Year celebration and she thought to herself that he might never become familiar with it now.

Moira said, "I'm so glad the two of you are here to help me as with this pregnancy I'm finding it challenging work to do the normal cleaning let alone do a special deep cleaning for the New Year. I think I've paid all the bills at the butchers, fishmongers, and bakery so I've cleared out the remains of the old year. There you are then, a clean break and we should be able to welcome in a young, New Year on a happy note."

Moira sank down into a chair as even this last speech had made her weary, "I'm going to have a little snooze as I feel so tired."

"That's fine, hen, ye have a rest. The house looks beautiful and there's nae else to do now except organise taking the steak and sausages to the bakery so that they can make the steak pie for New Year's Day."

"Oh, yes I'll cook the steak and sausage later and then tomorrow we'll go into town and deliver it to the bakery."

Robert and James had come in from school and Robert said, "Ma, how do the bakers know whose pie is whose, 'cos all the folks take their meat to the bakers to make their pies? It would be easy to muddle them up and then you might get someone else's meat that wasn't as good as yours."

"Well, they make a whole load of pastry and then they put it in the baking trays to make the bases and then one by one they put the filling in the pie and put the pastry over the top and carve the family's initials on the pie with a knife."

"Oh, that's clever."

"Yes, I wouldn't want to get the McDonalds' family's pie as they're poor and I bet they don't buy such good steak as we do."

"Well, you needn't worry about that as all the neighbours have clubbed together and bought them the meat for their New Year's Day pie, so they'll have a feast just like all the rest of us."

"Oh, that's good and Ma, listen, I asked Mr Robertson if I could be his delivery boy next year and he said I'd be old enough then, so I can deliver all the pies on my bike, and he said he would pay me a shilling."

Chapter Twenty-Three

The family all sat round the fire on New Year's Eve. Aunt Jeanie had bought a board game called Errand Boy, for the whole family as a present and they spent few hours laughing and squabbling over the game. There were accusations of "Pa you're cheating." and "Ronald's cheating now, Ma," hotly denied by any of the accused. At last, it was decided that James had acquired the most money and property and was the winner and the boys helped to pack the game away. Angus handed him a sixpence, and everybody chuckled when he said,

"Well, dash my wig."

Ronald said, "You haven't got a wig."

"I know that silly but one day at school I said, 'Bugger me and my teacher told me it was rude to say that, and a more polite expression would be to say dash my wig."

Angus said, "Your teacher was quite right" but thinking that he wouldn't take it any further as he knew the boys would start to ask why saying, 'bugger me' was rude and that it could lead into all sorts of areas best left alone. After they had put the game away, they played some parlour games. The boys loved 'Squeak Piggy Squeak' and after a boisterous half an hour of play with much shouting and laughter, Moira calmed the boys down by introducing a quiet game. She brought in a tray that she had already prepared from the pantry, covered in random articles and everyone had a few minutes to look at the items. Moira then took the tray away and gave everyone a pencil and paper. The room fell quiet as everyone concentrated on remembering what had been on the tray. There were many chuckles when Moira brought back the tray, with everyone comparing their answers and their mistakes.

"Pa, that wasn't a carrot, it was a turnip and there weren't six bottles of beer."

"Och well, a man can dream, can't he?"

There was more good-natured joshing and eventually Moira declared that Ronald was the outright winner. Angus gave Ronald a sixpence and there was more laughter, when not wanting to be outdone by his brother, he looked at the money and said,

"Well, dash my wig."

Moira commented, "Goodness that expression is fast becoming the family motto."

Then the boys begged the family to play charades, which they loved. Angus was the first and amused the boys by acting out the Nursery Rhyme 'Little Miss Muffat.' They laughed when he pretended to be a spider and then roared with laughter when he made a horrified face showing the heroine being frightened away by the spider. When it was their turn, Robert and James acted out a passable interpretation of 'Jack and Jill' guessed by Moira. She was going to do a charade of a book for the adults but thought it wouldn't be fair to the boys so did *'Babes in the Wood'* instead. Lana guessed the correct answer but all the books she could think of like *'Uncle Tom's Cabin'* and the newly published *'Alice in Wonderland'* were too difficult to portray so she grabbed her cloak and a spoon and large cooking pot from the scullery and messed her hair up. She told everyone she was a person and proceeded to dance around the pot and stir it. Everyone was bewildered until she grabbed the broom from the cupboard and pretended to fly on it.

The boys cried out, "We know what you are. You're a witch"

Angus laughingly said, "I always knew you were a witch."

Auntie Jeannie said, "Well, as it's my turn to do a charade, I'm going to choose a different game. Let's play the laughing game."

They all sat round in a circle and one by one each person said, "Hee hee" "Ho ho" and "Ha ha." The aim of the game was to make someone laugh to eliminate them and the last person in the circle who did not laugh was the winner. Angus made a funny face and Robert and James caught sight of his face as he crossed his eyes and grimaced. The boys collapsed into giggles and then Lana couldn't help herself as she too glimpsed his hideous grimace and she started to chuckle.

"Pa, that's not fair, you're supposed to just say, 'Ha Ha' or 'Hee hee,' not make a funny face." As soon as the boys said this, just the thought of one on her husband's funny faces made Moira let out a great cackle of laughter and when she looked at Angus, he made another one of his faces and she was gone. As she collapsed on the floor giggling her body relaxed and she let out an enormous fart. She tried to apologise but she was shaking with laughter so much that she could not speak. Lana who always found farts hilariously funny rolled around on the floor with her laughing hysterically. The boys used to their mother being decorous, thought their Mum's little accident was riotously funny and joined in shouting

"Ma farted" in between uproarious giggling.

Soon all four of them were in a heap on the floor clutching their stomachs and laughing. When they finally wiped the tears of laughter away from their eyes, it was deemed that Angus was disqualified because he had cheated and the winner of the game was pronounced as Auntie Jeanie, being the last to succumb to laughter.

At last, as midnight approached, everyone had a drink in their hands, whisky for the adults and lemonade for the boys. Angus put his glass down and got ready to be the family's first footer. He put a bottle of whisky and a lump of coal in one of his deep coat pockets and filled the other pocket with all the cash they had and a Dundee cake. He stepped outside just before midnight and walked down the road. When he heard the church bells ringing to welcome in the New Year he turned back and knocked at his own front door. The long-standing tradition of first footing meant that the first person who stepped over your threshold had to be tall, dark, and carrying whisky, money, coal and some sort of food. That ensured that the family would be prosperous for the coming year. If a fair-haired person was the first to enter the house, it brought bad luck for the coming the year.

They went through the same ritual each year as Moira knew that some of the neighbours and Angus's workmates would call round, but she didn't want to take the chance that a fair-haired person would be the first visitor. She felt relieved when Angus came in. She thought, to herself, it was especially important to have good fortune this year with all the duplicitous plans she had made with Lana.

Moira, Lana and Jeannie brought out the food from the pantry that they had prepared earlier. There was a good spread of sandwiches, pickles, sausage rolls and even oysters not to mention mince pies and several types of cake on the table and soon there was a knock at the door as the first guests arrived. There were cries of,

"Happy New Year to ye all." "We've come to first foot ye."

"You're too late, I sent poor Angus out in the cold before midnight so he could first foot us."

"Well, nae harm, in having two first footers, I'm tall dark and handsome and I've brought in some whisky, coal, salt, shortbread and some money."

"Thank you, thank you and come away in. Happy New Year to you too. What would you like to drink? We've got some whisky, or would you prefer brandy?"

When everybody had a drink, they had a quick gulp, put their glasses down and all formed a circle, joined hands and sang 'Auld Lang Syne'.

"Should auld acquaintance be forgot and never brought to mind?
Should auld acquaintance be forgot and auld lang syne
For auld lang syne, my dear, for auld lang syne,
We'll take a cup o kindness yet, for auld lang syne."

They all sung with great enthusiasm, pumping their arms up and down in time to the song and then there was much hugging and kissing. James had fallen asleep in an armchair and Angus carried him up to bed. Ronald followed him upstairs yawning and Lana went up as well to tuck him in. There was no need for a story tonight though as he was asleep as soon as his head touched the pillow. Lana came back downstairs where one of Angus's workmates waylaid her.

"Och Lana, you look so bonnie tonight with your rosy cheeks and shiny hair. It must agree with you living in Dundee."

He planted a big kiss on her cheek,

"Why thank you, yes, I have enjoyed my stay in Dundee and it's not too bad at the mill, at least on the finishing section where I work."

She helped herself to a sausage roll and sat down next to her aunt. She felt a stab of poignancy as they had planned that Stefan would stay for Hogmanay and thought how much he would have enjoyed it. She wondered if he would ever experience a Scottish New Year but bolstered by all the jollity decided that she must stay positive. After all she was the one who thought he was alive somewhere and would one day come back to her. She knew he would find the longstanding tradition of first footing fascinating and would want to know its origin. Lana didn't know herself and made a silent promise to do some research so that she could tell him all about it. She cheered up at the thought that at least she had Stefan's baby to look forward to and wondered if she would have a girl or a boy. She joined in the celebrations, laughed, and joked with all the partygoers so that no one could tell that she was hiding a broken heart.

Chapter Twenty-Four

Back at the mill, the days passed uneventfully. Luckily, for Lana the work in the finishing section was quite easy. She helped to crop off any surplus fibres and Jessie and Maisie made sure that they and the others lifted the jute onto the wheelbarrows. They pushed them over and put them onto the pressing machines so that all Lana had to do was to move a lever so that the jute was ironed at high pressure through heavy rollers to give it a smooth pressed finish. She helped to fold up the finished jute, but the work was not taxing her at all and she felt well.

The only blot that ruined her otherwise tranquil life was when Mr Campbell, the mill manager paid her a visit to her house, on Saturday evening under the pretext that he needed to see her about the murder investigation. Lana took him into the front parlour and after exchanging the normal pleasantries he said,

"I have to admit Lana, that I used an excuse to see you as I wanted to ask you to have supper with me."

Lana was surprised and a little apprehensive, as she just did not like the man at all. She thought there was something disturbing about him, but she couldn't quite put her finger on it and because he was the boss at the mill, she agreed.

"Thank you, Mr Campbell, I am at a bit of a loose end as I don't know if you know that my fiancé has disappeared, so I will accept your kind offer.

William Campbell knew very well that Stefan had disappeared as he had arranged to have him murdered and although he was thinking, 'Yes and I hope his body is at the bottom of the North Sea tied to a rock,' his face remained impassive as he said,

"Oh, yes, my dear, I had heard, and I am sorry about that. Have you had any news from Holland? I believe he was Dutch, wasn't he?"

"No, no apparently, he did not re-join his ship and they sailed back to Rotterdam without him. The captain was just as mystified as me and the police have not found any clues or his body."

Lana felt tears welling up in her eyes as she spoke the last words.

William Campbell thought to himself, "Well I have been very patient and waited a month for her to get over her beau but thought this will not do for her to be upset. Oh no, I want her happy and smiling." and he said,

"Now, now, it won't do any good crying so why don't we go out now, the fresh air will do you good and food will cheer you up."

She told her aunt that she was going out for a bite to eat, put on her cloak and bonnet and went outside and climbed into Mr Campbell's barouche. It was a sunny day, although cold and when they arrived at the inn just outside Dundee, Lana's cheeks were glowing. They went inside and Lana couldn't help feeling embarrassed as everyone was staring at her.

Mr Campbell noticed her discomfiture and said, "Don't worry about folk staring, it's just that we make such a handsome couple."

Lana gave a nervous laugh as the owner of the inn took them to their seats in a secluded corner, out of sight of the other customers, making Lana begin to feel better. Mr Campbell showed Lana the menu and asked her to choose what she would like.

"I'll have the grilled haddock with vegetables, Mr Campbell."

"You can call me William, never mind Mr Campbell"

Lana smiled cheekily, "But I'd better call you Mr Campbell at work, otherwise the other girls might get jealous if they think there is favouritism going on."

"No, that would never do, so you'd better call me Mr Campbell at work," he said with a satisfied smile thinking that she was doing rather well and getting the hang of how their relationship would develop.

He called the waiter over and ordered Lana's meal and a steak pudding with vegetables for himself. They had a pleasant time and Lana started to enjoy herself and even laughed and smiled. After they had eaten the main course, William looked at the menu again.

"Aah, they've got some late strawberries as a pudding, a rare treat, would you like to try them?"

Lana agreed quickly and the waiter brought two big bowls of the fruit swathed in double cream. When she had eaten the strawberries, to her dismay Lana suddenly felt that she was going to be sick and quickly got up and ran outside. She just got to the street in time and vomited into the gutter. Mr Campbell had followed her outside and it hit him immediately as his wife had been the same when she was pregnant but with her, it had been gooseberries.

"You are with child," he said to Lana.

She didn't know what to say but thought it would be useless to deny it as she would have to have a leave of absence from the mill to have the baby. Mr Campbell kept a poker face even though he was struggling with conflicting emotions. He was angry because this would ruin his plans but then he thought that it would be better for him as she would be vulnerable with a child to care for and might be agreeable to him setting her up in a small house and entering an arrangement with him. He didn't feel any remorse that he had organised the death of this unborn baby's father but only thought of his plans and that he must be patient and understanding.

Lana wiped away the tears that always came with being sick and Mr Campbell handed her the napkin he had been holding when he ran after her, to wipe her mouth.

"Yes, I'm going to have a baby, it's due in July but I want to come back and work at the mill."

"Well, congratulations my dear. The baby must be a comfort to you and of course we will give you time off to have the baby and then when you are ready you can come back to the mill."

"Oh, thank you for being so understanding. My sister is going to look after the bairn for me in the week and I'll go back to Anstruther at the weekends."

He dropped her off at her house and Lana ran in to tell her aunt her news that she had told Mr Campbell about the baby and that, he had told her not to worry and that she could come back to the mill and have her old job back after the baby was born. Auntie Jeanie was pleased for her as she had been a bit worried that Lana would lose her job but when she told Jessie and Maisie the following Monday they said,

"I don't trust that man; he's got something up his sleeve."

"Be careful, Lana, he's not the kind understanding man you think he is."

Mr William Campbell sat in his office staring out of the window thinking about Lana. There was something about that girl. She was unusual. She was special. On the one hand, she seemed like a naïve country girl but on the other, she was refined and sophisticated. Usually, his little peccadillos were just a bit on the side, but he would have to be careful he did not become too attached to Lana.

Chapter Twenty-Five

It was June already and the time had gone surprisingly quickly Lana thought, as she placed her bag by the door. Auntie Jeanie had borrowed her friend's horse and cart for the journey to stay with Andrea at the pub in Elie. It was a bright sunny day, and the ferry crossing was smooth and uneventful. They made timely progress from Newport to Leuchars and then on to St Andrews, where they took the road across country to reach The Ship Inn at Elie.

"It seems strange not to be going along the coast past Crail to Anstruther."

"Weel, this is better as ye don't want folk seeing ye. Ah know ye havenae put on much weight but ye know what folk are like for gossiping they only need tae see ye and that could be enough to start a rumour. We dinnae want that."

Lana had tried to eat lots of fruit and vegetables and had avoided fattening foods, so she hadn't put on much weight. She smiled to herself as she remembered one day when she had felt so starving that she just had to make herself a piece of bread and dripping, which she had devoured with relish. The thought of it could still make her mouth water as she remembered the taste of all the meat juices mixed with the fat melting into the home-baked bread still warm from the oven and she suddenly felt hungry.

"My, I'm starving."

"Well, I thought we could stop at the old coaching house at Lathones for something to eat. It will make a break in our journey. How would that suit you?"

"That would be wonderful."

When they arrived, the groom took care of their horse, giving him, some water and hay and he even rubbed him down. The inn was quite crowded as it served the local village of Largoard where there was a coalmine. As it was Sunday, it was full of miners with their wives.

They soon got talking to one of the families who pointed out the famous wedding stone placed above the fireplace as its lintel, and they related the story about Iona Kirk and Ewan Lindsay who ran the pub from 1718 until Iona's death in 1736. The miner told them solemnly that the couple were so in love that when Iona died the wedding stone cracked and Ewan died shortly afterwards of unknown causes. He pointed out the crack in the stone saying,

"Some say yon Ewan died of a broken heart."

"Oh, that is such a sad and lovely story."

They chose a table, and no sooner had they settled down than the waitress asked them what they would like to eat.

"What would ye recommend?" Jeanie asked

"Och folk come for miles around to have a go at the chefs' wee lamb stovies. They're famous."

They both took the girl's advice; Lana ordered some Sarsaparilla to drink, and Auntie Jeanie ordered a whisky. "Might as well push the boat out", she said with a broad grin.

Feeling rested and replete they carried on with their journey, down to Elie. They reached the lake at Kilconquhar and then took the left branch of the road, which led to Elie. The weather was warm, and Lana slipped her shawl off her shoulders enjoying the sun warming her bare arms. It wasn't long before they heard the gulls cawing and saw them circling heralding their approach to Elie as they turned along the coast road. When they reached, The Ship Inn Andrea was standing by the door, and she flung her arms around her sister.

"Moira has told me all about your troubles, you poor thing, you don't seem to be lucky with men, do you? Anyway, I'm happy to help and I'll show you where you'll be staying. Come round to the back door, as there is a back staircase. Lana, you'll have to stay hidden in the daytime, but you can go out by the back staircase in the evening, so come round to the back door now. We don't want folk to see you as you know what gossips they are, especially the old biddies, you can just imagine them saying, 'Och I clocked that Lana St Clair, an she looked as if she was expecting a bairn, ready to drap she was. It's a cock 'n' bull story that Moira St Clair has had twins, ye mark my words one of those wee 'Uns is her sister Lana's bairn.' Then the cat would be out of the bag."

Andrea had the accent off pat and pulled such a pinched a sour face when she was mimicking the old biddy that Lana couldn't help but laugh out loud,

"Oh you're a caution Andrea, you are. But it won't be difficult for me to stay in during the day. I've got books to read and I'm making some baby clothes, so I can sew. Moira gave me some paints for Christmas so I can even paint some pictures. I won't be bored at all, besides Moira will be here in a few days and I've got Auntie Jeanie to look after me."

"Yes, I'll bring your meals up to you on a tray."

"You see, I shall feel like the Queen. But what about your husband Andrea, is he all right with all of this?"

"Ben is fine. He likes a bit of drama and he's looking forward to having two babies here, as his own children are grown up."

"Well, the babies won't be here for long."

"Yes, he knows that, but I think he's secretly hoping that seeing your babies will make me feel broody. He'd like me to have a child."

"How do you feel about that?"

"Maybe but I'm so busy with all the work in the pub that I don't think he realises that he'd have to hire more staff, if I had a baby to look after."

"Well, he can afford it."

"Yes, he can, so maybe. We'll see what happens." Andrea smiled broadly.

Chapter Twenty-Six

The days passed quickly, and Lana got used to just popping out for some air in the evenings. She thought the better of shouting at the sea though in case she drew attention to herself.

One Sunday at the end of July, Lana woke up and went to the window, stretched her arms over her head and gave a cry as she felt a pain across her back and abdomen. She thought nothing of it and put it down to the mussels she had eaten the day before. Auntie Jeanie came bustling in with a cup of tea and a steaming bowl of porridge.

"I don't think I can eat anything; I've got a tummy ache but I'll drink the cup of tea." She took a sip, "Mmm, that's lovely."

Moira came in and said, "Are you not eating your breakfast today?"

"No, I've got a stomach-ache. It must have been those mussels from last night."

"It'll not be the mussels, it's the baby that's on its way."

Lana stubbornly refused to believe that she was in labour and said,

"No, no I've just got a stomach upset that's all."

She still refused to accept that she was in labour until about five o clock when she finally had to admit that her sister was right. "I didn't know that having a baby hurt so much." Lana moaned as a strong pain overtook her. Moira bathed her forehead with cool water and told her to grasp her hand if it helped. As the pains grew stronger, Aunt Jeanie told her to push. Lana pushed with each pain and then Aunt Jeanie gave a shout and said,

"I can see the wee head so just pant for a while and when the next pain comes push like mad."

Lana screamed as she gave an almighty push, and she felt a wet rush between her legs. The baby started to cry, and Aunt Jeanie said joyfully, "It's a girl." Lana felt the tears streaming down her face.

"Are you crying because the baby's not a boy?"

"No, I'm just relieved that it's all over."

Auntie Jeanie cut the umbilical cord and wrapped the baby in a clean sheet and handed her to Lana. Lana examined the baby's fingers and toes to reassure herself that she was perfect.

"She looks just like Stefan, look at her long dark eyelashes and dark eyebrows, except that she has my dark hair."

"Och all that dark hair will fall out and she'll be blond just like her father."

"I don't mind what colour her hair is, she's beautiful, my baby daughter Freya.

"Is that what you are calling her?"

"Yes, Stefan always said it he had a daughter he would call her Freya. Oh dear, I feel as if something else is coming out of me."

"That's Okay don't worry, it's just the after birth and I'll get rid of it."

Once Jeanie and Moira had cleaned up the church bells rang for evensong.

"I've just realised that Freya has been born on Sunday which means she'll be bonnie and blithe and good and gay."

"Well, that's good, if she's got a happy temperament perhaps, she won't keep you up all night crying. I just hope mine is born on a Sunday too."

Moira didn't quite get her wish as her baby arrived the next week, not on the Sunday but the Monday. Moira was delighted as she now had a daughter to complement her two sons. She was a pretty baby with blond hair like Moira who smiled as Lana recited the rhyme to her,

"Monday's child is fair of face."

Auntie Jeanie scoffed and said, "That's a load of rubbish, all ye three girls are fair of face and nae one of you was born on a Monday!"

"Well anyway I shall call her Alina as it means fair, and it goes with Freya as they both end in the letter 'a'.

Lana said, "Freya and Alina, that's perfect."

They put the babies in the cot together and Moira said, "Look how sweet they look one dark and one fair."

★ ★ ★

Lana and Moira were back in Anstruther when Freya and Alina were two months old and both babies were healthy and growing well. They had just started to smile at everybody when Auntie Jeanie had reluctantly returned to Dundee. She shed some tears when she left,

"Och, I'll miss ye two wee angels, but I'll be back soon."

Lana was quite overcome too when she left and shed a few tears herself,

"Thank you for everything you've done for me, I couldn't have managed without you. I'll be coming back to Dundee to stay with you in February of next year. I hope to start work at the mill then. Freya will be seven months by then, so I won't mind leaving her for a week at a time and seeing her on Saturday night and Sunday. So, you can come back to Anstruther with me then.

Aunt Jeanie smiled at Lana, "You're a brave lassie and I love you."

She got in her little cart, which they had put in the field behind the house together with the horse. Jeannie had borrowed her friend's horse and cart on a long loan, and she gave a wave as she gave a clucking noise saying, "Giddy up" to the horse and cheerfully declaring, "My friend will be pleased to see me with her horse and cart."

Moira and Lana decided to take the babies for a walk to try to dispel their sadness at Aunt Jeanie's departure. It didn't take long for them to cheer up as everybody they met stopped and wanted to talk to the babies. Freya's hair had gone blonde as Aunt Jeanie had predicted and so the babies looked similar. They were both little charmers and smiled beatifically at all their admirers.

"Will ye just look at them, they're so bonnie. They're off to break a few hearts when they grow up. I don't know which one of them is the prettiest. They're both so gorgeous."

Lana knew which baby was the most beautiful, Freya, of course, she looked just like a female version of Stefan with her dark blue eyes, thick dark eyelashes and blonde curls.

Lana would never have said this to Moira for although Alina was pretty, she looked pale in comparison to her cousin Freya.

"Why is it that everyone is so fascinated by twins?"

"I don't know but at least everyone has accepted that they are your twins, Moira and that I have just come back home to help you."

"Yes, it's really good that our plan worked, and no-one is the least bit suspicious."

"The only ones who are suspicious are Robert and James and only because you are always picking Freya up, but I haven't said anything to them. I just said that you like Freya because she was born with dark hair and looked like you."

"She's not dark haired like me now and she looks the image of Stefan. It breaks my heart that he's not here to share her with me and it's breaking my heart to have to leave her with you and go back to the mill.

Chapter
Twenty-Seven

While Lana planned her return to Dundee and work at the mill, Detectives Murray and McDuff were still investigating the serial killings.

"What do ye think about the witness reports of seeing a wee man lurking around the docks?"

"Well, we'd better take statements from those good folks. But it's mighty strange that the murders seemed to have stopped. We havenae found a dead body for well over a year. T'was after that mill lassie reported her betrothed had gone missing, Stefan van Uden, I think was his name. Something must have happened that night when he disappeared to frighten our murderer off."

After they had taken the statements from the various witnesses the consensus seemed to be that the man was foreign and seemed to be destitute as he was sometimes seen begging. The detectives told the rest of the police force to keep their eyes open for this man and to arrest him on sight as he was a person of interest.

A few weeks went by, and another report came in, this time from the cook at the Camperdown House, just outside Dundee. She reported a stranger, Russian she thought, who had come to the back door asking for food. He said his ship had sailed without him leaving him stranded. The cook thought that he had made a camp somewhere on the estate because the ghillie, Mr Robinson, had found rabbit traps and evidence of rabbit bones and old fires. The two detectives set off to the Camperdown Estate and after they had taken a statement from the cook, they spoke to Mr Robinson,

"'Tis one thing to come to the estate to poach but to set up a camp and live on the estate is a down right cheek; I will shoot the bugger if I find him."

"Oh nae, don't do that, we need to speak to him, he could be our serial killer."

"All right, if you're after catching him ye could lie wait for him by the vegetable garden as he's partial to our tatties. Ah suppose a cracking pure baked tattie goes well with rabbit especially if it's free."

"Fine we'll arrange a rota to stand guard over the vegetables starting tonight. Mind it's cold so we'd better tell all our lads to wrap up well and bring some whisky to keep the cold at bay. It can't be any fun for the poor man, he must be freezing."

"Well, the sooner we catch him the better it'll be for him then."

They didn't have to wait long as the two constables on the first watch grabbed the man that evening and there was a terrible commotion at the police station. Detectives Murray and Mc Duff heard loud shouting,

"*Ya Ruskii. Ya nye ponyimayu. Pojalsta, pojalsta. Ya nye ubiyitsa. Ya Ruski.*"

"All right. We know you're Russian. Do you speak any English?"

"Yes. Me Sergei Alexandrovich. Cook on ship the *Navki*. *Navki* she sail without me leave behind. I go to docks every day to see if *Navki* come back. I have knives to hunt food."

"Well Sergei, we're investigating the murders of sailors a year ago around the Dundee docks. Did you kill these sailors?

"No I no kill men, I kill rabbits to eat. No here year ago. I only here few months, *Navki* left in October."

"Alright, Sergei, we will keep you in custody for a few days while we check out your story. At least you'll be warm and dry, and you'll get three meals a day."

"Thank you. I like to stay in police station. Is very cold outside."

It only took a quick trip to the harbour to see the Harbour master and they found that their suspect was telling the truth. They also found that the *Navki* was due to dock in Dundee on the twentieth of March.

"What do you think?"

"No, he can't be our murderer. The murders started long before he was stranded. We'll just go and tell him the good news that he can re-join his boat."

"Well Sergei, the good news is that we believe you. You are not the serial killer we are looking for and your ship is due to dock on the twentieth of March so you are going home."

"*Oh spasiba*, thank you, thank you. I stay here until ship arrives?"

"Well as it's only a few days I expect we can accommodate you but remember to tell everyone in Russia that the Scottish police are very hospitable!!"

"Yes, yes, I do this."

Chapter Twenty-Eight

Lana had survived another Christmas and New Year without Stefan. She still thought about him every day. The other day she thought she caught a glimpse of him disappearing round a street corner and had run after the man. She shouted "Stefan" and the man turned round, his mouth curved into a round O of surprise. She had to explain that she had mistaken him for a friend and apologise. The man was quite agreeable and seemed amused when he said,

"Och, dinnae worry lass it's nae often that I get a beautiful woman running after me."

She walked despondently away shaking her head to dispel the image and return to reality. It was a cold and blustery day in March 1866 when she returned to work at the mill, and she was glad to escape from the bitter wind. All the girls made a tremendous fuss of her, and Mr Wainwright couldn't seem to stop bustling around her asking her if there was anything she needed. Lana soon settled down to a routine of working all week and going back to Anstruther for the weekend. Her breasts were still swollen and producing milk and she bound them with a bandage and a piece of cotton to soak up the milk.

Each time she had to leave her daughter; she was distraught. Freya cried when she said goodbye, but Moira had told her that she recovered quickly and seemed happy. Lana knew that she couldn't do this forever as she knew that she would lose her daughter to Moira's family, and she selfishly wanted Freya to herself. She dreaded the day that Freya called Moira 'Mama' as she would think that Moira was her mother and not her.

It was now the middle of Lana's fourth week back at work. March had come in like a lion and as the saying went, seemed to be going out like a lamb. It was nearly April; the weather had mellowed, and Lana made up her mind. She was going to leave the mill and return to Anstruther. She had found out that the Bakery down by the Quayside was short staffed and she had decided to ask if she could work there. She would not earn as much as she did at the mill but at least she would be with her daughter.

When she got back to Auntie Jeanie's house that evening, she sat down and wrote a letter of resignation that she would take in to give to Mr Campbell the next day, telling him that she would be leaving at the end of the week. She would be back in her home and with her old friends, why she might even go for a drink with Billy O'Neil. It would be good to go out and have some fun, and even flirt. She was happiest in the company of men and although she knew that she might never find another man she could love as much as Stefan, she could still hope that she could find some sort of peace. She thought that she was cursed as she had lost one husband and one prospective husband. Surely, she mused she might find a kind-hearted man who could be a father to Freya, and although there might not be passion if he was kind love could grow from quiet harmony. She decided that if she met another man who was agreeable to bringing Freya up as his daughter, she would give him a chance. Freya needed a father, and she would look for a man to fulfil that role. She would put all thoughts of being cursed from her head as she thought surely, she had been blessed with a healthy and beautiful daughter. She felt better now that she had made a decision and curled up in bed and had the best night's sleep she had had for a long time.

Chapter Twenty-Nine

It was just another ordinary day for Moira, but she did not realise that she would have two surprises and a shocking revelation by the time that night fell. She had cleared up the breakfast dishes and taken the boys to school, put the babies in the playpen and was hanging out the washing on the line in the garden, when she heard the clip clop of a horse's hooves approaching the house. She looked over the wall and saw a stranger tying his horse reins to the front gate. She quickly entered the house through the back door, splashed some water from the sink on her face and smoothed her hair.

She opened the front door as the stranger walked up the path, "Hello" she said tentatively.

"Hello, I'm sorry to trouble you. My name is William Campbell and I'm one of the managers at Cox's Mill. You may have heard Lana speak about me."

Moira did not say that Lana had said that she didn't trust him and that he made her feel uncomfortable, but instead said politely "Oh yes she has mentioned you."

She recovered from her surprise and remembered her manners "I know its early, but you must have ridden all the way from Dundee so would you care for a whisky"

"Thank you that would be most welcome."

"I'll have a glass of whisky too," Moira said, as she knew it had to be something serious for him to come all the way to Anstruther to visit her house and thought it might steady her nerves. She couldn't explain it but she had taken an immediate dislike to the man. He made her feel anxious and apprehensive. She poured the whisky and handed one of the glasses to Mr Campbell.

When he had received the letter of resignation from Lana, Campbell had been horrified and knew that he had to act quickly and so he had decided to see Lana's sister to see if she could persuade her to stay at the mill.

"I'll get right to the point no need to beat about the bush. I have come to see you as I have a proposition for Lana, and I know as her older sister that you may be able to influence her to accept my offer. I have always admired Lana and I would be willing to set her up in a wee house. She could have her daughter with her, and I'll pay for a nanny 'til she goes to school. Why will I even pay for her to go to a good school when she is old enough."

"But why would you do that?"

"I will do all of that and more if Lana will agree to becoming my mistress."

"How dare you think that I would persuade my sister to become anyone's mistress, let alone your mistress She would never do that. Why she doesn't even like you and she certainly doesn't have any feelings for you in that way. She loves Stefan and she is waiting till he comes back."

Willie Campbell realised that his long-laid plans had all come to nothing because in the end, Lana's sister Moira had told him that Lana would reject him, and he started to feel anger welling up inside him. Why, no girl had ever objected to his advances at the mill, he was the manager and had power over their livelihood. How dare this chit of a girl refuse him? He just couldn't contain his anger and shouted at Moira.,

"Ye and your sister are stupid lassies, Stefan is never comin' back. I told the smugglers that he was a rapist and paid them to murder him. They threw his body way out in the North Sea. Ye needn't think of going to the police as I've arranged for the Customs and Excise to lay in wait for them tomorrow night when they're taking delivery of some contraband. I wanted to get rid of them in case they can't keep their mouths shut. So, with any luck they'll all be shot or at least put in jail and who's going to take their word against mine. A convicted smuggler or an established and trusted member of society who is a manager at Cox's mill."

Moira was shocked and felt tears welling up in her eyes that someone could be so mean spirited to murder her sister's fiancé. Then her desolation transformed into rage, and she shouted back at him,

"Why, you evil foul little maggot. How could you stoop so low as to murder my sisters' husband-to-be just so that you could bed her? I'll make sure she resigns from her position at the mill. She won't ever have to see your ugly face again. You are as repulsive as a smelly dead herring. Get out. Get out now."

With these words, she threw the rest of her whisky in his face. Mr Campbell eyes were stinging with the whisky, and they were pouring with tears as he staggered out of the house.

★ ★ ★

Moira collected herself and realised that she would have to find the smugglers and question them to find out the truth. She put the two girls into the pram and set off from pub to pub looking for the smugglers. She had gone to all their local haunts without success, but someone told her about Jock's favourite bench at the quayside. She was out of breath, her hair dishevelled, and she felt mentally exhausted. She saw Jock sitting alone staring out to sea and rushed over to him,

"Hello, I'm Moira Lana's sister and I've just had a disturbing conversation with a certain Mr Campbell from Cox's mill. He said that you paid him to kill Stefan."

"What are ye talking about lassie, I've nae murdered anybody, and I don't even know who Stefan is?"

"Well Mr Campbell told me that he paid you to murder my sister Lana's husband-to-be Stefan. He said you killed him and threw his body into the North Sea."

"Now will ye hauld yer horses a wee minute there, I didn't know he was Lana's sweetheart, or I would never have agreed to do it. A man asked us to kill a sailor but we didnae recognise him as Mr

Campbell from the mill, because he was wearing a balaclava. The man said he had raped his sister and that's how come we agreed to do the dirty deed as we all thought that rapists deserved to die. But as it happens, we rescued him from the Dundee Slasher and when we saw what a handsome laddie, he was we doubted that he would ever need to rape any lassie, why he probably had lassies queuing up to walk out with him. So, we thought there was something fishy about that man's story and decided to save the sailor's life, so we gave him to the press gang.

We recognised him from some of the taverns we frequent, and we thought he could have recognised us as fellow drinkers. So, we coudnae release him but we coudnae murder him either.

"Tell me what happened I want to know everything."

"I remember Michael saying to me, when I saved the sailor from having his throat cut, 'What did ye do that for, that was the Dundee Slasher, and he could have done our job for us.' So, I hit the laddie over the head to knock him out while we decided what to do. Then I said 'Well, it was just a natural reaction but now that we've rescued him from the murdering varmint it would be a shame to kill him. It's a pity that there is nae a press gang now. That way we could've made a bit more money and we needn't commit a murder. He's such a fine-looking laddie that I thought he deserved a chance to live.'"

It was then that Michael said, "Hold your horses a wee minute, I heard that the captain of that new steamer ship in the harbour was looking to recruit crew for a boat that's off to New Zealand, The HMS Brisk. I know where the able seamen drink. I know that captain and he won't be above paying dosh for a recruit for the navy, even if it's a bit illegal *See Notes 6. HMS Brisk

The man who paid us will never know, as this handsome laddie will just disappear. It'll keep him safe; otherwise, the man might try to murder him again."

So, then Robbie said, "Come on then, load him into the wheelbarrow and we'll go to the pub. It's nae far from here. We'll ask for ten shillings and we can go to the pub and that'll buy the three of us a good night and we'll nae have blood on our hands."

Michael said, 'We'd better be quick, or this fine laddie will wake up." and then I said,

"Och, don't worry yourself he's out for the count. I hit him hard, and he'll nae wake up until tomorrow. Then I remembered that Michael had bent down and picked up a wee blade that the murderer had dropped on the quayside, and I said to him,

'Ye should give that to the police. 'Tis evidence and it might help them to catch the murderer. Look 'tis real silver, ye can see the hallmark and it has initials engraved on the handle.'

So, Michael said, 'Well, I'm no going to the Police, they might think that I'm the murderer' and I said,

'Keep it then and you might be able to hand it over later'"

Moira frowned and said to Jock, "But how do you know that you didn't kill Stefan when you hit him over the head?"

"Och, he was aye breathing, and he was OK. He likely just woke up with a bad headache. We coudnae kill him and we coudnae release him. That is the whole sorry tale hen, as far as I know he's sailor in the Royal Navy. He was impressed into the HMS *Brisk*, sailing out of Portsmouth in December last year."

"So, you didn't murder him and he's still alive."

Moira threw her arms around Jock and kissed him on both cheeks. "Oh, thank you, thank you, I'm so relieved for my sister. But I was forgetting I had to tell you that Mr Campbell wanted to get rid of you and your friends in case you would incriminate him and so he has told the Customs and Excise men to lie in wait for you tonight by the Wemyss caves in East Neuk, as he knew that you were expecting a cargo."

At Moira's words, all of Jock's surprise and delight when she had kissed him changed to anger and fear.

"Why that dishonourable wee bam pot, how could he betray us when we supply him with rum and baccy every week? I'll go and find Michael and Robbie and warn them about the trap the night. We'll have to go and signal to the men bringing the cargo to abandon the drop so that they don't get caught and all."

He jumped up, shook Moira's hand and with these parting words he sped off down the road,

"Lana is a brave lassie but tell her to stay away from that evil Mr Campbell as ye know it takes a long spoon to sup with the devil."

★ ★ ★

Moira was unaware that there was another stranger visiting Anstruther, Ton Van Uden from the Netherlands. He walked slowly down the gangplank of his ship onto the quayside in Anstruther. He had no idea where to start looking for his son Stefan. He didn't even know the first name of the girl Stefan wanted to marry let alone her family name. He just knew he had to find him. They had to resolve their disagreement.

When Stefan hadn't come back on board the Zeeland, he had thought he was just angry with him after their quarrel and that he would come back home when his money ran out and agree to marry Antoinette. However, it was now well over a year, why it was eighteen months so why hadn't he come back? Where was he? He had a small *carte-de-visite* of Stefan, which he showed to passing people and asked if they had seen this man. but everybody said the same,

"Naw ah don't know him." Or "Och a handsome laddie like that I'd remember him if I had seen him."

In the house where they did know Stefan, Moira and was sitting at the kitchen table telling her husband about the visit from Mr Campbell and the news she had found out from the smugglers about Stefan when Robert and James came in from school. Moira didn't want them listening in and so she asked the boys to take Alina and Freya for a walk in their pram. The boys didn't mind, in fact they enjoyed taking the babies out as everyone made such a fuss of them and often gave the boys sweets or fruit, saying,

"Och, ye're good lads to take the babies out. Ye must be a good help to your Ma."

Ton Van Uden had almost given up his quest when he saw two boys pushing a pram along the narrow road. Everybody that passed the boys stopped and talked to them and Ton thought to himself that there was a chance the boys might know Stefan.

He came alongside the pram and saw that there were two babies and not one, dressed in matching outfits. He was about to ask the boys if they knew Stefan when he looked at the twin girls and one of them gave a wide smile and held out her arms to him. He was shocked as she was the image of Stefan when he was a baby. It was the eyes, a deep blue fringed with dark lashes with dark brows highlighting their perfection.

Ronald said, "Och, that's Freya, she's a flirt and it looks as if she's trying to add you to her list of admirers."

Freya gave a wide smile and carried on holding her arms out to Ton. He was captivated and began to wonder if the baby was his granddaughter.

The other baby girl smiled at him and as if she wasn't going to be outdone by the other one held her hands up to him too.

James commented, "Och well. There she goes, that's Alina and she's just trying to make sure she doesn't miss out on your attention. She copies Freya all the time."

Ton thought idly that they must be non-identical twins as the other baby who was pretty with blonde curls and pale blue eyes was different from the other twin. Freya's likeness to his son mesmerized him and that he almost forgot to ask the boys if they knew Stefan. He recovered from his shock and showed them the photograph.

Ronald said, "We don't know him, and we have never met him, but we've heard of him."

Ton was elated as at last he thought he had located Stefan, but his joy turned to disappointment and fear when Jamie said, "Stefan is the name of my aunt's betrothed. They were to be married but he disappeared mysteriously, and no-one knows where he is."

He knew Stefan would never leave the girl he intended to marry voluntarily and began to fear the worst, that Stefan must be dead.

Chapter Thirty

Ronald and James ushered Ton into the house. "Mum we've met this stranger who says he is Stefan's father and he's looking for him just like Lana.

Ton stepped into the room and Moira recognised him immediately as he resembled Stefan.

"Oh, you must be Ton Van Uden, Stefan's father. Hello, I'm Moira, Lana's sister, Lana is the girl Stefan intended to marry."

Moira impressed Ton, as she seemed cool, calm and collected.

He replied, "I'm pleased to meet you Moira and I've come over from Rotterdam to find out what has happened to my son."

"I've just had some fantastic news that solves the mystery of his disappearance. He's been pressganged into the Royal Navy and the name of the ship he is serving on is the HMS *Brisk*."

Both the babies had started to cry. While Moira took Alina into her arms, Ton had a sudden revelation that the other baby was Lana and Stefan's baby, his granddaughter. His heart went out to Lana as he empathised with the stress this girl had experienced when Stefan disappeared, and she was left alone and pregnant. Moira noticed Ton's expression when the truth had dawned on him and quickly told the boys to go outside to play before supper. They would have to explain to them later that Freya was their cousin and not their sister, but she did not want to have that conversation right now. There were more critical issues to resolve.

Ton quickly discarded his overcoat and picked up Freya, "I know this baby is my granddaughter and I will bless Lana's marriage to Stefan when he returns."

Moira gestured for them to sit down and told them all about the conversation she had had with Jock, the smuggler. Ton, Moira, and Angus were astonished that Stefan had survived two attempted murders, once by the Dundee slasher and then by the smugglers. She told them that instead he had been press-ganged into service on HMS *Brisk* a Royal Navy ship.

Ton said, "I have my ship moored in the harbour and it's the new type which runs on steam, so we don't have to rely on the wind. It means I can make good time down to London and I will go to the Admiralty to find out where HMS *Brisk* is stationed. When I find out where she is I'll go in one of my ships to rescue Stefan and bring him home."

"I'm not going to tell Lana that Stefan may be alive as I don't want to get her hopes up for them to be dashed. She's suffered enough. I'll wait till we are sure he is coming home. She has given in her notice at the mill and will be moving back with us next week."

She went into the kitchen and made a pot of tea. The four of them discussed what they should do about the manager of Cox's Mill, Mr Willie Campbell.

"I don't think we can go around accusing him of plotting to commit murder. We have no proof; it would be his word against the smugglers, and I know whom the police would favour. We'll have to let it go for now and just concentrate on bringing Stefan back. "As you sow so shall you reap and that wee weasel will get his comeuppance, ye mark my words." Angus thumped the table as he spoke.

Freya wriggled on Ton's lap and tried to copy Angus's banging the table with her small hands and uttering baby talk.

"Aye ye tell them hen." Angus said.

They all laughed at Freya's antics and Ton said, "I'd best be going then; give me your address and I'll send you a letter from London when I find out where on earth Stefan is in the world."

Chapter Thirty-One

Jock had been shocked when Moira told him that Campbell had been such a traitor and reported him to the customs men. He was horrified to learn that, but he had also named the beach they used to bring the contraband brandy in from the Netherlands and that they stored it in Jonathon's cave, part of the Wemyss caves at East Neuk. Galvanised into action Jock went to find his fellow smugglers, Michael and Robbie, in the pub and sat down with them to impart his bad news to them.

"He buys our brandy right enough and is all smiles and polite then he goes and betrays us."

"There was aye something about his sly weasel face that made me think ye coudnae trust him. So, I was right all along.

"Never mind about him, we'll have to shift all the bloody barrels of rum that we've stored, out of the cave. Can ye git some of your mates to help? Then we'll have to stay at the beach tonight and give the signal to abandon the drop. They should know that if they see three lanterns that means danger, the coastguard or excise men are nearby, and they can't land on the beach. We can't have our Dutch suppliers getting caught. It would ruin our kinship with them nae to mention any future business. It's a good job that we weren't meeting them down by the Dreel tonight as it'll be easier for us to get away at Wemyss."

The smugglers often took in the contraband in Anstruther at the Dreel and brought it up the Dreel River to an inn that had a seaward door down to the burn but if they were expecting a large delivery, they operated at the Wemyss caves so that they could store the barrels of rum called *anks*.

"But we might get caught on the beach or worse even shot and killed."

"Yeah, the excise men are quick to use their rifles. Ah think there was a report in the newspapers the other day about how they shot and murdered some smugglers up in Montrose."

"Well, we'll have to take our chances that we can make a quick getaway after giving the signal to our friends. We'll stand on the high bank by the path and escape on horseback. There's a path that leads to the coast road and we can do a fair gallop down the road to Anstruther. Now I'll go and get the cart and catch up with ye back here in half an hour with all the pure tough men ye can muster to help us shift the brandy We'll take it to the White Swan in Elie as I know the landlord there will hide it fur us. Ye know Lana, well her wee sister Andrea is married to tae the chap who owns the pub, so I know they'll help us."

The smugglers scrambled to their feet and went off in different directions. When Jock returned with the horse and cart, he found that Michael and Robbie had rustled up four other men. Once they had just about fitted in the cart, they set off to Jonathon's cave, part of the Wemyss caves in East Neuk. They walked down the track to the beach and with so many helpers they made short work of loading the nine-gallon barrels onto the cart. The four men that had helped them walked behind the cart until they reached Elie and then helped to unload the barrels. Jock spoke to Ben the publican and then turned to Andrea. He told her that Moira was well and that she had warned him that Campbell had reported them to the Customs and Excise men.

"Och, that man is an evil monster. I think from what Lana has told me that he was planning to persuade her to become his mistress. I wouldn't be at all surprised to learn that he had something to do with the Dutch sailor's disappearance."

Jock was jolted out of his reverie with the problems he was facing with the revenue men and his face turned red as anger swept over him realising immediately how and why Campbell had tricked him. He was embarrassed as well as angry as he knew that Andrea, Lana's sister would find out about the part that the smugglers had played but was so relieved that they had only sent Stefan off to join the Royal Navy and hadn't murdered him.

"You're right. He certainly is a wrong 'un and I expect he'll get his comeuppance one day", already thinking of revenge for himself and Lana if he managed to avoid capture by the customs men. The men piled into the cart, and they made their way back to Anstruther. Jock gave the men who had stepped up to help them a generous payment and heaved a sigh of relief that the barrels had been saved so there was no evidence of smuggling but thought to himself, 'The next part would not be so easy.'

Later that night the three smugglers tied their horses to a fence post by the path and waited for darkness to fall. They took their positions on the high bank as birds began to sing their evening chorus, waves made a shushing noise as they broke on the shore and gradually the light faded. When they could see the stars lighting up the sky, they searched the horizon for the lights of the boat that they knew was coming.

"Look there she is. I can just see her."

"Quick light up the lanterns then."

Usually, the boat came as close to the shore as she could without running aground and then sent a small dinghy to carry the contraband to the shore.

They held up the three lanterns and waved them frantically. The boat returned their signal with their own three lanterns, and they saw it turn around and speed off into the night. A Customs and Excise boat that must have been lying in wait in a nearby cove appeared and gave chase, but the Dutch ship was too fast and outran the smaller vessel.

Michael laughed as he said, "No chance, they're just too fast. Tis good they got away." His laughter faded as they all heard the noise of ten burly Excise men scrambling out of one of the caves.

"Quick, Jock and Robbie, ye get away on the horses and I'll distract them by running along the beach, so they'll chase me."

"But what about ye. They'll catch ye for sure."

"Aye that they will but I've got some evidence that I can trade for my freedom. Remember the wee silver knife the Dundee slasher dropped. I'll offer to give it to the police and make a statement about where I found it. Now go on, leave me, go, go, go."

With that, Michael ran down to the beach and Jock and Robbie disappeared into the darkness and led their horses up the pathway. They resisted the urge to mount them and gallop away until they reached the road where they knew the noise of galloping hooves would not carry so well. Even so, they kept looking over their shoulders every so often expecting a mob of Revenue men to come charging after them.

They arrived in Anstruther with sweat pouring off the horses and took them back to the stable they used, rubbed them down and gave them some hay. Once the horses had been cared for, they headed for the nearest tavern and ordered glasses of whisky. It was only when they began to relax that their ordeal began to take its toll and Jock started to shake uncontrollably. The Innkeeper noticed that Robbie was as white as a sheet when he went to the bar to buy Jock another whisky, and he said,

"You look as if ye've seen a ghost."

"No, more like the devil or over ten devils who were waiting for us at Jonathon's cave."

"Och, ye mean the Revenue men lying in wait for ye, well in that case the whisky is on the house. We're no friends of the excise men and they are nae wanted here. There was a batch of them hanging around the Dreel, so someone must have told them that ye sometimes used the Dreel to bring in the barrels of rum. Ah made quite sure that they knew they were not welcome in my inn and they coudnae call in for a wee dram here."

And beyond

Chapter Thirty-Two

As suspected, Stefan was on the other side of the world in New Zealand. There had been times, in the past eighteen months when he had felt he was going out of his mind, worried about Lana, their baby and confused as to what had happened to him and why. When at first, he had found himself in the hold of a ship he did not know what had happened to him and often had recurrent nightmares when he would wake up in his hammock sweating and shaking. In these nightmares, someone grabbed him, and he felt a knife slicing through his neck.

He knew that was true because he still had the scar, but the rest was a jumble of confused memories. He thought he could remember a voice saying something about murder but try as he might he could not recollect any more. He thought he recognised some of the faces of the men but could not remember where he had seen them. It niggled at him, there was something but every time he tried to grasp it, it just eluded him. It was like a crafty, sly old fox slipping away into the dark just as he thought he had it. He lay back in his hammock trying to make sense of it all. What had happened, why was he here on a Royal Navy ship as a member of the Royal Navy?

He had relived the memories he did have a hundred times or more to see if anything could explain his situation. Nothing came to him, but he drew some comfort in going over the events in his mind, so he tried once again. When Jock had knocked him unconscious, he had woken with a jolt and tried to sit up. Everything had come back slowly. Awareness, senses, memory, and pain. He remembered he had felt antagonising pain in his head and had gone to hold his head in his hands but had found that his hands were bound to a berth of some sorts. His eyelids were gummy and difficult to force open. He could not use his hands to rub the crust that had formed while he slept and blinked rapidly to clear his vision. He had groaned and tried to remember what had happened. His thoughts had been a confused jumble of impressions, someone jumping out at him with a knife and then men shouting. He had seemed to remember that it was a woman holding the knife, but he wasn't sure as everything seemed chaotic.

He had thought someone, one of the shouting men hit him over the head with a club and then he remembered nothing. He cursed himself for his indecisiveness, as he couldn't help thinking that if he had married Lana quickly and whisked her off to Rotterdam that this would not have happened. He had a faint recollection of something that Maisie had said about a man at the mill, but his past life had retreated into a haze. Perhaps this man was the cause of all his troubles, or he was imagining phantoms that didn't exist in the real world.

The pain was no phantom though and had unwillingly pulled him back to consciousness. Stefan had felt a rocking movement and he had known he was aboard a ship. He had heard faint cries of men shouting commands,

"You twos have got the anchor detail" and "You twos make sure the masts are upped" and he knew that the ship was preparing to set sail. The steam engines roared into life, and he had felt the ship start to move, slowly at first as it negotiated the harbour exit and then it had sprung into life and moved faster and faster. He had wondered where it was going and what he was doing tied up in the bilge. He didn't wonder for long as he had heard footsteps and a sailor had appeared by his side.

"Aye, you're awake, I see, here's a drink of water for you. You look as if you need it."

"Thank you. Where am I? What am I doing on this boat? Moreover, where are we going?"

"Why you've been empressed into Her Majesty's Royal Navy. I'll take you up to see the captain and he'll explain what's what."

Stefan had seen a new Royal Navy state-of-the- art steam clipper in the harbour, the SS *Agamemnon* and had admired the boat. Why he had even thought about asking to look it over so he could tell his father about the new steam clippers. He thought his father could consider converting one of his fleet or buy a new steam-propelled ship.

He had said to the sailor, "Fine, take me to the captain of this ship, I believe that pressing men, as it is called, into the Royal Navy has been made illegal and as I am a Dutch citizen it is also illegal to recruit a foreign national in this way. My father, Ton Van Uden, is a well-known Dutch trader in jute and other commodities and can pay to have me released."

Stefan had not been worried as he thought he would be able to persuade the captain to contact his father but when they reached the captain's cabin in the stern of the ship, he had realised that he had been too optimistic.

"Here ye are captain, here's the fellow that was delivered. He's a good catch an nae mistake, already a seasoned sailor. He says his father is a rich merchant and can buy him out."

"Thank you, Able Seaman Cox." The captain dismissed the sailor and studying Stefan had said,

"Well now, here's the thing, you now have a choice. You can either sign up as a volunteer, receive an advance payment, and purchase clothes and a hammock or remain a pressed man and get nothing."

Stefan had been angry. He could not remember much about the previous night, but he had not lost his memory completely and he knew who he was,

"I am Stefan Van Uden, the son of a rich Dutch trader and I know my rights. You cannot do this; pressganging is now illegal."

"You're right it is now illegal to pressgang men into the Navy, but I've been asked by a good friend of mine Captain Charles Webley Hope to find him some crew for his ship the HMS *Brisk* that is sailing to New Zealand from Portsmouth in a few days to relieve the HMS *Miranda*. I owe him a favour and as I have you as a prisoner, I am afraid that you are the favour."

"The addition to his crew of a Dutch-speaking experienced sailor will be a godsend because a Dutch man named Abel Tasman, in the 1640's, was the first to "discover" and map New Zealand, a good century before Captain Cook of the Royal Navy and it will therefore be extremely useful if old Dutch documents need be deciphered."

He had given a great bellowing laugh, "Look on it as a great new adventure, laddie."

Stefan had glared at the man, "At least send a message to my fiancé in Dundee, she is expecting my child and we were to marry so you must send her a message."

"Give me her address and I will send her a note to tell her what has happened to you."

The captain wrote down Lana's address, although he did not intend to carry out his word, as that would compromise his plans for Stefan. He had known that what he was doing was not strictly legal and he did not want any trouble. Besides, he had thought, "Possession is nine tenths of the law."

"Now we'll find you a cabin and a bunk and I'll send Able Seaman Cox with some breakfast for you. I expect you are hungry by now. It'll take us two days to reach Portsmouth but don't worry; we'll look after you well."

Chapter Thirty-Three

When HMS *Brisk* had set sail from Portsmouth, it had been a cold and blustery day in December but as the ship travelled, further south it became warmer and warmer. Stefan settled down into the routine of life aboard the ship and all the other sailors were friendly. His duties were not arduous, and he happily painted and chipped the rust on the superstructure of the ship, caulked the planks of wood on the decks with tar and helped to clean the wheelhouse and quarterdeck. He especially enjoyed when it was his turn to stand watch from the bow of the ship or wing of the bridge to look for any obstruction in the path of the ship.

Stefan often talked to the captain, and he was picking up many facts about navigation. The captain had told him that he had faced the choice of sailing the HMS *Brisk* through the Canary Islands or passing them to port or starboard and he had chosen to go round them because the mountains could create a wind shadow for several hundred miles which he said would mean 'snail pace sailing'.

So, Stefan had to be satisfied with just a glimpse of the Canary Islands. Their interesting volcanic mountains piqued his curiosity and he thought that one day he would like to come back and explore the islands. The captain enjoyed educating Stefan, found his eagerness to learn commendable and told him that they would now make good speed thanks to the trade winds, but he warned Stefan that they had to face another challenge, the dreaded doldrums with fickle winds and sudden squalls. He said they would have to use the propeller with its steam power to navigate them through this hazard. The ship approached the Saint Peter and Saint Paul rocks about 20 degrees west, heralding their approach to the equator, Captain Webley Hope used a trumpet and announced that Neptune would visit the ship the next morning and all the sailors who had never crossed the equator would take part in an initiating ceremony. The sailors made the ship snug, the tops sails closely reefed, courses hauled up and top gallant sails furled.

Stefan had made friends with a Yorkshire lad called Ben who had been in the Navy since he was fifteen and was a seasoned sailor. He had a mop of brown curly hair that seemed to grow as fast as the grass on Stefan's lawn at home in Rotterdam and he was forever having it cut by the ship's barber. There were laughter lines all around his blue eyes as he was always smiling and chuckling. His mouth matched his eyes and was permanently set in an amused upward curve.

"Eh up, it's that time again, well, Stefan you'll enjoy the experience and it's all genuine fun, an' we get an extra tot of rum as well. I'm a Shellback, or a son of Neptune and you are a Pollywog. Tomorrow you will take part in a ritual to become a Shellback. But tonight, is Wog Day, all of you Pollywogs are allowed to capture and interrogate any of us Shellbacks you can find, and you can tie us up, whip us or pour water on our heads. It's a sort of revenge in advance for the ordeal you will go through tomorrow."

After dinner men appeared in costumes depicting Davy Jones, bears, and police. They all bore a striking resemblance to the senior officers on board. They read out a list of men charged for their crimes who were to be summoned at the ceremony the next day.

When they had departed, Stefan joined in all the mayhem chasing various crew members round the decks, catching some, tying them up, and tickling their feet till they cried for mercy. It was all enjoyable and they ended up laughing their way to their hammocks. Stefan thought it was a clever way to keep up the spirits of the men, helping them to forget their confinement in a floating prison for a long time and being unable to walk on firm ground. It was an effective way for the men to let off steam.

The next day when he went up on deck, he saw an amazing sight. During the night, a swimming pool had been fashioned using a new sail secured to the gunwale of the barge on the booms and the other edge to the hammock netting making a hollow of eight feet that was filled with seawater.

Gunfire saluted the southern hemisphere and a procession emerged from the Fo 'castle. Captain Webley Hope was dressed as Neptune and was sporting a long grey horsehair wig and an equally long beard. He was wearing a long flowing robe over a pair of short pantaloons and a ruffled shirt. There was a tin crown on his head, and he was carrying a trident. Accompanying him was his wife her highness Amphitrite, who was in fact the ships doctor and was wearing a dress and a nightcap, stolen from some poor girl in Portsmouth. Their cheeks and lips were painted vermillion and their arms blackened with soot.

There were some other officers covered in Papier-Mache costumes representing sharks and other fish. Stefan and the other sailors all laughed and cheered at the sight of all their superiors dressed in silly costumes. The pageant commenced with them all sitting down on chairs on a specially erected dais, opposite the makeshift pool. There was a chair facing them with its back to the pool. Then, all the so-called Pollywogs were ordered below decks to be summoned to the deck one at a time by the same bears and police that had announced their names the evening before.

When it was Stefan's turn, he was ordered to sit in the chair facing Neptune and Amphitrite and his crimes were read out. Neptune, alias the captain, shouted out in a booming voice,

"You have disregarded the traditions of the sea and have taken liberties with the piscatorial subjects of His Majesty Neptunus Rex."

Stefan's' face was lathered with pitch and paint and some of it was scraped off with a piece of roughened iron hoop, after which the barber tipped his chair backwards into the water. He came up spluttering, coughing and several of the sailors standing by in readiness for this task, hauled him out of the temporary pool. Stefan stood dripping on the deck, which he didn't mind in the least as it was so hot.

All the newly initiated Shellbacks were presented with a certificate, which read,

TO all sailors wherever ye may be - to all subjects of the Realm of the Raging Main, to all Sharks and Swordfish and other Finny Folk; to all Sea Serpents and Whales, to all mermaids, Naiads, Sirens and Luring Beauties of the Bays.

GREETINGS and know ye this 5th of January 1865 on board the good ship HMS Brisk in Latitude 0'00' 00' in the Atlantic Ocean Stefan Van Uden attempted without due authorisation or making the customary obeisance, to enter the royal domain of his oceanic majesty and was accordingly subjected to the trial and inquisition of the fathomsless deep.

WHEREAS the said intruder having endured these ordeals with courage and fortitude, WHEREFORE he is now deemed worthy by His Majesty to be numbered as one of his Shellbacks. Wherefore, we Davy Jones, Viscount Atlantis, Baron of the boundless seas, etc, etc, etc, His Majestys principal scribe,

REQUEST and require in the name of HIS MAJESTY, NEPTUNE, RULER OF THE MIGHTY OCEANS, all of those to whom it may concern to allow the bearer to pass freely without let or hindrance and to afford every assistance and protection to which Stefan is entitled by virtue of this freedom of this Raging Main.

Stefan was proud of his certificate and rolled it up to keep it safe so that he could show it to Lana.

Chapter
Thirty-Four

The ship then made its way to Rio de Janeiro where they stopped for two days to load more coal on board and to replish their food supplies. Once again Stefan was amazed at all the the strange shaped mountains especially the Corcovado mountain that overshadowed the whole city. He helped to load all the cargo that the Captain had ordered but was not allowed ashore. He could only admire the glimpses of lush green vegetation, study with interest the teeming population on the docks and puzzzle over the incomprehensable Portugese language when the dock workers shouted to each other. Once again he thought he would like to come back to this fascinating place as a visitor.

If the truth be told, Stefan had begun to enjoy his adventure, although he would have hotly denied it. He missed Lana but he thought that when she received the letter from the Captain of the *Agamemnon* that she would make sure his father came to rescue him and return him safely to her arms. He wasn't too worried as he thought he would be home by April or May, well before the baby was born.

Upon leaving South America the ship turned eastwards toward the distant shores of Africa straight into the trade winds and the long rolling swells of the South Atlantic. Stefan was enchanted to see albatrosses swooping above his head. When he was on lookout duty one day with Ben, suddenly Ben shouted to him,

"Look Stefan, over there there's a school of whales."

Stefan was enthralled to watch the whales as they leapt out of the water and seemed to twist and twirl around. When later in that week he was on the night watch duty he marvelled at the clarity of the night sky and he saw the Southern Cross for the first time. Every day he was having new experiences and learning new things about ships and navigation, so he didn't have time to dwell upon Lana.

They arrived at Cape Town on the tip of South Africa and the Captain chatted to Stefan while they waited for a pilot to be brought on board to take the ship into the Table Bay harbour. He told him that the old harbour had been notorious for violent winter storms and that there had been a particularly vicious storm in 1858 when 30 ships were blown ashore and wrecked with a huge loss of life.

He added that before 1860 the harbour had been closed during the winter but since then the British Colonial Government had constructed a breakwater which developed into the Victoria and Alfred Basin, so it was now a safe harbour. Stefan had heard a lot about Cape Town as the Dutch had used the port when they traded with the Indies. He remembered from his history lessons at school that Jan Van Riebeeck and other employees of the Dutch East India

Company had been sent to the Cape to establish a way-station for ships travelling to the Dutch East Indies and many Dutch people had settled there.

Originally in the hands of the Dutch, the ownership of territory went back and forward between the British and the Dutch. Britain captured Cape Town in 1795 but it was returned to the Dutch by Treaty in 1803 and then the British occupied the Cape again in 1806 following the Battle of Blaawberg and in the Anglo-Dutch Treaty of 1814 Cape Town was permanently ceded to Britain.

He was impressed by the Table Mountian with its near vertical cliffs and flat topped summit and Ben pointed out the thin strip of cloud, which was called colloquially 'the tablecloth' sitting on top of the mountain. His own country, Holland, was so flat that he wasn't accustomed to mountains and one of the sailors noticed his fascination with the mountains and lent him his telescope to look at some of the other peaks surrounding the city.

Stefan was glad that the temperature had dropped from the stifling heat at the equator, Cape Town had a Mediterranean climate and because it was in the Southern hemisphere it was summertime so the temperature was a pleasant 70 degrees Farenheit.

Ben had told Stefan that the markets in Cape Town were amazing, full of fruit and vegetables and local African arts and crafts and Stefan thought he might be able to buy a gift for Lana and the baby but when he had asked the Captain if he might go ashore to do some shopping the Captain had said,

"I'm not letting you go ashore because there are too many Dutch people living here who could spirit you away and you're too much of an asset to me to let that happen. Why I'd be one man short. No, that would never do. Give Ben some money and he can buy you something to take home as a memento."

"I don't need to jump ship as I gave a letter to the Captain of the *Agamemnon* to send to my fiance so I know that my father is on his way to buy me out of the Navy. His ship is probably only a few thousand miles behind us."

Captain Webley Hope didn't tell him that his friend had told him that he hadn't sent the letter and that no-one was coming to rescue him. He had seen that Stefan had got over his original despondancy and was now an established and useful member of the crew and he did not want to see him dejected and in despair.

When Ben returned the next day he confessed that he had spent Stefan's money on drink and women but promised to pay him back. Although Stefan wanted to punch him on the nose he decided that it was not a clever idea as fighting on board ship was a punishable offence so he did nothing and had to just make do with his memories of Cape Town's beautiful scenery. The purser had bought fresh supplies and all the crew were treated to fresh oranges and grapes. The mess meals showed a significant improvement with more interesting vegetables and even fresh meat for a few days.

The HMS *Brisk* sailed out into the waters of the Cape of Good Hope and Ben warned Stefan that this was where the Roaring Forties started and they would face fierce winds and large ocean swells of 80 feet, bigger than buildings. When they passed the Kerguelen islands to starboard, Ben told him that this was the worst bit of their journey as they sometimes met intense gale force storms and that although it was summertime it could sometimes be chilly as the wind might be coming straight up from the ice of Antarctica.

When the gale hit them, Stefan realised that Ben had been right when he experienced seasickness for the first time in his life. As he brought up the dinner he had just eaten, he hoped it would be the last time as well. The storm had come up suddenly after the evening meal and the Captain had given the order to batten down the hatches. Most of the crew stayed down below while others manned the ship tied to the masts by ropes so that they could be hauled to safety if they were blown overboard.

Just as suddenly the weather conditions changed from brutal to mild as they reached Western Australia. Then the Captain pointed the bows of the ship south, out of the Indian Ocean and back to confronting the Roaring Forties, where fortunately they did not prove to be so challenging. They reached the eastern Australian seaboard and huge ocean swells carried them to the port of Sydney.

As the HMS *Brisk* sailed into Sydney harbour, which was a great meandering waterway full of inlets and coves, all the crew gave a great cheer that they had survived the often gruelling and demanding journey. It was midday and Captain Webley Hope went ashore but returned only an hour later with orders to sail immediately to New Zealand. All the crew were dismayed as they had hoped to stay in Sydney for a few days of rest and recuperation.

Stefan was not bothered by this turn of events as he was not allowed on shore leave so it made no difference to him whether he was afloat on the sea or in the harbour, except that he did not want to experience any more storms. Luckily, the onward journey to New

Zealand was uneventful and the ship put into the western harbour of Manukau, Auckland on New Zealands North Island on the 5th February 1865. Stefan would have been dismayed if he had known that this was to be his home for the next year.

Chapter Thirty-Five

As soon as they had docked, the HMS *Miranda,* the ship they had come to relieve, left the harbour in great haste as if she couldn't get away quick enough. Life went on as usual on board and early in the morning of the First of March Stefan heard marching boots on the quayside and orders being barked out.

The gangplank was lowered and troops of about 300 or 400 soldiers boarded the ship, the men sitting down on the deck where they could and propping up their rifles next to them or against the mast or bilges. Stefan spoke to some of the men and they told him that they were the 2nd Battalion, 14th regiment under Colonel W.C. Trevor. A couple of the men joked with Stefan and told him that their nickname for him was the Crapper because of his unfortunate initials. When the last man came aboard, Captain Webley Hope gave the command to "weigh anchor" and Stefan learned that they had been assigned the job of transporting these men to Wanganui further up the west coast.

By the end of the month, Stefan had guessed that the Captain of the *Agamemnon* had not sent his letter and that probably no one was coming to rescue him. Nobody would know what had happened to him or would know where he was. He realised that Lana would be frantic and knew he would have to send a letter to her himself. He wrote the letter and all he had to do now was to find a ship that was returning to London to deliver his letter.

He had written.

My dearest Lana,

I am writing to tell you that I have not deserted you but have been sold into the British Navy. I have so much to tell you that I do not know where to begin. I was taken to Portsmouth on board a fast steam ship, given to Captain Charles Webley Hope to make up the number of sailors he needed on his ship the HMS Brisk. As soon as I had boarded the ship, we set sail for Australia, so I had no time to write to you from London. I did ask the first Captain of the HMS Agamemnon to write you a letter but as I have received no news from you, I presume that he sent no such letter. We sailed around the Cape of Good Hope and on arrival in Sydney; our orders were to proceed immediately to Auckland where we arrived in February to relieve the HMS Miranda who left the same day. I would have given the Captain of the Miranda a letter, but they left in such haste that I did not have the opportunity. We are now undertaking escort duties in the New Zealand Wars. New Zealand has two islands, North and South and our first assignment was to take troops to Wanganui on the west coast of the North Island.

That's all about me but you, my darling sweetheart, I hope and pray that you are well. I hope the pregnancy is going well and that you will deliver our precious baby safe and sound. I miss you terribly and long for the day when I can hold you in my arms again. I do not understand why this has happened to me but please believe me that I did not run away from you. Can you contact my father, explain what has happened to me and see if he can go to the Admiralty in London and arrange for my release from the British Nav

You can write to me at HMS Brisk, Auckland New Zealand and send it via the Admiralty, Whitehall, London. They will arrange to send the letter via the next ship that is sailing to Australia or New Zealand. I do not know how long this letter will take to reach you as ships can take up to four months to reach London, although sometimes with a fair wind it only takes two months. It is now March and so you should receive my letter by June, and I hope to receive a reply from you by October. Perhaps my father, armed with a release letter, will get one of his ships to come and pick me up. I know I argued with him about my marriage to you, but I hope he has forgiven me by now and when he meets you, he will understand why I wanted you for my wife. I am giving this letter to the Captain of HMS Orpheus to take back to London.

I love you, Lana, my darling Anstruther lass and I hope we will soon be together.

All my love Stefan

He was angry and so disappointed that he had missed spending Christmas and New Year with Lana and her family, especially as she had told him all about the customs and celebrations that the Scottish people carried out for Hogmanay.

He had even thought seriously about jumping ship the next time they went into port. The trouble was that if you were caught the punishment was severe and being so far from home it was doubtful if he could find a Dutch ship, or any ship for that matter, that would be willing to take the risk of hiding a fugitive and taking back to Holland or Britain.

In the past Stefan knew that the British Navy had shot deserters and although the death penalty was no longer used, he had seen a couple of sailors who had been caught deserting ship and lashed fifty times with the cat o' nine tails until their blood ran along the decks. He knew how easily wounds could become infected in this hot climate and sailors sometimes died. He weighed up the chances and decided that it was not worth the risk. His main aim was to get back to Lana in good health and so he had begun to save up his meagre pay so that he could purchase his freedom.

But once Stefan had found a ship sailing for London, he felt more positive. He had given his letter to the purser's mate who had passed it to the purser's mate on the HMS *Orpheus* when they were both ashore buying provisions. As it was March and he calculated that the letter should reach Lana by June at the latest, with a month's grace to contact his father and another four months for the ship to reach New Zealand, he worked out that he would have some news by October or November at the latest. Of course, it would then take another two to four months to sail home, but he reckoned that he could be home by March next year and he did have his back-up plan of saving money to buy his release from the Navy.

Chapter Thirty-Six

Stefan had become used to the food on board, which had improved a great deal when they reached Auckland. Before that, it had been a diet of salted meat and ship's biscuits but now the purser was able to buy fresh meat, mostly mutton or lamb and some vegetables although there was a predominance of potatoes and cabbage. These two vegetables were indigenous to the island, but the settlers had planted seeds and some of the settlers sold their surplus produce of carrots, beans, beetroot, broccoli, and onions. Sometimes there were also apples and oranges available and even peaches, plums, raspberries, and strawberries.

The crew were divided into messes for eating, usually consisting of eight men although this number was not fixed. The way it worked was that each sailor in the mess group took a turn at being the mess cook and the mess cook for the day collected the day's ration for all the mess from the purser's mate or steward's mate.

Stefan had found this a problem because they had a cook at home, and he had never had to cook in his whole life.

"Ben, I don't know how to cook as we always had cooks and servants at home."

"By 'eck, I didn't know you were a toff. Don't worry I'll show you what to do."

Stefan was a quick learner, soon had the hang of boiling all the food in a large copper and even started to enjoy the experience.

Stefan and Ben soon began to be creative with the meals they prepared, adding herbs and spices bought locally. When Ben went ashore, he found parsley, rosemary and sage for sale grown by the settlers and then there were the indigenous spices of New Zealand, namely piri piri, a useful source of chilli flavour, piko piko and harakeke seeds and oil used for flavouring. The dishes served up in their mess became legend and many sailors were asking to join their mess. It was allowed to change messes at the beginning of the month, but the popularity of their mess caused such uproar that the captain had to step in and forbid anyone else from joining their mess.

"Ah told ye Stefan that I'd make a master chef of you."

"He's not a master chef he's more like a master mess."

Stefan was happy and enjoyed all the joshing as it reminded him of his crew on the *Zeeland*. Mealtimes were one of the highlights of the day and they were sacred. A ninety-minute break was allowed for the meal, and this was never interrupted except in an emergency. There was also a limitless supply of beer for the crew, and they were allowed two separate rations of rum, watered down with water per day, with lemon or lime juice added to prevent scurvy.

The tots of rum were served at midday and then again between four and six. The time that the rum ration was distributed was called 'Up Spirits' and each mess had a 'Rum Bosun' who would collect the rum from the officer responsible for measuring the right number of tots for each mess. The tots of rum certainly helped to relieve the monotony and helped the ordinary able seamen to bear being cooped up on the boat.

The boredom of the crew was alleviated a little when they took Governor Grey to Kawau on 1 May. Later in the month, there was more activity and although they were dismayed to hear of the demise of the clipper *Fiery Star*, they immediately set sail for the Chatham Islands to the east of New Zealand's South Island to search for any surviving passengers and crew. However, when they arrived, they found that the *Dauntless* had already rescued the few survivors from the ill-fated ship and so they returned to Auckland.

As they were in the Southern hemisphere, the months of March, April and May were New Zealand's Autumn, where the temperature hardly ever fell below 60 degrees Fahrenheit. The temperate climate meant that in New Zealand's winter months of June, July and August the temperature was always around 53 degrees Fahrenheit. During that winter of 1865, in August, they took 300 soldiers for the 70th Regiment from Taranaki to Napier but apart from that, the crew had extraordinarily little to do and spent time repairing, painting, and caulking the ship.

In October, the middle of the New Zealand Spring, Stefan was suntanned from being outdoors all the time. He was physically fit from all the loading of cargoes and stowing cargo-handling gear, stationary rigging and running gear but inside he was miserable. He was making the best of life as a sailor and trying to be happy and optimistic, but he had been really counting on receiving a reply from Lana or his father. His moods swung up and down and like earlier in the year, he thought morosely that Lana and his father too, deemed him a coward who had run away from his problems. Why, if there was no reply to his letter, they must hate him.

Then two things happened to cheer him up. The first was he spoke to Ben about his worries and Ben reassured him with his words,

"They may not have even received your letter. The HMS *Orpheus* could have sunk, many ships are wrecked around Cape Horn, so don't you worry lad. From what you've told me about your lass, she would never forsake you. Besides which she will have had your baby by now, so she'll need you to support her. You mark my words it'll all turn out good in the end."

The second thing that happened was that Able Seaman Hartley, who found him half-way up a ladder painting some wood, told him to meet the captain on the bridge. Stefan climbed down from the ladder, wiped his hands on a rag and followed him. He knew that the captain liked him as he often explained naval procedures to him, and he wondered if he had committed some infraction or if the captain had received a letter from his father. It was neither of those things, but it was a life changer.

"Ah, there you are, Van Uden, I have some good news for you, I am promoting you to be the ship's purser although the official title is paymaster. I know that you are honest and trustworthy and what is more I know that you complete any task given to you competently. You told me that you were the purser on your father's ship and although this is a much bigger ship, the basis is the same.

It is an important post; you will now be a commissioned officer and you will have a white strip between the gold rings on your arm of your jacket. You will manage the delivery of equipment, accommodation, and food to ensure the smooth running of the ship. A major aspect of your new post involves managing people and those in your department that includes caterers, stores accountants and stewards. Do you think you can manage all that? Of course, there will be an increase in your pay and I'm sure you will be pleased about that as I know you are saving up to buy your way out of the Navy."

"Thank you, Sir, I am delighted to be given the opportunity to ensure the smooth running of the HMS *Brisk*."

"I have every confidence in your ability to carry out this important duty. There is one more matter, before the purser became ill, he was looking for a new purser's mate as the current mate has reached the end of his enlistment contract and is returning to London on the next available ship. I thought you might like to appoint someone."

"I would like Abel Seaman Ben Crossley to be my mate."

"Yes, I thought you might suggest Crossley, an excellent choice, he will do perfectly. Very well, Van Uden that will be all, Able Seaman Hartley will take you down to the stores and you can start immediately."

The captain handed him a sheet of paper, "This is your first job as we are landing the Hawke Bay cavalry to their station at Hawkes Bay. There have been further conflicts with the Hau Hau. They will only be on board for a day, but we will have to feed them and that means lunch, dinner, and breakfast on the day they disembark. I do not want to hear any complaints from the Army that we treated their boys badly and that the food was not up to scratch. Therefore, that means we must lay on a virtual feast. Do you understand me?

Stefan made his way down to the mess to tell Ben the good news, singing a sea shanty he had learned from the other sailors,

> *What will we do with the drunken sailor*
> *What will we do with the drunken sailor*
> *What will we do with the drunken sailor*
> *Early in the morning?*

Ben heard him coming and joined in with the chorus,

> *Weigh-hay and up she rises*
> *Weigh-hay and up she rises*
> *Weigh-hay and up she rises*
> *Early in the morning!*

"By 'eck you sound happy all of a sudden."

Stefan told him the good news that he was to be the new purser and that he was to be his purser's mate and they both broke into the next part of the song together,

> *Put 'em in the scuppers with a hose pipe on him*
> *Put 'em in the scuppers with a hose pipe on him*
> *Put 'em in the scuppers with a hose pipe on him*
> *Early in the morning!*

Eventually when they had finished singing a few more verses they collapsed with laughter and stopped to get their breath back.

From that time on, Stefan did not have time to be miserable, his new job kept him so busy that he did not have so much time to dream or worry about Lana. There was hardly a day that went by when some member of the crew put in a request for candles, clothes, tobacco and more coal for the single-screw steam engine or other miscellaneous items.

He had a new crew made up of several stewards, steward's mates, stores accountants and of course, his own purser's mate Ben. Strictly speaking, he should have eaten in the officers' mess in the wardroom, but this was not compulsory, and he preferred to eat with his own men. The officers were supplied with fresh food from the chickens and pigs housed aboard the ship but since reaching Auckland, there was no difference in the quality of food served as Stefan made sure he bought chickens and other meat for all the crew on the ship.

The first time that he went down the gangplank with Ben and walked on firm ground had felt wonderful. It was a revelation to him. He knew that the Māori name for Auckland was Tamaki Makaurau meaning, 'the maiden sought by a hundred lovers' in reference to its natural beauty, but he was stunned when he got his first glimpse of the city.

The HMS *Brisk* was moored in the southwest harbour of Manakau, the surrounding hills covered in rainforest and the landscape dotted with dozens of dormant volcanoes. He knew that the city was interesting, built on an isthmus, the only port to have two harbours, the Manakau harbour on the Tasman Sea and the Waitemata harbour on the Pacific Ocean.

Stefan was fascinated by the bustling market and loved the choice of all the different fruit and vegetables. It had a distinctive smell of fresh fruit and vegetables mixed with all the exotic spices on sale. He was entranced by the markets but found the extraordinary mixture of different races in Auckland even more captivating. There were Polynesians, the native Māori and many European settlers from different countries, Germany, England, Scotland, France, Italy and Holland. He was stunned when he first saw Maoris as their faces were covered in tattoos and each one was unique. He was used to seeing flat tattoos on sailors, but the Maori tattoos had grooves rather than a smooth surface. Besides sailors did not usually have tattoos all over their faces so Stefan could not stop himself from staring at any Maori he came across. He was intrigued.

One day while walking through the market he was delighted to hear Dutch being spoken and stopped in amazement and to introduce himself. The man's name was Herman De Groot and he and his wife had two young children who had immigrated to New Zealand the previous year. They had sold their farm in Holland and had been going to buy some land to farm in New Zealand but had been dissuaded by the recent killing of the missionary Carl Volkner at Opotiki, earlier in March that year.

Volkner had been hanged from a willow tree near his church, his head had been cut off and as a final insult, the Maori, Kereopa Te Rau, swallowed his eyes, dubbing one 'parliament' and the other 'Queen and the English Law'. Herman told Stefan that his wife had begged him to stay in Auckland where she felt safer. He had agreed, as there had been some other incidents of the massacre of settlers on farms. So instead, he had gone into partnership with another immigrant from Scotland, both investing money in a sawmill. Later that year in August, they invited him to dinner and Stefan who was allowed shore leave for one evening until midnight, was delighted to accept.

He spent a very pleasant evening as Herman's wife Lisa, had cooked a special Dutch meal of *hutspot*, a colourful mashed potato dish together with *klapstuk* a piece of braised beef, together with some accompanying vegetables of local grown carrots and peas. After the first course, Lisa proudly presented Stefan with a Dutch apple tart,

"Some friends of ours from the church who have been here for five years have been successful at growing some apple trees and they gave us some apples. So, I have made a Dutch apple tart especially for you."

"This is my favourite dessert, and it reminds me so much of home, I love it."

Herman's partner Duncan McCuskey and his wife Josephine were also at the dinner and Stefan told them his story. He told them all about Lana and that they had been going to get married and that she was expecting his baby at the end of July. Josephine clucked sympathetically,

"So, she will have had the child by now and you don't know if you have a son or a daughter"

"Yes, that's right. I've written to her, and I sent the letter on the HMS *Orpheus* in March, and I was expecting a reply by now, but I've heard nothing."

"We'll hide you if you want to jump ship and we can arrange for your safe passage on a ship back to London."

"No, it's kind of you to offer but I've been saving up and I should have enough money to buy my release from the Navy by August of next year and pay for my passage home. I prefer to do it legitimately as I don't want to run the risk of being shot and killed."

Duncan had brought a bottle of whisky and they all sat down in comfortable chairs while Herman poured everyone a glass. The conversation went on to the latest New Zealand Wars with the Maori and they told Stefan about the Treaty of Waitangi,**** which had been a source of much debate and controversy ever since 1840. They also told him about how a General Assembly had been established consisting of a legislative Council appointed by the Crown and a House of Representatives elected every five years and that in this parliament of seventy-six members there were only four Maori seats.

Stefan had heard about the Māori's massacring settlers, but he felt some sympathy for them and said, "I don't blame them for fighting, I would fight too if someone tried to take over all the land in Holland and destroy my house."

Stefan's remark led to a heated discussion and when Stefan took his leave, the four were still arguing and he could hear raised voices all the way down the road. In fact, Stefan had also made friends with some of the Maoris and indeed with one Maori, whom he had met when he had gone to the local markets to buy supplies for HMS *Brisk*.

**** See notes 5 Maoris and the Treaty of Waitangi

He had stopped to buy the usual potatoes and cabbage from one stall and noticed that the stallholder was selling some other vegetables, which he did not recognise so he asked what they were. The man replied,

"Him is sweet potato and him there is yam and him ti pore. All good. Jolly nice."

"Alright, I'll take all of them. I expect my friend Ben will know how to cook them."

"You, no British sailor?"

"No, I'm Dutch, my name is Stefan. What's your name?"

"My name Tani."

"Pleased to meet you Tani"

Tani helped Stefan load all the vegetables into his cart and Stefan noticed a box of apples under the stall. "I'll take those apples too, if I may."

Stefan laughed as he handed Tani more money, "You can go home now; all your goods are sold. It's a short day's work for you Tani."

You, good fellow, Dutchman Stefan."

From that day on, they became friends and Tani always called him Stefan Goodfellow. Stefan admired Tani, as he was well built, athletic and tall. He was as tall as Stefan and similar in build. Stefan knew that the Dutch were renowned for being large, broad shouldered and big boned but Tani matched him in size.

They were both a little over six feet in height and Stefan thought he was a good-looking man. He had high cheekbones, brown eyes and curly hair and Stefan noticed that his teeth were good and looked startlingly white against his bronze-coloured skin. Like all the other Maoris, he had tattoos that covered his entire face, but this did not detract from his good looks but made him look more handsome.

One day after he had known Tani for a week, Stefan asked him,

"Why do all the Maoris have tattoos on their faces?"

"Is called Ta Moko and not all Maoris allowed to have Ta Moko Is only for Maoris of high rank. Is important step between being a child and becoming an adult."

"Why are all the tattoos different?"

"Each Ta Moko***** shows what man has done, his family, his position in his tribe, if he married."

"Oh, I see, so if I could understand the designs, I could tell a lot about you. Like the name of your tribe."

"I from the Ngai tai tribe."

"Where is your village?"

"Kianga now at Otahuhu, old Kianga was further north, but settlers wanted land for farming. Good land, good soil. We say no, so government troops come one day and destroy all *wharepuni*, this Maori name for sleeping houses. Took land, so move south. Lose everything. Cattle, tools, *wharenui*, This Maori name for large house. Many friends and family killed.

"That's terrible; you must hate all the settlers."

"No, Maori now have *hauhau*, mean goodness and peace, it says Maori people will get back their land, Maori believe new faith. Is good. War no good."

***** See notes 6 Ta Moko

"I see but I've heard that the government are worried about Hauhau, and they see it as a threat."

"Yes, is problem Maori want keep land, Government want take land, so will be more fighting."

Stefan felt tremendous empathy and admiration for this man. Not only was he strong but he was also stoical and philosophical too about the whole situation. He felt it made his own predicament seem insignificant and trivial. He thought he should not complain so much for after all he hadn't lost his home and livelihood for good. He could learn a lesson from Tani.

Chapter Thirty-Seven

S tefan was happier with his life now that he was allowed ashore, and he even began to love HMS *Brisk*. The ship had a distinctive smell, a mixture of the wood heated by the sun, the hessian ropes and the soap used to scrub the decks. She made creaking and groaning noises as she settled in the water in the harbour, and he thought it was easy to understand why sailors referred to ships as 'she' as they were like living beings.

However, these feelings did not stop despondency overcoming Stefan again as the Christmas of 1865 approached. He had already missed one Christmas with Lana and he was in despair as he realised that time had marched on and by now, his baby would be five months old. The sailors in his charge all knew and liked Stefan and called him pusser, the nickname for purser used throughout the Navy. They had found out about his story from Ben. They were all pleased when he became their officer in charge but even their friendship and affection could not ease his mood.

His friends the Dutch couple had invited him to celebrate Sinterklaas with them on the 5th of December and he had spent a pleasant evening with them. They had given him a leather-bound diary as a gift, and he spent some time every evening writing about his life and experiences in Auckland. He would give it to Lana to read when he managed to buy his release from the Navy and return to Scotland.

He had bought some silver wine goblets from a family, returning to England because they had not settled down in this new country and they missed their family back home. They had had to sell some of their belongings to pay for their passage back home. Stefan had thought the goblets would make an excellent present for his friends for Sinterklaas. It was more difficult to find a present for Tani, but he paid Tom, the blacksmith or armourer as he was called on the ship, to make some metal pots and pans. When Stefan went to collect them, Tom had also made some tools, a hammer, pliers, a wrench and a spade with wooden handle. Stefan planned to give these gifts to Tani after Christmas in January of 1866.

Stefan had found out that although the *hangi* or earth oven was the traditional Maori method of cooking, some food was cooked over glowing embers, in which case he thought Tani could use pots to boil water and cook food. He was impressed at the inventiveness of the *hangi,* hot rocks and water used to create steam in a shallow pit dug into the earth. Food was layered of top of the rock, the meat first and then the vegetables and covered with leaves, flax matting, then the soil replaced to trap the steam for a few hours. He hoped Tani would use the pots and pans and he knew the tools would be useful.

For Christmas, the stewards had decorated the mess and even found red tablecloths. Ben asked him to find some capons and Brussel sprouts for all the crew and Stefan managed to buy these from some of the settlers.

"You've done well, Stefan, I'll make a feast on Christmas day. Just you wait and see. Capon, roast potatoes, Yorkshire puddings, you have never seen Yorkshire puddings like mine, carrots, Brussel sprouts. No one will be able to move after lunch. Oh yes, we even have Christmas puddings that old pusser Jim bought in London before the ship set sail. You missed Christmas last year, so miserable you were that you stayed in your hammock most of the day and missed all the festivities. Never mind you can make up for it this year, we'll all cheer you up."

Stefan smiled at his friend but thought, "I don't even know what Yorkshire puddings are, let alone tasted one." He was surprised to find that he enjoyed Christmas with his crew. When he finally left them, they were all singing songs and drinking their rations of rum, doubled because it was Christmas.

He marvelled at the way in which the sailor's enjoyed life with all its difficulties, remembering the fun involved in the 'Crossing the line' ceremony when the HMS *Brisk* had crossed the equator contrasting with the terrible storm when they had been cooped up below decks not knowing if they would survive.

After Christmas, in early January, when he and Ben made a usual visit to the market, Stefan heard his name being shouted out. "Stefan Goodfellow, Stefan Goodfellow" and he saw Tani grinning at him, white teeth gleaming in the sunlight.

"I come find you, you and Benmate, come celebration in village, next Saturday. Meet wife, children. Whole village want meet you. Especially important."

Stefan was given permission for himself and Ben to stay on shore until midnight. It was a beautiful New Zealand Summer's evening, a slight breeze wafting the particular New Zealand smells of spices mixed with the trees and flowers native to the country. Stefan and Ben made their way to Queen Street where they had arranged to meet Tani with his horse and cart, his mode of transport to and from the market. There had been sunshine all day and so the sky was clear of any clouds and the night sky was sparkling with stars. Stefan had been studying a book on astronomy that he had found on the ship. He knew that sailors of old had used the stars to navigate and thought the knowledge would be helpful to him in the future. He was pleased when he recognised the Southern Cross and Canis Major, the Great Dog. He pointed them out to Ben and showed him Sirius, the dog star.

Ben laughed and said, "By 'eck, you're becoming a right boffin."

When they spotted Tani, Stefan and Ben scrambled into the cart, avoiding stray potatoes, an old cabbage and sat on some empty sacks.

"Is good *Hakari*, this night. Brother Tiki has daughter Heeni she dedicated to a god in ritual, now we have feast."

"Have you already had the ceremony?"

"Yes, ceremony only Maori, no others, now feast and dance."

"As long as we're not the feast." Ben said sardonically.

When Stefan looked back on the evening all he could remember was being continually amazed. The Maoris greeted their arrival enthusiastically, many the tribe all shaking hands with them, and they experienced the traditional Maori *Hongi* greeting. They both found it a curious because the Maoris pressed their foreheads and noses at the same time against Stefan's and Ben's forehead and nose. Tani told him that in the *Hongi*, the *ha* (or breath of life), is exchanged and intermingled. The breath of life was also interpreted as the sharing of both parties' souls.

He noticed that most of the men had tattooed faces and that each one was different. Afterwards he remembered that all the women were beautiful, or had that been an illusion? There was no alcohol, Maoris did not drink, so there had been no chance of drink influencing his perception. They all had long flowing black hair, golden skin and dark eyes fringed with black lashes. Some of them had tattoos around their mouths and chins, which seemed to add to their allure.

Tani introduced his wife Aki and his son Rangi, which he told them, meant sky in the Maori language, then his daughter Aroha, which meant love. The houses in the village, the *wharenui*, were rectangular, made of timber, rushes, some sort of tree ferns and bark, with thatched rooves and earth floors but all tidy and immaculate.

The food was piled up on huge pyramid or cone-shaped structures. Several of the women began to serve the food sharing it out to the guests and the members of the tribe, on large wooden plates. Half of the time Stefan did not know what he was eating but he recognised mussels, whitebait patties, prawns, and seafood kebabs.

He was given some *rewena* and Tani told him it was Maori traditional bread made from potatoes. This was served with some sort of pate, which he enjoyed until Tani told him it was shark liver pate. Next came wild pork with baskets of potatoes. There was *whio*, which was a native duck and *kereru* that Stefan identified as wood pigeon but when they were served up with *kiore* and he was told it was Polynesian rat and *kuri*, Polynesian dog, he refused both dishes politely. He did try the *hu hu* grubs; although uncertain to try them at first found that they were very tasty.

The food all eaten, and leftovers cleared away, the chief of the village announced that his men would perform a *haka* in honour of their guests. The men appeared, including Tani, dressed in traditional costume, bare-chested, wearing a wide bead belt with strings of beads hanging down, head-dress of a band with two feathers at the back and necklaces of leather with a single piece of jade, bone or shell.

The costumes alone astounded Stefan and Ben. The men began the war dance, with threatening gestures, legs wide apart and knees bent, stamping their feet, slapping their thighs, shouting, and ending in sticking their tongues out. The tattooed faces made them all look fierce. The two men did not understand what the men were chanting:

> *Ka mae, ka mate,*
> *Ka ora, ka ore*
> *Kei te tangata,*
> *Puhuruhuru,*
> *Nana I tiki mai,*
> *I whakawhiti ti ra,*
> *U pane, kau pane,*
> *Wiri t era.*

But they did not need to, as the aggressive postures and grimaces explained it all. It was a war dance.

Ben said, "If I saw them lot coming towards me, I'd run."

"Me too."

It all went quiet after the display and an old man, with long white hair and an equally long beard appeared and sat down next to Stefan and Ben. Tani reappeared and introduced them to Anahera. He told them that his name meant angel and he was a Tohunga Matakite. He explained to Stefan that this man was able to see what was yet to come and he would foretell their future. The old man began to speak in Maori and Tani translated in his broken English.

"He say Stefan Goodfellow go in boat to South Seas and then Stefan no come back. Older man comes for Stefan in small boat from far away; take him home to cold land. He have happy life and many children. Other man Ben stay here marry Maori girl, many children, exceptionally good life, make good business."

Tani said, "Tohunga tell me you go so I make presents for goodbye." He handed Stefan a set of wooden bowls, beautifully carved. Then he gave him three necklaces and said,

"One for wife, one for you. One for wife sister. Anahera say she good woman look after your Lana"

Stefan's pendant was a carved ox bone in the shape of a fish.

"You always be with sea Stefan Goodfellow."

The one he gave him for Lana was made of New Zealand Mountain jade, a round curved shape.

"Is *koru* meaning new life and harmony."

Then he gave him a necklace for Moira and said, "This one *toki* it means strength and courage."

Feeling overcome, Stefan thanked Tani with a big hug.

They said goodbye to all the village with lots more hugs and Ben even received a kiss from one Maori girl. Waving their last goodbyes, they travelled back to the city in Tani's cart, and he took them back along the quayside to the HMS *Brisk*. Stefan had left his presents for Tani in the cart and handed them to him, explaining that they could use the pots on an open fire.

"Thank you, Stefan Goodfellow, many changes for Maori now, in future, so is good. I like and tools very good. Hope one day you come back with wife and baby to visit Tani."

"I haven't gone yet so I will see you next week."

"No, Tohunga right, you go South Seas and no come back. No see you again."

With that, he flung his arms around Stefan and gave him a hug. Once again, Stefan was overcome and felt tears forming in his eyes. Turning away quickly, he walked up the gangplank. Ben followed him and when they went below decks, he said,

"By 'eck, why did you get all the presents and I got none."

"Didn't you listen, it's because you are staying here and I'm the one who is leaving."

"Mmm, my contract is up in four months, and I thought about staying here. I like the climate and the life; did you see all the Maori girls. They are gorgeous. There was one I liked, and she took a shine to me, at least she kissed me goodbye."

"Well, there you are then."

Stefan felt a twinge of disappointment as he had hoped that he could persuade Ben to go back to Holland with him. He could have worked for his father as a manager at the warehouse, or even accountant for the business. He felt a twinge of envy that Ben was free to settle in this beautiful county. However, he smiled at his friend, pleased for him that he would be happy settling in this new country.

"Now I'll definitely have to come back to New Zealand to see you as well as Tani."

Chapter Thirty-Eight

It was no surprise to Stefan when the captain announced the next day that HMS *Brisk* was going to sail around the South Seas after first going to transport some more soldiers to Taranaki. Ben was excited,

"By 'eck, that geezer, the witch doctor or whatever he was, it looks like he was right, so I hope he's right about me an' all."

It was a beautiful sunny day in February, as they both leaned on the rails watching all the activity on the quayside and were both surprised when a line of Maoris appeared.

"Why it's Tani, Aka, their children and all the other members of their tribe."

The group started singing a Maori song as the ship slipped out of the harbour heading for the South Seas, their voices carrying in the still air. The sailors could still hear the beautiful melody until they reached the open water and it faded away. Stefan felt a great sadness. He had learned to love New Zealand and loved his new Maori friends. He would miss them. The gesture of singing farewell had made it more poignant, and he felt a tug on his heartstrings. He felt a great empathy for plight of the Maoris and wished he could do more to help them. He had no more time to feel sad as Captain Webley Hope came down from the bridge and addressed him,

"I've never seen that before, you are certainly popular with the locals; I should recommend you to Governor Grey, you'd make an excellent diplomat and could help with his political negotiations with the Maoris."

"Thank you but I'm going home, my father is coming to secure my release from the Navy."

"How do you know that?"

"I have it on the absolute best authority from the Maori Tohunga."

"You surely don't believe all their mumbo jumbo."

"We'll see. He'll be here by September when we go to Sydney for a refit."

★ ★ ★

As time progressed and February became March, the HMS *Brisk* had visited many of the islands of Polynesia. Stefan thought that each island was more beautiful than the last with miles of silver sands and water so clear you could see right to the bottom. He marvelled at the strange statues on Easter Island and met all the natives and some European settlers in Tonga, Samoa and the Cook Islands, Tuvalu and the Wallis and Fortuna Islands.

By the time that May arrived, the HMS *Brisk* turned to the northeast to Micronesia and Stefan continued to be amazed at all the hundreds of small islands that made up Micronesia. He had thought he had his fill of beautiful islands but when the ship arrived at Bora Bora, surrounded by coral reefs Stefan thought that this was the most beautiful island of all.

On the other side of the world, his father, Ton Van Uden, was also visiting an unknown and unfamiliar territory although it was not so exotic, namely the Admiralty in London.

Part Three

The rescue and the arrest

Chapter Thirty-Nine

Stefan would have been delighted, if he had known that his father, a veteran sailor, and captain, had made good time to London in his new steam propelled ship and moored in the new Royal Victoria Dock in East London, as it was the deepest dock built for steam-propelled boats.

He had set off early on a Tuesday morning at the end of April and had arrived late on Wednesday evening so by the time he had completed all the necessary procedures there had been not time to go to the Admiralty. Besides which, he was feeling physically and mentally exhausted. The shock of first believing his son to be dead and then hearing the news that he was serving on board a British naval ship in New Zealand, not to mention that he had a granddaughter, had all taken its toll and he fell sound asleep as soon as he curled up in his comfortable captain's bunk.

The next morning, he rose early and leaving his crew to look after the ship he made his way to the Custom House railway station as he knew there were always cab stands outside railway stations. On the way, he passed a group of flaxen-haired sailors chattering in German, a Black sailor with a cotton handkerchief twisted around his head like a turban and another sailor with a green parrot in a wooden cage. As he walked along the quay, he smelt tobacco and nearly felt overpowered with the fumes of rum. Then the stench of hides and huge bins of horns, sickened him and was thankful when the atmosphere became fragrant with coffee and spices.

He popped into the Customs House to ask the address of the Admiralty and they told him it was in Whitehall. The customs man he spoke to told him that it was about eleven miles away, which was extremely helpful, as the driver of the hansom cab needed to know this so he could estimate the fare. When Ton explained to the man the reason for his visit, he even gave him the name of the man he would need to see, the First Naval Lord, the Honourable Sir Frederick Grey.

Ton found a hansom cab, gave the cab driver the address of the Admiralty and told him the distance was eleven miles.

"Okay, gov, I charge eight pennies a mile so the fare will be eighty-eight pennies, that's seven shillings and fourpence, you won't find a cheaper ride than mine."

"That's fine by me. It seems a fair price."

As they left the dock area and the forest of masts disappeared into the distance, they passed courts and alleyways full of run-down looking lodging houses and public houses called The Jolly Tar or The Old Sea Dog or other maritime names. The open streets all had a maritime character with sailmakers, sailor's cheap shoe-marts, rope-makers, doors blocked up with hammocks, shops selling canvas trousers, bright red and blue flannel shirts, and rough pilot coats and of course, grocers that were provision agents advertising that all their goods were warranted to keep in any climate. Gradually as the hansom cab left the dockland area, the streets were no less busy but became more gentrified. There were tree-lined avenues, neat and cared for houses, commercial properties displaying names of insurance companies and law firms, smart hotels, men on horseback, police officers in top hats and ladies walking out in beautiful dresses wearing extraordinary concoctions on their heads that passed for hats.

Soon they reached the busy centre of London and the cab driver, a very chatty Londoner, pointed out The Tower of London as they passed it, the cab driver said,

"That's where the old bugger; Henry the Eighth chopped his wife Anne Boleyn's 'ead off. Oi fink 'ee chopped a few other poor blokes 'eads orf an' all. Well. Of course, 'ee didn't do the dirty deed himself 'ee just gave the orders." He gave a laugh, "I 'spect 'ee just said 'off with their 'eads" and he laughed again.

As they passed St Paul's Cathedral, he kept up his running commentary and told him it was built by Sir Christopher Wren and said that the views were fantastic from the dome.

"If you climb another 259 steps in the dome, you'll find the whispering gallery, I took me kids there an' they all thought it was magic. They spent hours sending messages to each other at either end of the gallery. I couldn't get them to leave, so I 'ad to bribe 'em with sweets."

They went up Ludgate Hill and the cab driver continuing his observations said,

"Aye, aye, watch out this is where the traffic gets terribly busy. It's always packed out in Fleet Street no matter what the time o' th' day."

Ton saw buildings displaying the names of famous newspapers jostling next to old-style taverns. They reached The Strand at last after they had negotiated their way past all the omnibuses. broughams and carriages. Ton smiled wryly at the name displayed on the first building that they passed because in Dutch, the word "strand" meant the beach. It was certainly not a beach now, although it had been in days gone by when it bordered the Thames. Ton glimpsed gentlemen's clothes shops displaying shirts and silk cravats in their windows, ladies fashion shops selling ball-gowns, hat shops, coffee-houses, and theatres. Passing the newly refurbished Eleanor Cross outside Charring Cross railway station, they reached Trafalgar Square and Ton had a splendid view of Nelson's column with its four lions in the centre of the Square.

The cab turned left into Whitehall and the cab driver drew up outside The Admiralty. His seat was high up in the front of the cab, with the passengers sitting behind, so he leaned through an opening in the roof to take Ton's payment for the fare. Ton had found the cab driver so entertaining that he gave him a guinea. He was glad that he had the foresight to bring enough English money with him for his quest to find Stefan, so he could afford to be generous.

The cab driver doffed his cap and said, "Why thank ye kindly Sir. You're a gent."

Ton surveyed the Admiralty and thought it was a strange looking building. It looked as if it was cobbled together from different structures. He went through an arch into a courtyard and approached the large door with twin pillars either side. He found himself in a spacious hall where a man in naval uniform was sitting behind a desk.

"I would like to see Admiral Sir Frederick Grey."

"Do you have an appointment, Sir?"

"No but I need to see him on a very urgent matter. You see my son has been press-ganged into the Royal Navy by mistake and I need to get him released."

"I see sir, it's all very irregular and usually the Admiral only meets people by appointment, but I'll see what I can do."

He beckoned a younger man over to him and had a whispered conversation with him. The young man ran up some stairs and the older man told Ton to take a seat. Ton spent a few minutes taking in the opulent surroundings. There was a chandelier, two suits of armour stood by one wall and two others faced them on the other wall. The staircase had two pillars each side of it and there was a large marble stature in an alcove. The waiting seemed interminable although it was probably only ten minutes before the young man careered down the stairs. Ton could tell he was a sailor by the way he took the stairs sideways as if on board a ship. A sailor's own safety measure so that if there was a wave surge, he would be flung sideways into the wall and not headfirst down the stairs.

He had a few words with the older man who addressed Ton, "You're lucky, Sir Frederick Grey has agreed to see you immediately. Lieutenant Jones will take you up now."

Ton followed the young lad up the stairs, who ushered him into a large room that was even more magnificent than the hall. There was a long table with a grand chair at one end and Ton saw a distinguished man wearing a naval uniform, who motioned him to take a chair on the side of the table next to him.

"Now, my good man, what's all this about?"

Ton told him the whole story and that he wanted him to write him a letter releasing his son Stefan Van Uden from service on the HMS *Brisk*.

"Yes, yes, A terrible business but we can't go off at half cock. I will have to check first that he is on the HMS *Brisk*. They send us reports regularly so it will not be difficult to find out if Stefan is serving on the HMS *Brisk*. Now it is the end of April so if you can leave it with me until the 15th of May, see me then at two o' clock. I think that will give me enough time to investigate matters and organise a solution to your problem. I'll tell my secretary to put you in my appointment's diary, so you won't have to wait around as you did today."

Ton thanked him and made his way down the stairs and out into Whitehall. He thought about catching the train back to the dock but decided to take another hansom cab as he enjoyed seeing all the sights of London. When he returned to his ship all his crew wanted to know what had happened and he told them that his story had been listened to, believed and he was going back to the Admiralty on 15th May. He was optimistic that he would be successful in gaining Stefan's release from the Navy. The crew who all knew Stefan cheered and Ton said,

"I saw a Tavern nearby and from what I could see the food looked good so we're all going out to celebrate. I will buy you all a pint of ale and pay for the dinner but if you want more drink, you'll have to pay for it yourselves. I am not paying for all you lot to get drunk, in fact, I am imposing a curfew and you all must come back with me after dinner. I don't want any more sailors going missing."

Chapter Forty

While he was waiting to go back to the Admiralty Ton had not been idle, had gone the local chandlers and to buy charts to help him navigate the ship all the way around the Cape of Good Hope and on to New Zealand. He had also visited some of the local grocers to buy provisions for their long journey. He knew it would be a long and sometimes dangerous journey, but he was looking forward to the voyage and thought, 'I haven't had such an adventure since I was a young man and sailed to the West coast of Africa.'

The day for his appointment came round and Ton went back to the Admiralty. The officer at the desk recognised him straightaway and ushered him upstairs himself. Ton entered the same grand and impressive room and Sir Frederick Grey greeted him like an old friend.

"Ah Mister Ton Van Uden, I have good news and unwelcome news for you. The good news first, we checked the reports we received from the HMS *Brisk* and we can confirm that your son Stefan Van Uden is indeed serving on board that ship. Captain

Webley Hope has sent glowing reports about him, and his behaviour has been so exemplary that when the serving purser was taken ill, the captain promoted him to the ship's purser, or paymaster as the job is now called. This post carries a lot of responsibility and is an officer status, so Stefan is now an officer in the Royal Navy.

I have here a letter securing his discharge from the British Navy signed and sealed by the Lord High Admiral, Sir John Pakington.

Now the bad news is that the HMS *Brisk* is sailing around the South Seas and we do not know her exact location. We do know that she will be in Sydney, Australia on the 26th of September to have a refit and so you can catch her there. When you meet Captain Webley Hope, you can tell him that there will be an investigation into this matter.

I have here another letter for you from Sir John apologising for all the trouble this has brought you and for all the distress caused to your son's fiancé. I understand that you told me she has given birth to their child, a girl you said. When I conveyed this information to Sir John, he insisted that we give the baby a gift of twenty guineas and there is a cheque for this amount inside the letter.

We could send a Royal naval ship to bring your son back home, but I understand that you will undertake the journey in your own ship, to ensure Stefan's speedy homecoming but if you can write to us on your return with a list of your expenditure, we will repay all the costs in full.

The journey around the Cape of Good Hope generally takes between two to four months and as it's the 15th May by my reckoning, you will reach Sydney by 15th July if you make good time. If it takes you 4 months you will arrive by 15th September so I am afraid, whatever happens, you will have to wait for the *Brisk* in Sydney. I am sorry about this, as I know you must be anxious to bring Stefan back home but at least it allows some leeway in case you must break your journey for some repair to your ship. I think you will find that we have covered everything and all that remains is for me to wish you "Bon voyage."

Ton gave his thanks and could not help but smile beatifically at everyone he met as he travelled all the way back to the dock. When he reached the ship, he immediately sat down and wrote a letter to Lana to apprise her that he had confirmed that Stefan was in New Zealand and that he would set sail immediately to bring him home.

Chapter Forty-One

Lana shut the front door carefully so she wouldn't wake the two babies. It was 4 am and still dark as she ran down the road to the town. She enjoyed working at the Bakery and did not mind the early start as it meant she finished work at 11 am and could spend the rest of the day with Freya. She entered the bakery through the back door and ran down the stairs into the basement where she found Mr Kerr, the baker dressed in his white jacket and trousers turning on the ovens.

Lana said, "Good morning, Mr Kerr, are there any special orders today", as she donned her own white coat and tucked her hair into her white hat.

"Nay lass, just the usual bread, Scottish breakfast rolls, scotch pancakes, scotch pies and I thought we would make some tea cakes today. Folk's like them."

Lindsey, the other girl clattered down the stairs, out of breath, and grabbed her white jacket and hat from the row of pegs on the wall.

"Sorry I'm a wee bit late this morning. My little one is teething and kept me awake half the night."

"Dinnae worry lassie, ye're aw right."

Lana and Lindsay started to mix and knead the dough for the bread in giant containers, Lana knew that in some bakeries they kneaded the dough with their feet, but Mr Kerr said he thought this was a disgusting practice and he wasn't going to make his bread that way. Why he had said folks sometimes found toenails in their bread and besides the bread tasted of sweaty feet. Once they had spooned the dough into the bread pans, on the racks, Mr Kerr checked that the temperature of the oven was hot enough and loaded the racks into the oven. Then the girls made the special dough for the Scottish breakfast rolls that were so popular, spooned the mixture into the sixteen-hole cake tins and put them in the oven.

When the third lot of bread had been baked it was swelteringly hot in the basement kitchen. Lana felt as if she was witting like a flower and could feel sweat running down her neck and back. She was glad it was time to go upstairs and open the shop. She and Lindsey loaded the bread from the cooling racks into the dumb waiter and operated it between them until they had moved all the loaves upstairs. Lana flung open the doors of the baker's shop and the smell of delicious new baked bread wafted down the street. There were people queuing outside and the girls were kept busy for the next hour selling the bread and rolls. Mr Kerr, the baker stayed downstairs and baked the scotch pies, scotch pancakes and currant buns, for the lunch time trade,

Suddenly, Lindsey gave Lana a dig in the ribs and nodded her head towards the street outside,

"Here comes Donald, I told you he was sweet on you. That's the fourth time this week he's come to work early. He comes into the shop to see you; he can quite easily collect all the goods for sale and delivery from the back entrance."

Donald was the delivery person for the shop and drove a small cart pulled by a horse to deliver bread and cakes all over the town.

"Away with you, he just comes in to take the left-overs from yesterday for his lunch."

"Hello Lana, how are you this fine morning?"

"I'm well, thank you Donald, and how are you?"

"I'm fine too, but I've come to ask you a favour. The local football team I support are playing a match on Sunday and all the lads have bet me that you won't come with me. They think you are too stuck up to come to a football match."

"That's rubbish, I'm not posh at all, and I'll be happy to come with you to the football match on Sunday."

"That's great I'll call for you at One O clock."

Donald made his way downstairs into the kitchen and Lindsey giggled as she said. "See, I told you, he'll be asking you to walk out with him next."

Lana smiled enigmatically, thinking that it would not be a bad choice to end up married to Donald. She still loved Stefan and thought about him every day, but it had been two years now since he had disappeared. He could be dead, and she could be waiting for him to come back forever, so it was quite fair that she should make plans for her and Freya's future.

When Lana got home, she had given Freya her lunch and as usual curled up with her on her bed and had a catnap. After her siesta, Lana took the two girls into the garden to play. Angus had adapted the boys swing on the old apple tree. He had made a seat with wooden sides and a bar at the front. The two babies could sit in the seat safely without the risk of falling out. As they were still very small, they could fit in the seat together. Lana was pushing the swing and they were shrieking with laughter. Their little legs were sticking out of the front of the chair, their hands clutching the bar and their hair streaming out behind them in the breeze. Lana was happier than she had been for a long time, she had a job, could spend time with Freya and now she might have a new beau.

Lana heard a knock at the door and ran inside to open it. There standing on the steps were Jessie, Masie and Auntie Jeanie. She gave a surprised yelp and flung her arms around each of them in turn.

"What on earth are you all doing here?"

"We came tae see your wee babby and we wanted tae tell ye that the police have caught the Dundee Slasher, cheers to the knife that the smugglers gave them." "Yes, and we wanted to tell ye aboot Mr William Campbell."

"'And we've brought yer Auntie Jeanie to stay for Yule and Hogmanay. We'll take the horse and cart back to her friend tonight because we've only taken the day off work from the mill and we would'nae like to impose on ye by staying the night. We thought that Jock would be able to take her back home in the New Year."

Lana went back outside and picked up both the babies. Alina and Freya seeing that new people had arrived began to make baby noises. Jessie, Maisie and Auntie Jeanie all swooped on the two babies.

"Oh, they've grown so big." Auntie Jeanie said. "They're both so bonnie. Can I take Freya? I know this one is Freya as she looks just like Stefan." Jessie said taking her out of Lana's arms.

Freya rewarded her with a wide smile and a chuckle. Alina not to be outdone held her arms out and Auntie Jeanie took her from Lana. They all sat around the large kitchen table, passing the babies round and dandling them on their knees. Eventually both Alina and Freya fell asleep in their mother's arms, tired out by all the excitement and they placed them at either end of the downstairs cot in the front room, sleeping peacefully.

Lana said, "Now you can tell us all the news from Dundee." Jessie recounted all she knew about the Dundee Slasher, how the Police had narrowed their search down by identifying the initials and family crest on the knife and had then watched the house and followed a black cloaked figure down to the docks where they caught them in the act, about to commit murder. She related how the local newspaper had dramatically announced the name of the murderer to be Lady Mary MacDonald. Everybody had been shocked that the killer was a woman and even more shocking was that she was their own local benefactress, Lady Mary.

She went on to tell them that she had been pronounced as completely insane and sent to the madhouse at the Royal Edinburgh Asylum. She recounted the entire story that the newspaper had printed about Lady Mary being raped by a sailor, becoming pregnant and eventually giving birth to a stillborn son, on her own.

Both Moira and Lana, having both given birth to healthy babies, said they felt sorry for her, and Lana exclaimed, "But why didn't she go to the police to report the rape or ask someone to help her when it was her time to give birth."

"She didn't want to bring disgrace to the family and her father was extremely strict so she thought he would blame her and have her locked up. You know how it is. Look what we had to do to hide your pregnancy."

"Yes, I suppose but she has ended up being locked up in the madhouse anyway, it's just very sad."

Jessie spoke up, "Well, don't forget that she did murder loads of sailors and Isla too. She admitted murdering her and she said she was after a good-looking blond sailor, but that Isla got in the way."

Lana gasped, "Good heavens, that must have been Stefan but why was Isla following him?"

Maisie joined in, "Ah can tell ye that as one of her friends admitted to me that she had confided in her that she was seeing Campbell and that she was in love with him. Her friend said that she had made her promise not to tell anybody but now she was dead there was no need for secrecy. She told me that Isla was very pure upset for Campbell had ended their relationship, but she was determined to win him back. Now Jessie and Isla clocked that he was after ye as his next conquest, and she was following Stefan so she could add the name of his ship to the report she would give him about your beau."

"I've got a new beau now, Donald who is the delivery man for the bakery. I went a football mahc with him and I'm hoping he amy ask me to marry him. Will you come to my wedding?"

Maisie gave a sharp intake of breath and Jessie kicked her under the table. Moira had written to Auntie Jeanie and told her all about

Campbell's visit, her talk to Jock the smuggler, his revelation about Stefan and that they had discovered Stefan's whereabouts. She had also told her that Ton, Stefan's father had come to Anstruther to find his son and that he had gone to the Admiralty, obtained a letter for Stefan's release from the Royal navy and was on his way to New Zealand to rescue him. Auntie Jeanie had told Lana's two friends and that Moira had decided not to tell Lana that Stefan had been found yet, in case something happened. She did not want to get her hopes up only to be bitterly disappointed and heartbroken again, especially now as she was in better spirits.

"Of course, we will," the two, said in unison. Maisie looking at Jessie with a shocked expression as she said,

"There might be one or two other lasses that would like to come; will that be all right with you? They can share our rooms or go back to Dundee the same day. Let us know and we can put the word around.

Moira, ever the practical one said to Lana, "Hold on a wee minute, he's only asked you to go to a football match and now you are planning a wedding. The poor man doesn't know what he has let himself in for."

"Well, I'm only saying it could happen, and besides, I know he likes me I can tell," Lana replied.

Moira got up and said, "I'll make some tea, Auntie Jeanie and Jessie do you want to help me?

Once they were in the kitchen Jessie whispered, "What are you going to do now? It would be terrible if she married Donald and then Stefan came back."

Moira whispered back, "Ton, said he will be back by December, and I'll just have to talk to Donald and explain the situation so that he does not ask Lana to walk out with him, or start courting her."

"But that might make him keener, if he thinks he's got to act fast before Stefan returns."

"Oh well, I'll think of something."

Just at that moment Lana appeared in the kitchen saying, "What are you three all whispering about?"

"We were just asking Moira about Donald, to make sure he was not a rogue. We didn't want you to be tricked", Jessie said quickly.

Lana studied all their faces, she was sure there was something funny going on, there was something they were not telling her, but she shrugged it off and said, "You don't need to worry about Donald, he's a decent and kind man."

Chapter Forty-Two

There was great excitement at Moira's house when a letter arrived from London. Moira sat down at the table to read the letter, as Angus had gone to work, and the boys were at school.

"Dear Mrs Law,

I have found out the HMS Brisk is stationed at Auckland in New Zealand and I have managed to establish that Stefan is indeed a member of the crew. I explained the story to the Admiralty who were extremely concerned and apologetic. They said that the practice of press-ganging is now abolished and is illegal and they have given me a letter to demand that Stefan is discharged immediately. They have also said that they will investigate the men involved and take further action.

There is one problem; the ship is sailing round the South Seas. Although I expect Stefan is enjoying seeing all the lovely islands, we cannot sail all around the South Seas looking for him, but we know that the HMS Brisk is going to

Sydney for a refit on 26ᵗʰ September and we will have to rendezvous with the ship then. This does mean a delay. I will set off now, in May and I estimate that with my new steam ship it will take 60 days or at the most 90 days to reach Sydney.

I will be there by mid-August at the latest and will have to wait for the HMS Brisk to arrive in late September. Again, it will take the same number of days to return to London and then a few days more to sail on to Anstruther. I should return to Scotland with Stefan, all being well, by the end of November or beginning of December, just in time for Christmas and your Hogmanay celebrations.

Meanwhile, I enclose a letter from the Lord High Admiral Sir John Pakington with a cheque for twenty guineas. The Royal navy have sent Lana this gift to compensate for all the distress she has suffered due to the press ganging. I'm sure Lana will find the money useful although I also feel that money could never offset the anguish and misery she has experienced.

I hope this letter finds you, Lana, and baby Freya well and I look forward to seeing you at the end of the year.

Yours sincerely Ton Van Uden

"Well, that's that then", Moira said, "Your Papa is coming home."

"Pa pa pa." Freya repeated. Then Alina started to say "Pa, pa, pa."

Moira started to giggle wondering what Angus would say if both the babies started to call him Pa. She knew he would just make a joke of it, as he did with everything. He hadn't been incredibly pleased at being part of the conspiracy over Freya's birth, but he had gone along with it. He had even made the two sisters laugh when he mimicked some of the old ladies in the village congratulating him about fathering twin girls.

Later that evening after supper when the children were all in bed Moira handed Ton's letter to Angus, who read it quickly.

"We can tell Lana everything now that ton has confirmed that he has located Stefan."

They asked Lana to sit at the table with them, opened a bottle of wine, poured out three glasses and began to tell her the whole story. When Lana heard that Mr Campbell had asked Moria to persuade her to become his mistress, she nearly choked on her glass of wine.

"Why the great fat toad, to think I would ever even give him the time of day, let alone kiss him. I always knew he was a scheming bastard. I wouldn't be surprised if he had something to do with Stefan's disappearance."

Moira carried on telling Lana about how Mr Campbell had tried to pay the smugglers to murder Stefan and because they were on the quayside to carry out Mr Campbells request, they rescued Stefan from the Dundee Slasher

Lana's eyes grew wider by the minute as she gasped in horror at the tale. And when she heard that Stefan had been pressganged into the British Navy and he was alive and coming home, she leapt out of her chair and screamed with joy. Tears were streaming down her face and Moira got up and flung her arms around her.

"Don't cry my darlin' girl, everything is going to be fine."

"I know, I am just crying with happiness."

They showed her the letter from Ton and explained that he had come looking for Stefan and met the boys with Freya and Alina.

"But why didn't you come and find me at the Bakery? I would have loved to meet Stefan's father. You should have told me as I have a date with the delivery man at the bakery and I would not have encouraged him if I had known that Stefan was alive and well."

"Wel, you will meet him when he brings Stefan home and you'll have plenty of time to get to know him before the wedding."

"You mean he has agreed to Stefan and I marrying? I thought he wanted Stefan to marry Antoinette one of his business partners daughters."

"No, it's all changed now, He has given his blessing to your marriage."

"And what did he think of Freya. Was he shocked?"

"He loved her, and she even sat on his knee. He said she looked just like Stefan when he was a baby. He said he was pleased to have such a beautiful granddaughter."

Moira told her how she had warned the smugglers about the Customs trap that Mr Campbell had set and how they had escaped apart from Michael who had traded his evidence to the police in return for his freedom.

"Thanks to my warning, Jock and the others moved all the contraband, they did not find any of their brandy or rum so there is no proof of smuggling activities although they know fine well that Michael is part of a gang. They tried to get him to give the names of the others involved but he refused.

However, in the end, Michael told them that he had evidence that would help the police in Dundee to catch the Dundee Slasher. Detectives Murray and MacDuff came down from Dundee and Michael gave them the knife that the murderer had dropped. It has initials engraved in the handle, so the detectives were excited as they said that was a good lead for them to follow up. He told them that his men were at the scene because Mr Campbell had paid them money to kill Stefan and they had managed to save him from the Dundee Slasher, who had dropped the knife and run off.

The detectives would see what they could do about Campbell although there was no evidence, and it was all hearsay. On the other hand, the knife was good solid evidence and as Michael had provided it, they have let him go and if they find the murderer, they'll forget all about the smuggling charges and selling Stefan to the Royal Navy. They might even be given a reward!"

"Well, that would be something, wouldn't it? Folks would be pleased as Jock, Michael and Robbie are popular." Angus grinned.

Moira returned his grin with a wide smile, "Of course they are as they supply half the town with cheap brandy and rum."

Lana felt dazed and could hardly believe than Stefan was coming home. Although she had always believed he was alive it was still a shock that she would see him soon. Angus brought out the bottle of whiskey and Moira found some glasses.

They raised their glasses and clinked them together.

"Here's to Stefans safe return."

They threw back their heads and drank the amber liquid smiling at each other. Lana felt exhausted as she had gone through an entire range of emotions, Incredulity, disgust, horror, shock, jubilation, but revived by the whisky her smile mirrored the absolute joy she now felt.

Chapter Forty-Three

They were not the only ones who were smiling. Back in Dundee, the two detectives in charge of the murder investigation grinned at each other. They had just identified the initials on the knife handle as being James MacDonald and they had found a crest on the other side of the handle that confirmed their discovery.

They had been sceptical when the customs men had contacted them about the knife handed over to them by the smuggler, they had in custody but when they had travelled to Dundee, interviewed Michael, and listened to his story they were convinced they had the evidence they needed.

"Let me see, aren't the MacDonald's that wealthy family who live in Glen Lyon House in Broughty Ferry. I seem to remember that the father Lord James MacDonald died a few years ago leaving a daughter, Lady Mary Macdonald."

"Where's the mother?"

"I think she died in childbirth, when Lady Mary was born, leaving the father to bring his daughter up on his own."

"I dinnae think our killer will be Lady Mary, it must be one of the staff who works at the house."

"We'll have to set up a watch on the house to see if anybody willies around at night and we'll have to have a gang of us to catch them in the act. But the Russian sailor being around frightened them off. They could think it's too dangerous and we might nae catch anybody."

"We'll just have to see; we'll ask if we can have some more help to set up to set up the operation as we'll need bobbies at the front and back of the house."

"It is odd how we've just eliminated our Russian sailor who was lurking around the docks and now we have a fresh suspect."

"Och, that's how things go, ye can be waiting for a hansom cab for an hour and then three turn up all at once!"

The two detectives and their team of men kept watch on the house all through the rest of March. By the beginning of April, they were wondering if this was a false lead, it was cold, and damp and they were getting very disheartened.

"I'm getting fed up sitting in the cold watching the house. Maybe this knife is a red herring. and the weather is off to get even more miserable, it's always raining. I can't even feel my hands they're so cold even in though I'm sporting gloves," Detective Murray said glumly as he rubbed his hands together to warm them up.

"Ah I know but tis the only lead we've got, and I think it's a good one. Think about it man, the murderer dropped the knife when he was about to murder that sailor. Think about how good we'll feel if we can catch the killer and take him or her off the streets. Ye won't be feeling blue then; we'll be celebrating with a pint of heavy."

"Never mind my feelings being blue tis my hooter that's blue and I coudnae half do with a pint of heavy right now."

"Our shift is due to end in an hour so when we're relieved, we can go back to my house. Mah missus will have the fire going so we can warm up and better than a pint of heavy, I'll give ye some whisky."

Just then, one of the police officers watching the back of the manor house came running round the corner. "Quick, we've juist seen a wee body in a black cloak creep out of the back door. They're traveling down the road so ye can follow them."

"That's us then. Here we go. You two get down to the docks and wait for us there. It may take a few of us to apprehend the villain."

Chapter Forty-Four

Lady Mary McDonald had dismissed her housekeeper for the night and when she was sure she had left, she carefully placed her dress on a chair and donned a pair of old riding breeches and a shirt. She tied her hair back into a ponytail and wrapped her black cloak around her. She took her silver knife engraved with the family's initials, from the drawer and hid it in the pocket of her trousers. It was the second knife she had taken from the cooks set of knives in the kitchen, as she had dropped the first one on the quayside down at the docks. She smiled to herself as she remembered the cook's annoyance.

"Och, this house is haunted, my wee pointy knives on that stand keep disappearing. I swear there must be a poltergeist. Or else there is a thief about."

She had been so grateful when the housekeeper had replied to the cook, "Don't be so dunderheaded ye've likely dropped them down behind one of the cookers or cupboards."

She did not want them to call the police about lost knives as that would never do. She remembered the night she had dropped the first knife all too vividly. She had been trying to get that blond sailor. She remembered it was the second time she had gone after him as the first time the girl got in the way, and she had killed her by mistake. That had made her feel bad as she only wanted to kill sailors. Then her second attempt had failed, and some men had rescued the same sailor once again. She had abandoned her mission for over a year, panicked by that last attempt. However, time had soothed her worries and she felt compelled to resume her task.

She walked stealthily out of the house, for it would never do if someone saw her for the servants were inveterate gossips. It would only take someone to mention seeing her slip out of the house and she could be caught which would be terrible as she would be unable to complete her mission. She ran lightly down the drive to the road that led into the town and the docks. She had been watching a certain sailor and tonight he would become her victim. She wanted to cause as much pain as she had suffered at the hands of a sailor. She could still remember the afternoon that the sailor had raped her. He had grabbed her as she walked past an alleyway, pulled her into the narrow passage and had taken her standing up pressed against the damp wall. He had just held a knife to her throat, pulled up her skirts and pulled down her drawers. It had happened so fast, and she had felt so dirty afterwards. No number of baths had washed the feeling away but when she had discovered she was with child she had wanted to die and had considered killing herself, she felt so ashamed.

She had managed to conceal her pregnancy from her family as her father would have blamed her and would have sent her to a lunatic asylum. She knew her father was a hypocritical religious bigot, dogmatic and strict. She knew without question that he would have said it was her fault and that she had disgraced the family name. Mary realised, in her heart, that it was not her fault as it happened in broad daylight and she and simply been in the wrong place at the wrong time. She knew the fault was with sailors, not with her and that was why it was her mission to kill as many sailors as possible. She had heard about girls, certified as mad because they performed the cardinal sin of having sex before marriage. It was thought they must be insane and so they were committed to asylums.

When her time had come, she had managed to creep into one of the greenhouses at the back of the estate, far away from the house and had given birth on her own. The baby was stillborn and at first, she had been happy about that as she had thought of it as the spawn of the devil and had planned to suffocate it anyway. But when she looked at the small body, she was unprepared for the rush of love she felt and the sorrow that her son had died. That was another reason for punishing the devils; they had not only degraded her but had killed her son. All sailors were dirty evil men and they deserved to die. It was her calling to ensure that as many of them as possible met this fate.

She was so intent on reaching the quayside and docks that she did not notice the two detectives following stealthily behind her at some distance. When they reached the town, it was easier as the police officers were not in uniform, and they blended in with the crowds.

The figure slipped into a dark alleyway by the side of a public house and Murray and MacDuff carried on walking and hid themselves in the alley at the other side of the pub. They soon spotted the other police officers sauntering along the quayside, whistled to them to get their attention, and then signalled them to join them.

They did not have long to wait as Lady Mary had been stalking her intended victim and knew what time he usually left the pub. There was a burst of light, noise as the pub door was flung open, and the police saw a sailor stagger out drunkenly. They saw the dark cloaked figure tiptoeing after the sailor and as the figure grabbed him from behind the four police officers ran out from their hiding place and snatched the knife from her hand. They grabbed the figure and held her down. She fought like a wildcat, and it took all four of them to restrain her. Detective Murray pulled the hood of the cloak from her head and exclaimed.

"Why she just a wee lassie." He pulled out a pair of handcuffs from his deep pocket and clamped them on her wrists.

"You can't do that, I'm Lady Mary MacDonald of Glen Lyon House."

"We know who you are, Lady Mary and we have proof that you have been murdering sailors for the last two years, so I'm arresting you for the murder of at least nine sailors and one woman.

Lady Mary wailed, "But it's my mission to kill as many sailors as I can. God told me too. He whispers in my ear every night, so you see you cannot stop me. It would be a sin for you to stop me." She started to struggle wildly.

A police wagon pulled by two horses came round the corner, stationed nearby to be at the ready in case they apprehended the murderer. As they bundled Lady Mary into the wagon, Murray called to one of the police officers left behind,

"Make sure the sailor is fine and take him back to his ship." He had noticed that the sailor was swaying on his feet looking quite bemused by the events.

He had also noticed that some of the crowd who had gathered to see what all the excitement was about were shouting threats at the wagon as they realised that the police had caught the Dundee Slasher at last.

"We'll get ye, ye murdering wee whore." "You need a taste of your own medicine." "See how ye like having your own throat cut."

Murray quickly took charge of the situation and told the police officers to form a line and to keep the crowd back so that the wagon was able to drive along the quayside with Lady Mary shaking her fists at Murray and MacDuff and spitting and shouting.

"You spawn of the devil. God will punish you for interfering with my mission."

As they held onto her, Detective Murray locked eyes with Detective MacDuff over Lady Mary's head and made the universal sign of madness twisting his finger round by his forehead. "She's no right in the heid."

"I'm afraid to say you are right and we'll have to get a doctor to see her when we reach the police station. I think it will be the madhouse at the Royal Edinburgh Asylum for her."

"Well at least tis all over now and we've caught our killer, so there'll be no more murders in Dundee, for the moment."

"I'm not mad, it's you two that's mad and I shouldn't be surprised if God is so angry with you that he'll strike you down with a bolt of lightning."

MacDuff rolled his eyes in an expression of disbelief and Murray nodded to him in agreement.

Chapter Forty-Five

After visiting Micronesia, The HMS *Brisk* had headed to the southwest corner of the Pacific to the islands of Melanesia, including Fiji, the Solomon Islands and Vanuatu. Their adventure continued when they visited New Caledonia. Captain Webley Hope told Stefan that Captain James Cook had discovered the island and named it for Scotland as the north-east coast reminded him of Scotland.

It didn't remind Stefan much of the Scotland he knew as he had only visited the Lowlands and he thought one day he would explore the Highlands of Scotland. He smiled ruefully to himself as he had such a list of places to re-visit already that he wasn't sure if he would ever get the time.

The voyage around the South Seas over HMS *Brisk* headed for Sydney in early September. Once more, they had to wait for the pilot to arrive to navigate the ship into her allocated berth. Stefan stood at the rails, as they were piloted in, looking at all the boats moored in the harbour and studying all the different flags fluttering from the masts. There were many different ones and then Stefan caught a glimpse of the Netherlands horizontal tricolour of red, white and blue.

His stomach did a double flip and his heart started to beat faster as he craned his neck to get a better look at the ship. "Can it be, one of my father's ships?" They drew closer until the HMS *Brisk* was level with the ship, but they were still some distance away. Stefan could see a lone figure of a man standing on the deck. He seemed to be shielding his eyes from the sun looking at the HMS *Brisk*. "Was it his father?" Stefan hardly dared to hope.

Then the man seemed to recognise the HMS *Brisk* and began to wave and finally Stefan was sure that it was his father. He noticed that the ship had funnels and he was glad that his father had followed the modern trend, especially as it meant they could travel home faster. He felt like running down the gangplank when they berthed to find his father and his father's ship but the harbour was quite large and he thought they could miss each other. HMS *Brisk* was quite large so his father would find it easy to find him. Stefan called to Ben and told him that his father was waiting for him in the harbour. Ben slapped him on the back,

"I told you it would all come good and that old Maori foretold that your father would come to take you home."

They both stood at the top of the gangplank scanning the quayside and sure enough after a few minutes, Ton appeared. Stefan ran down the gangplank and threw himself into his father's arms.

They both shed some tears and Ton said,

"I'm sorry that I quarrelled with you. I have met Lana, your fiancée and she's a fine girl. You have a daughter now and Lana has named her Freya."

"Lana must have remembered that if I had a daughter, I said I would call her Freya. Are they both well?"

"Yes, they are in good health and Freya is adorable. She looks just like you did as a baby."

They boarded the ship and the sailors on the deck surrounded them, curious to see what was going on. Stefan was bombarded with questions.

"I forgot my manners; let me introduce my good friend Ben. He helped me when I was despairing and thought I'd never go home. Ben this is my father, Ton Van Uden."

"Pleased to meet you, Ton. I've heard all about you."

"Oh dear, I suppose he told you I was a spiteful old man and wouldn't agree to let him marry the girl he had chosen. Well let me tell you that is all in the past now and I want him to marry Lana."

Captain Webley Hope had seen all his crew milling about on the deck, slapping Stefan on the back, shaking an older man's hand, and had come down from the bridge to see what was going on. Stefan quickly introduced them to each other and said,

"My father has come to take me home."

The captain ushered them both below decks to his cabin and indicated that they should both sit down. He took out a bottle of whisky, poured three glasses and handed one each to Stefan and Ton, taking a large gulp from the other that he had poured for himself. Ton had been keeping the letter from the Admiralty in the inside pocket of his jacket and he pulled it out and handed it to the captain. The captain read it silently and then addressing Stefan said,

"That's quite clear, Stefan you are discharged from service in Her Majesty's Navy, and you are free to leave immediately."

He turned to Ton, "I have to tell you that I shall be sorry to see your son leave, he has been an asset to me, his conduct has been exemplary, and you should be proud of him. He's a credit to you."

"Thank you."

Stefan and Ton left the cabin and Stefan told his father that he had to say goodbye to his charges. He ran down the stairs to the mess room and found all his friends talking excitedly about the event. They were all pleased for him and there was a lot of back-slapping as Stefan told them he was leaving immediately as he wanted to start his homeward journey as soon as possible.

He gave Ben his address in Holland and told the others to write to him too if they wanted as he would like to hear how they were getting on. He had a special hug for Ben who promised to write to Stefan. Stefan promised that he would journey back to New Zealand to see him if he decided to settle there and told him to come to Holland if he decided against it. Amid loud cheers Stefan left the mess and his men with good memories of the time he had spent on board the HMS *Brisk*. He quickly made a detour to his bunk to retrieve his meagre belongings and the presents from Tani.

Ton and Stefan boarded the Dutch ship named, '*The Rocket*,' which Stefan supposed referred to its fast steam-powered engine. Stefan could hardly believe that he was free at last and that he was going home. He was longing to see Lana and his daughter. He had supressed any thoughts of Lana for the last few months as they only caused him pain but now, she was only a few months away he could dream of her again.

The journey back to London was uneventful but seemed interminably slow to Stefan. As they navigated the Cape of Good Hope without experiencing any storms, Ton told him not to be so impatient,

"We've been very lucky, and we've had fair winds and a following sea. We've passed through the worst part of the journey and we're just a hop away from Rio de Janeiro where we can refuel and then it's the home run across the Atlantic"

"I know we've been lucky, it's just that I'm longing to see Lana and my baby daughter."

They made good time, partly due to HMS *Brisk* arriving early in Sydney for her refit so they had been able to set off in mid-September and they arrived at the Port of London at the end of November. After a few days delay, buying provisions and more coal, they set off once again around the east coast of England and north to Scotland. They finally arrived in Anstruther on the fifth of December and Stefan smiled to himself as he thought this was the best Sinterklaas gift he had ever had.

He was dressed in his Royal Navy Officer's uniform, a navy-blue frock coat with epaulettes, gold braid and gleaming brass buttons. He was also wearing a bicorn hat and with his suntanned face, he was a handsome sight. As he walked from the quayside through Anstruther with his father by his side, people stopped to stare at him.

He walked up the path to Moira's door and said hello to Ronald and James who were kicking a ball around in the garden. They gawped at him open mouthed. Stefan knocked at the door and after a few minutes, Lana opened it. She didn't recognise him at first, in his uniform and was astonished,

"Hello, I think you must have the wrong house."

"Lana, it's me, Stefan."

She was speechless, then burst into tears and flung her arms around him.

Stefan hugged her back and kissed her, his own tears running down his face mingling with hers.

At last, they broke apart and just gazed at each other in wonder as if they could not believe what they were seeing. Freya broke the spell, as she ran to the door. She had her breakfast plastered all over her face.

"This must be Freya", Stefan said as he swooped down and picked her up. She started to laugh delightedly.

"This is your Papa, Freya."

She repeated "Pa pa pa." and tried to pull his hat off.

Stefan removed his hat and flung it onto the table and his daughter laughed even more.

"She's got your laugh, Lana."

"Yes, but she looks like you."

"She's got your eyes though, slightly tip tilted. She's perfect."

Stefan kissed his daughter all over her face, while she giggled in delight and made enchanting baby sounds. Ronald and James came in and Lana introduced them to Stefan. Then Ton came in through the door, Moira started to bustle around telling everyone to sit down and she would serve up tea and scones.

Stefan sat down with Freya on his knee and Alina not to be outdone started to laugh and giggle and held out her arms to Ronald saying,

"Pickie up pickie up" and he put her on his knee.

Ton had brought a bag with all the presents from the Maoris in New Zealand and Stefan handed them out to Lana and Moira, telling them the meanings of their necklaces. The two sisters admired each other pendants and put them on. Moira was especially affected by the gift and its meaning of strength and courage.

"I don't know if I deserve this."

"You've been a tower of strength to me." Lana answered and Stefan turned to Moira saying,

"An old Maori fortune teller, told my friend Tani about you and so he bought you this special necklace for me to give to you to thank you for looking after Lana for me. So, you certainly deserve it."

Lana was amazed at the workmanship of the carved wooden bowls and Stefan told everyone about the Maoris. Ronald and James were fascinated when he told them about their houses and the feast. When he said he ate the *hu hu* grubs, Ronald said,

"Zooks, you wouldn't catch me eating grubs."

James, who was more adventurous, said, "What did they taste like?"

"Mmm, they were like mashed-up peanuts. Very nice. I was surprised."

"I'd eat some then because I love peanuts."

Both of the boys were enraptured when he regaled everyone with his description of the *haka* war dance where the Maoris stuck out their tongues and they exclaimed excitedly,

"Mum, can we go to New Zealand and visit the Maoris. I want to watch their war dance."

"Yes, and I want to go to a feast and try *hu hu* grubs."

Everyone laughed and Moira said, "Ask Stefan if he is going to sail back there and, he'll take you too."

When all the tea was drunk and the scones eaten, Moira and Lana took the babies upstairs for a nap. Then Stefan and Lana sat in the front room, and everyone left them alone to catch up. Stefan told her all about the places he had visited. He showed her his certificate of Crossing the Line and she laughed with him as he told her about Pollywogs, the mock shaving, the captain dressed as Neptune and the ship's doctor dressed as his wife and the unceremonious backward tumble into the home-made swimming pool.

They talked and talked and after dinner that night when Ton had gone back to his ship and Moira and Angus had gone to bed, they sat up for half the night talking. They both shed tears of happiness and they sat on the old settee clutching hold of one another as if their very life depended upon it.

"You remembered that I said that if I had a daughter, I would call her Freya. She's beautiful and I love you both."

Ton had told Stefan about the plans Mr Campbell had made to have him murdered and how the smugglers had rescued him from the Dundee Slasher. Lana explained that the smugglers had had him press-ganged into the Royal Navy, so that the man who had paid them to murder him would never know that they had not carried out their task. It was a blessing in disguise as it had kept him safe from another attempt by Mr Campbell to murder him. Stefan had wanted to set off immediately to Dundee to have it out with Mr Campbell but when Lana had explained that the smugglers had carried out their own revenge he was placated.

She recounted all she knew about the Dundee Slasher, how the Police had narrowed their search down by identifying the initials and family crest on the knife that one of the smuglers had given them and had then watched the house and followed a black cloaked figure down to the docks where they caught them in the act, about to commit murder. She related how the local newspaper had dramatically announced the name of the murderer to be Lady Mary MacDonald. Everybody had been shocked that the killer was a woman and even more shocking was that she was their own local benefactress, Lady Mary.

She went on to tell him that she had been pronounced as completely insane and sent to the madhouse at the Royal Edinburgh Asylum. She recounted the entire story that the newspaper had printed about Lady Mary being raped by a sailor, becoming pregnant and eventually giving birth to a stillborn son, on her own.

Lana, having given birth to a healthy baby, said the felt sorry for her, and wondered why she didn't go to the police to report the rape or ask someone to help her when it was her time to give birth."

Stefan said "I suppose she didn't want to bring disgrace to the family and I think her father was old fashioned and extremely strict so she thought he would blame her and have her locked up. You know how it is. Look what you had to do to hide your pregnancy."

"Yes, I suppose but she has ended up being locked up in the madhouse anyway, it's just incredibly sad. But she did murder loads of sailors and Isla too. She admitted murdering her and she said she was after a good-looking blond sailor, but that Isla got in the way."

Stefan gasped, "Good heavens, that must have been me but why was Isla following me?"

Lana told him, "One of her friends admitted to me that she had confided in her that she was seeing Campbell and that she was in love with him. Her friend said that she had made her promise not to tell anybody but now she was dead there was no need for secrecy. She told me that Isla was very pure upset for Campbell had ended their relationship, but she was determined to win him back. Now Jessie and Isla both clocked that he was after Lana as his next conquest, and she was following Stefan so she could add the name of his ship to the report she would give him about your beau."

"Apparently now he was attacked and savagely beaten up and both his legs were broken. According to the gossip around the mill, his guidwife told someone that the police had called at their house and advised him that he would be better to leave Dundee, as they coudnae guarantee to protect him. She doesn't know what's going on, but she says that she's not going with him down south as she doesn't want to leave all her folk in Dundee, so he's on his own. The rumour is that he is off to find work in the cotton mills in Lancashire."

Lna continued, "It must have been Jock and the smugglers. They were extremely annoyed that he informed on them to the Customs and Excise."

Stefan was incredulous that he had escaped the murderer twice and expressed his sorrow that Isla died to save his life. When Lana explained that Isla had been Mr Campbell's mistress and the reason, she was following him was to provide more information to her ex-lover, Stefan had grown angry again and wanted to find him to beat him up.

Lana had managed to calm him down and then Stefan had declared that it was his entire fault, that he should have married her sooner and that this would then not have happened. Lana had said it was all her fault as she naively had not realised that Mr Campbell had designs on her. There were many tears and Stefan declared that he would not be so indecisive in the future. Lana acknowledged that she would not be so trusting. Then they had both clung on to each other and agreed that it wasn't either of their faults and that Stefan had had a lucky escape from the Dundee Slasher and they should both put it all behind them and look to the time ahead.

Even at breakfast the next day they were still recounting tales to each other, in between laughing and kissing, until Moira said,

"Come on you two lovebirds, stop kissing and canoodling, we've got a wedding to organise."

Chapter Forty-Six

The Parish church at St Monans seemed almost ethereal, as it was so close to the water that it looked as if it had risen out of the sea. Lana had chosen this church, a few miles from Anstruther along the coast, as the setting was so picturesque. She wanted everything to be perfect for her wedding and beside it was near to Elie where they were holding the reception at The Ship Inn, her sister Andrea and her brother-in-law Ben's pub. Moira and a few of her friends had helped to decorate the church that morning with fresh flowers and so she knew the church would look and smell lovely. The church started to fill up as people arrived either walking along the coast road or driving up in hired carriages, broughams, and phaetons. Soon Moira, Angus, Jessie, and Maisie arrived and waited outside for the bride to arrive.

Lana had been grateful that Angus had gone with the bridesmaids. As her father was dead, he was stepping into the role of giving her away and he could have gone with her in the wedding carriage. But the last few weeks had been a maelstrom and she needed some time to become calm and collect her thoughts.

She got into the brougham, decorated with flowers and ribbons and sat back with a sigh of relief. Alone at last, she thought back to the day that Stefan had come back. They had both shed tears of happiness and Lana remembered how they had sat on the old settee hanging on to each other as if they thought they would lose one another again.

Lana broke out of her reverie as they approached the church and adjusted her tiara and veil. Moira had helped her choose them when they had made a trip to Edinburgh to a wedding shop to buy the bridesmaid dresses. It was beautiful and delicate with seed pearls and as she put it on, she knew that she looked her best. She had borrowed Moira's wedding dress because she thought it would be unlucky to wear her old dress, which she had kept as a sentimental memento of Robbie. She thought of Robbie and imagined him smiling that she had found happiness again and she was incredibly happy, happier than she had ever been in her whole life.

She had survived all the grief over the loss of her Robbie and the anguish of Stefan's disappearance. She knew that all the past unpleasant episodes had made her stronger and she could now face anything. The carriage drew up at the church and Angus was there to hand her out. There was a crowd of people standing around the church entrance and she heard cries of,

"Aah, don't she look lovely."

Angus said, "You look beautiful Lana."

Lana smiled at him expecting him some teasing banter but to her surprise, he kept quiet.

"You don't look so bad yourself in your kilt."

He took her arm and led her into the church and the organ music started to play. She saw Stefan waiting at the altar still looking suntanned and handsome and she could hardly believe that he was here and wondered if she was hallucinating until she saw his beaming smile, lighting up his face and crinkling his eyes at the corners.

She suddenly felt terrified at having to walk down the aisle past all the people that she had deceived about the baby and her heart was fluttering. Moira, Jessie and Maisie were following behind her as her bridesmaids, looking attractive in their deep pink dresses with flowered circlets on their heads. Jessie had seen the expression on Lana's face and Lana unexpectedly felt a pinch on her bottom and turned her head to see Jessie, giving her a wink and smiling widely,

"Ye'll be all right lassie."

Maisie whispered forcefully, "Jessie you're a caution."

Lana smiled at her friend, brought down to earth she no longer felt nervous and sailed down the aisle confidently smiling back at everyone.

The minister's voice rang out, "We are gathered here in the sight of God and in the face of this company to join this Man and Woman in holy matrimony. Into this holy estate, these two persons present come now to be joined. If any man can show just cause, why they may not lawfully be joined together, let him now speak or else hereafter for ever hold his peace".

The minister then asked each of them "Wilt thou have this Woman to thy wedded wife and wilt thou have this man to thy wedded husband? After the exchange of vows when they both said,

"I will" the Minister asked, "Who giveth this Woman to be married to this man"

Angus replied, "Her family and friends gathered today do."

He stepped back so that only Lana and Stefan were standing facing the minister. The minister then said the words "I take thee Lana, to my wedded wife and to hold from this day forward, for better or for worse, for richer for poorer, in sickness and in health, to love and to cherish, till death us do part, according to Gods holy ordinance; and thereto I plight my troth." The minister then repeated the words to Stefan using to my wedded husband and Lana and Stefan both repeated the words to each other.

Stefan's groomsman, who had come over from Rotterdam, handed the minister Lana's and Stefan's ring and Lana handed her bouquet to Moira, her maid-of -honour. The minister blessed the rings, put them on each on their fingers and said,

"With this Ring I thee wed, and with all my worldly goods I thee endow in the name of the Father and of the Son and of the Holy Ghost. Amen. I now pronounce you man and wife."

They went outside with the church bells ringing and the smell of the sea in the air. Ton had brought some of the new-fangled confetti with him and had distributed it to the people waiting outside and Lana laughed as she was pelted with the small, coloured discs. The confetti swirled around carried by the breeze from the Firth of Forth.

Stefan had paid a photographer to take photographs and he had set up his tripod with the camera looking like a pair of bellows a few yards from the church entrance. He asked everyone to line up for a group photo. Lana, Stefan, Auntie Jeanie, Jessie, Maisie, Moira,

Angus, stood in the middle with Ton Van Uden and Lucas behind them.

The photographer placed the pageboys, Robert, and James in their kilts in front of the adults. When he was happy with the composition, he told everyone to keep as still as possible as it took a few minutes for the photograph to develop. Then he took another photograph of just Lana and Stefan and by this time, Lana was growing impatient to get to the reception at Elie, as she knew that Freya was waiting there.

Moira had arranged for a friend to look after Alina and Freya during the ceremony and then to take them to the reception at Elie. Both girls had looked sweet and pretty in their new pink dresses bought for this special occasion, but Lana thought that by the time they got to Elie the two babies could be covered in food and drink. But she needn't have worried as Andrea had looked after her nieces well and when Lana arrived the two babies were sitting on a rug in the corner playing with coloured bricks and some wooden animals, looked after by two of the barmaids from the inn.

Andrea and Ben had made a splendid spread for the wedding buffet, and everybody filled their plates from the central table and sat at side-tables. Each wedding guest had a wedding favour of homemade shortbread tied up in a small box with a ribbon, made by Andrea.

The food looked scrumptious and there was a whole cooked salmon, a turkey breast, roast beef, roast pork with crackling, roast mutton and a ham hock with various bowls of salads, meat pates and fish pates, scotch pies, cheese tarts, new potatoes and baskets of bread and salvers of fresh butter. There were dishes containing mouth-watering vegetables with butter melting over them, mustards and pickles, mint jelly, cranberry sauce and applesauce. Waiters were going round with bottles of wine filling everyone's glasses when they saw they were empty.

When everyone had eaten the savoury course, the chefs brought out the desserts from the kitchen and people queued up, spoiled for choice between chocolate tart, lemon syllabub, apple charlotte, trifle, orange custard, layered lemon jelly, rhubarb jelly, blancmange, raspberries and cream or a slice of sandwich cake with lemon curd and vanilla bean buttercream.

The top table had Lana, Stefan, Ton, Lucas, Moira, Angus, Jessie and Maisie, Robbie and James and of course Alina and Freya in their highchairs, at the end of the table. Alina was a little more demanding and Moira had picked her up and was holding her on her knee. Lana looked at Freya who was chuckling and making baby talk with the barmaid who was looking after her and she smiled and waved to her. She supposed Freya had become used to separation from her as she seemed quite happy.

Stefan announced that his father, best man, and brother-in-law were going to give their speeches, and everyone quietened down. There was a lot of laughter as they each told tales about the wedding couple. Then Andrea brought in the wedding cake which they cut announcing that each guest was be given a slice of cake to take home.

The tables were cleared away to make way for the fiddlers and the dancing and Lana was able to circulate. She was pleased to see little Jack and his mother, from the mill and went to have a word with Leslie. She felt a little guilty because she had not invited Jack to be a pageboy or even sent him and his mother an invitation to the wedding and reception. However, she smiled wryly when she heard what Leslie had to say as she learned that Jack had not been deterred by the lack of a formal invitation.

"Och, he pestered me to death to come to the church and reception when Jessie announced that anybody from the mill would be welcome at your wedding and so I arranged for a friend to mind the wee 'Uns for a day. We're staying the night in Jessie's room and will go back with her in the morning. T'was a bonnie do and I wish ye all the pure happiness in the world. The food was marvellous - ah havenae eaten so well in years."

Lana carried on circulating and looked around for Stefan's sister Mariella. She needn't have worried about her as she was sitting amongst a crowd of Angus's friends from the docks holding court, laughing and flirting. Lana wondered if her daughter Freya was like her aunt Mariella as she was displaying the same characteristics.

Sure, enough when she looked around, she saw Freya sitting on the blanket in the corner surrounded by several of the village children, pointing imperiously at one of her toys while the children all scrambled to give it to her.

She saw that Jessie was dancing with Lucas and that Maisie was laughing and chatting with one of the men from the dockyard. Moira and Andrea were dancing with their husbands. The violinists were tirelessly playing different waltzes, the whole room filled with music, laughter, and conversation. Everyone was happy, and Lana was content that the reception was a success. She spotted Ton and thought how wonderful it was that he had seemed to abandon his objections to his son marrying a Protestant and had welcomed Lana into his family with open arms. His concerns had been resolved because of all the arrangements they had made.

Stefan had obtained a special dispensation to permit him to have a non-Catholic ceremony and although Lana had decided not to convert to Catholicism, she had agreed that Freya would be baptised and brought up in the Catholic faith. She had made her own proviso that Freya should attend the Protestant church when they were in Anstruther and that she could make her own mind up about which religion she wanted to follow when she was twenty-one.

She stopped to talk to Ton, and he told her that he and Stefan had bought the house that Lana wanted down by the harbour in Anstruther, also that they would start to build her a house on the family estate in Rotterdam as soon as they arrived so that she could help to design it. The idea was that the family could live in Rotterdam with regular visits to Anstruther. Lana was overcome and was thanking Ton when Jack ran up to her,

"Well done on your marriage. Ah was off to ask ye to marry me when I was older, but I've spoken to Stefan, and I think he's a good man so you're alright there."

Lana laughed aloud as Jack sounded so grown up but then he always had, ever since she had first met him, and he had warned her about Mr Willy Campbell.

Jack sighed and said, "I'll just have to find someone else now."

She heard Ronald calling to him, "You're missing your turn." and he ran back to where Ronald and James were sitting at a table.

She was pleased that they had befriended Jack and she presumed they were playing a game of snap.

"Who is that?" Ton asked

Lana explained that he was one of the boys that the mill employed, and he was working to help support his younger brother and sisters, as his mother was a widow. Ton seemed interested and so Lana told him about all the children that worked at the Mill and how little the children were paid.

Ton remarked, "He's a good lad, then, looking after his family at such a young age."

The music started up and Lana went to find Stefan so they could dance. Then she danced with Ton, Lucas, Angus and even the smugglers, Jock and Michael. She only stopped when she went upstairs with Moira to put Alina and Freya to bed. Then there was more music, dancing, fun and laughter.

Ton had put money at the bar, so the drink was flowing freely, and Lana felt a little tipsy and stopped to ask Stefan to check his pocket-watch for the time. She was surprised that it was 11 o clock and was about to say, "Goodness, where has the time gone?" when Jack came running up to her in great excitement,

"Lana, I'm off to be a cabin laddie on Ton's ship, so I can train to be a sailor and I might even be a captain one day, Ton said. He has talked to my mother, and he will pay me three times the money I earned at the mill so he'll give two thirds of it to my Ma, and I can have the rest, it'll be the first time I've ever had any money of my own, so it feels wonderful. Ton says I'll have to pay for my clothes and a hammock but that's all right. I'll be able to visit ye in Rotterdam and in Anstruther when you're here and I'll see my Ma and my wee brothers and sisters when the ship docks in Dundee. This is the best day of my life. I'm so glad ye came to the mill and I met you. Ta for being my friend."

"I'm happy for you and you must come and see me to let me know how you are getting on."

"Aye, I'll definitely do that cos you're the best friend I've ever had"

He ran back to where his mother was sitting and she raised a hand to wave across the room at Lana and mouthed, "Thank you." Lana felt overcome and when Ton appeared at her side she said, with tears in her eyes,

"Thank you for offering little Jack a place as a cabin boy."

Stefan put his arms around her and said, "Now then Mrs Lana Van Uden, you can't cry on your wedding day. I forbid it."

Lana tears turned to laughter as she said, "I'm crying with happiness. I never thought I'd be this happy again." Just at that moment, someone announced that by popular demand, the last dance would be the Gay Gordons and there was mad scramble as everyone rushed onto the dance floor. Stefan put his arm around her shoulder, and they joined the circle of dancers. As he twirled her around, she started to giggle,

"I remember the first time you danced the Eightsome Reel you were all left feet and nearly fell over but you were good at the Gay Gordons, so you'll be all right."

Stefan laughed good naturedly, "Just wait till I teach you some of our Dutch dances. It'll be you that has two left feet then."

"Do you have special dances in Holland, then?"

"No, I was just teasing you. We don't have any traditional dances."

Stefan guided her into the centre where couples whirling, and dancing surrounded them. There was a lot of noise from the loud music and people laughing and talking. There was the smell of fresh flowers, with undertones of sweat from all the crowds of people mixed with the smell of peat burning in the fireplaces. They looked into each other's eyes and Lana said,

"This has been the very best day and I love you Stefan Van Uden."

"I love you too Lana Van Uden and I hope there will be many more days like this one. You are the sweetest most beautiful girl in the world. I know all my family will love you and you will be the toast of Rotterdam."

THE END

Appendices

1. The Spanish Armada and Anstruther

There was great surprise and consternation in Anstruther when the townsfolk woke up one morning in 1588 to find a strange ship, barely afloat in the harbour. The captain of the *El Gran Griffon*, the flagship of the Spanish Armada, had decided to put into the Firth of Forth. Escaping from the battle, they had lost in the English Channel he realised that his boat was not going to make it sailing round the tip of Scotland on past Ireland and France to the Atlantic to reach their homeland. Fears of a Spanish invasion were rife in Scotland and the citizens of Anstruther became alarmed when they found out that the boat was indeed a Spanish ship with 270 sailors aboard.

However, James Melville, who was one of the founders of the Protestant Church of Scotland, had a ministry covering Anstruther and the town officials approached him for advice on how to treat the sailors. Melville announced that although the sailors were Catholic, the townsfolk should treat them with decency and integrity to demonstrate the goodness of their own Protestant religion and so the sailors were welcomed with kindness and generosity. The favour was returned when chief Spanish Admiral, Juan Gomez, interceded on their behalf to free an Anstruther vessel that was impounded by the Spanish Authorities in Calais. The ship was returned with his regards to the Minister, Laird and townsfolk of Anstruther.The Spanish sailors were treated to a period of Scottish hospitality while their repatriation to Spanish Flanders was negotiated. Some of the sailors married local girls and were happy to stay in Anstruther. All this is a matter of historical fact and is well documented but as the story *The Anstruther Lass* is a work of fiction, I have romanticised these facts and invented a Spanish commune living in Anstruther in the mid-1800's. I do not know if such a commune existed back in the 1800's, or indeed exists today but I like to think that there may be some townsfolk of Anstruther that are proud of their Spanish ancestry. One thing is certain, the townsfolk of Anstruther should be proud of the way they extended hospitality to the shipwrecked Spanish sailors back in 1588.

2. The Beggars Benison

The Beggars Benison was a Scottish gentleman's club devoted to, 'he convivial celebration of male sexuality.' It was founded in 1739 and closed in 1836. The word 'benison' means blessing and according to its founders, the club's name came from a story about King James V, who disguised as a bagpiper was journeying to the East Neuk of Fife. Failing to cross the Dreel Burn, when it was in full flow, a buxom lass came to the rescue, tucked up her petticoats and lifted her king across her shoulders to carry him to the opposite bank. The King was grateful and gave her a gold sovereign and in return, she gave him her blessing which was,

"May your purse ne'er be toom [empty] and your horn aye [always] in bloom."

The clubs rather rude motto thus became, "May prick nor purse ne'er fail you." The club was estimated to have 500 members many of whom were influential and powerful figures in landowning, business, law and customs. It is said that the members drawn from the upper classes of society dined and drank together, exchanging obscene songs and toasts. Much of their discussion revolved around sex and there were often lectures on sex and anatomy. The club had a stock of pornography and there were sometimes naked 'posture girls' for the members to look at. Its evocative name was often toasted with a knowing wink at polite dinner parties and referenced in the erotic literature of the day.

It is suggested that the club was a fellowship that grew from its smuggling origins to serve the business interests of its members.

The coastline of Fife was a haven for smuggling especially after the 1707 Act of Union when Scotland was hit by English taxes on trade, causing smuggling to be viewed as an acceptable occupation. So, according to your point of view, the Benison members were libertine and enlightened free-trade heroes or local wealthy protectionist tax evaders. Whatever the case, the rituals of the club were used to strengthen bonds and commit to the cause and one clue to the club's nature is its symbol of a purse tied to a phallus.

3. Hogmanay and Yule

One of the most surprising things about Christmas and New Year in Scotland is that Christmas was not celebrated as a festival and was virtually banned in Scotland for 400 years, from the end of the 17th century to the 1950s. The reason for this, dates back to the years of Protestant Reformation, when the strait-laced Kirk proclaimed Christmas as a Popish or Catholic feast and as such needed banning. Indeed, there are records of charges being brought against people for keeping 'Yule'. Christmas Day was not declared a public holiday until 1954 and Boxing Day only became a public holiday in 1974, so at the time of the story there would not have been a Christmas holiday closing of the mill but just a holiday for New Year's Day.

It is believed that the Vikings originally brought many of the traditional Hogmanay celebrations to Scotland in the early 8th and 9th Centuries. These Norsemen, or men from an even more northerly latitude than Scotland, paid particular attention to the arrival of the Winter Solstice or the shortest day and they fully intended to celebrate its passing with some serious partying. In Shetland, where the Viking influence remains the strongest, New Year is still called Yules, deriving from the Scandinavian word for the midwinter festival of Yule.

The origin of the name Hogmanay is not clear. It may have been introduced to Naval Lord Middle via French. The most commonly cited explanation is a derivation from the Northern French dialectal word hoginane, or variants such as hoginane, hoginono and hoguinettes, hoginono and hoguinettes, those being derived from

16th-century Middle-French aguillanneuf meaning either a gift given at New Year, a children's cry for such a gift, or New Year's Eve itself.

Other people think the origins may have been from Gaelic and yet others reject both the French and Gaelic theories and instead suggest that the ultimate source both for the Norman French, Scots and Gaelic variants of this word have a common Norse root. There are a number of traditions and superstitions that have to be taken care of before midnight on the 31st of December. These include cleaning the house and taking out the ashes from the fire. There is also the requirement to clear all your debts before 'the bells' sound midnight, otherwise you will be in debt all year.

Immediately after midnight, it is traditional to sing Robert Burns "Auld lang Syne." Burns published his version of this popular little ditty in 1788, although the tune was in print over 80 years before this.

> *"Should auld acquaintance be forgot and never brought to mind?*
> *Should auld acquaintance be forgot and auld lang syne,*
> *For auld lang syne, my dear, for auld lang syne,*
> *We'll take a cup o kindness yet, for auld lang syne."*

One of the chief parts of the Hogmanay party, which is still continued with equal enthusiasm today, is to welcome friends and strangers with warm hospitality and of course lots of enforced kissing for all. 'First footing' (or the first foot in the house after midnight) is still a common tradition across Scotland today. To ensure good luck for the house the first foot should be a dark male and he should bring with him symbolic pieces of coal, shortbread, salt, black bun and a wee dram of whisky. The dark male part is believed to be a throwback to the Viking days, when a big blonde stranger arriving on your doorstep with a large axe meant trouble and would not have been auspicious for a happy New Year.

So you can see that traditionally, in Scotland the celebration of the New Year was of greater significance than Christmas. The Lowland Scots called the feast of the birth of Christ, Yule and the season from 25th December to 6 January was often known as Yuletide. The Scots word 'Yule' comes from the old Norse 'jol' which was a midwinter a pagan celebration of the winter solstice, in part to brighten the darkest days, in part to appease the gods to allow the sun to return!

The end of Yuletide on the 6th of January has long been known as 'Uphalyday'. The most well-known of this feast still takes place in Shetland where the name has taken on the local form 'Uphellya' and is celebrated on the last Tuesday of January and combines both a pagan fire festival with Christmas rites.

The use of the word Christmas did come into fashion during the Victorian period, in some parts of Society, when the feast became very commercialised with gifts, cards trees and decorations. However, most of the Scots still referred to Christmas as Yule and it is still quite common in modern Christmas cards produced in the Scots language to see the message, 'A Blithe Yule' meaning 'Happy Christmas' or even 'A Cantie Yule' meaning 'Cheerful or pleasant Christmas'. Also in the Victorian period, there was a more relaxed attitude to Yule and although it was not conspicuously celebrated in Scotland, people exchanged Christmas presents.

4. The New Zealand Wars and the Waitangi Treaty

It is in no doubt that, the indigenous Maori tribes of New Zealand were treated badly by European settlers who simply immigrated to New Zealand and settled on land belonging to the Maoris. They took their land, and the Maoris were unable to grow crops to support themselves and they were made homeless. There were a series of armed conflicts that took placed between 1845 and 1872 and most were triggered by tensions over disputed land purchases, and they escalated dramatically from 1860 as the government faced a united Maori resistance to further land sales and a refusal to acknowledge Crown Sovereignty.

The colonial government summoned thousands of British troops to mount major campaigns to overpower the movement and acquire farming and residential land for British settlers. Later campaigns were aimed at quashing the so-called *Hauhau* movement, an extremist part of the Pai Marire religion, which was strongly opposed to the take-over of Māori land and was eager to strengthen Maori identity.

At the peak of hostilities in the 1860s, 18,000 British troops, supported by artillery, cavalry and local militia battled about 4000 Maori warriors in what became a gross imbalance of manpower and weaponry. Although outnumbered the Maori were able to withstand their enemy with techniques that included anti-artillery bunkers and the use of carefully placed pa or fortified villages, that allowed them to block their enemy advance and often inflict heavy losses, yet quickly abandon their positions without significant loss. Both sides in later campaigns often fought in dense bush used guerrilla-style tactics. Over the course of the Taranaki and Waikato campaigns, the lives of about 1800 Maori and 800 Europeans were lost and total Maori losses over the course of all the wars may have exceeded 2100.

The Treaty of Waitangi was a treaty first signed on 6th February 1840 by representatives of the British Crown and various Maori chiefs from the North Island of New Zealand. The Treaty established a British Governor of New Zealand, recognised Maori ownership of their lands, forests and other properties and gave the Maoris the rights of British subjects. In return, the Maori people ceded New Zealand to Queen Victoria, giving her government the sole right to purchase land.

The Maoris and the English interpreted the Treaty differently and this led to many grievances particularly with regard to land claims, which continue to this day. From the late 1960's Maori began drawing attention to breaches of the Treaty emphasising problems with its translation. Almost 150 years after signing the treaty the government tried to give judicial and moral effect to the document by writing another new version, the 'Spirit' or 'intent' of the treaty through specifying it's principles. This move highlighted that the original document was not a firm foundation for the construction of a state.

Nowadays the Treaty is generally considered the founding document of New Zealand as a nation. However, there are still many disagreements between Maori and non-Maori New Zealanders, which are taken to the Waitangi Tribunal, set up in 1975. The Crown, in most cases, is not obliged to act on the recommendations of the tribunal but nonetheless in many instances has accepted that it breached the Treaty and its principles. Settlements for Treaty breaches, to date, have consisted of hundreds of millions of dollars of reparation in cash and assets, as well as apologies and so it could be said that the Maoris have fared better than the indigenous Red Indians of North America.

In 1974, the date of the signing of the Treaty was declared a national holiday and is called Waitangi Day.

5. Ta Moko

The people of Eastern Polynesia brought the art of the Maori tattoo to New Zealand in 1769. It was a rite of passage between childhood and adulthood, accompanied by many ceremonies and rituals. It signalled status and rank and showed a person's accomplishments, ancestry and marital status. The person's ancestry is indicated on each side of the face, where the left side is generally the father's side and the right side the mothers. No two tattoos are alike and the moko could be used as a kind of identification card, other Maoris could recognise a person's power and position by his moko. It was also traditionally used to make a person more attractive to the opposite sex. Men had full facial tattoos, while women only had their chin, lip and nostrils tattooed.

Having a Ta Moko was an extremely painful experience as deep cuts were incised into the skin with a range of uhi (chisels) made from albatross bone. This manner of tattooing leaves the skin with grooves after healing, instead of the usual smooth surface left after needlepoint tattoos. The inks that were used by Maori were made from all natural products. Burnt wood was used to create black pigments, while lighter pigments were derived from caterpillars infected with a certain type of fungus, or from burnt kauri gum mixed with animal fat.

Due to the sacred nature of the Maori tattoo, those who were undergoing the process, and those involved in the process, could not eat with their hands or talk to anyone aside from the other people being tattooed. Those who were receiving tattoos made it a point not to cry out in pain, because to do so was a sign of weakness. Being able to withstand the pain was a very important in terms of pride for Maori people. There were other rules and regulations around being tattooed, for example, many Maoris had to abstain from sexual intimacy while undergoing the rite and had to avoid all solid foods. The person was fed from a wooden funnel to prevent foodstuffs from contaminating the swollen skin. A person would be fed in this manner until the facial wounds had fully healed. The leaves of the karaka tree were often used as a balm that was applied after the tattooing to help the healing process. The tattooing was often accompanied by music, singing and chanting to help soothe the pain.

In recent times. The Maori people have revived the old methods of tattooing as a way of preserving their cultural heritage. The art organisation known as Te Uhi a Mataora was recently established by traditional Maori tattoo practitioners. They strive to propagate the art form by reviving old traditions and preserving old designs, and state that Maori tattooing is a cultural symbol.

6. HMS *Brisk*

HMS *Brisk* was a wooden-hulled screw sloop of the Royal Navy, launched on 2nd June 1851 from Woolwich Dockyard. She served in the Crimean War and as part of the West African anti-piracy patrol, as well as during the New Zealand land wars. Her captain was Charles Webley Hope when she went to New Zealand and all her movements there as recorded in this novel are correct. The only thing that has been changed is that in order for Stefan to be on board, I have put that she left Portsmouth at the beginning of December 1864 and as she arrived in Sydney on the 15th of January 1865 it means that the journey was far shorter than the usual three months that it took. Many apologies for this discrepancy, which I have counted as poetic licence.

Bibliography

Archibald, Malcolm, 2012, *A Sink of Atrocity, Crime in 19th Century Dundee*, Edinburgh, Black and White Publishing Ltd.

Gourlay. George. 1888. *Anstruther or Illustrations of Scottish Burgh life.* Culpar-Fife. Westwood & Son.

Killrenny and Anstruther Burgh Collection. 1999. *Historic Anstruther: People and Places.*

Mackie, Charles, 1836, *Historical Description of the Town of Dundee,* Glasgow.

The Factory Act of 1883: eight pamphlets 1833-1834, New York.

King, Michael. 2012. The Penguin History of New Zealand, London, Penguin.

Orange, Claudia. 1996. The Treaty of Waitangi, London, Allen and Unwin.

About the author

Vivien Carmichael is the only daughter of Scottish parents, Anna and Alex Carmichael. She was born and brought up in Brighton but has always loved Scotland. She went to Varndean Grammar School for Girls and then undertook a Teachers Training Course. She spent a year living in Paris and then returned to London where she met and married her husband. She has two sons, Nick and James.

Vivien decided to attend Brighton University as a mature student when her youngest son went to school, gaining a BA (Hons) degree in Library and Information Studies. She worked for some years in special libraries in London. Disenchanted with commuting, Vivien studied for a CELTA certificate and taught English to foreign students in Brighton. Vivien has written two other novels for children and adults aged 8 to 80 years: "The Skimming Stone" and "The Grail of the Unicorn Planet".